DEATH IN THE ATTIC

A TWISTY AMATEUR SLEUTH MURDER MYSTERY

THE BREAKFAST CLUB DETECTIVES
BOOK 5

HILARY PUGH

Housemouse Press

Copyright © 2024 by Hilary Pugh

All rights reserved.

No part of this book may be reproduced in any form or by any electronic or mechanical means, including information storage and retrieval systems, without written permission from the author, except for the use of brief quotations in a book review.

❀ Created with Vellum

PROLOGUE

There was just a hint of red in the sky as daybreak crept over the horizon, causing the driver of a silver-grey car to blink away the first rays of sun that sparkled on the road ahead. It was a brand-new car, only a few miles on the clock and still with the showroom tang of polish and new leather. Its purchase was the result of a well-deserved bonus. They were worth it, weren't they? It had been a tough year, but they had turned it around and last night they had celebrated its success dressed to kill in the latest designer gear. A night of boozy speeches and self-entitled camaraderie at one of the most exclusive restaurants outside the M25.

The party had lasted well into the small hours of the late June night, the shortest night of the year. A night when some people celebrate the solstice, daubing their bodies with woad and dancing naked at Stonehenge, perhaps, with twigs in their hair. As uninhibited but a lot less sophisticated than their own company-sponsored party. It seemed only an hour or two since they had watched the sun setting over the lake and someone had cracked open the first bottle of champagne. That was after the aperitifs, bottles of wine – both red and white – and liqueurs; no one was counting the empty bottles and used glasses, or the number of explosions from champagne corks. No one cared about the alcohol content or the cost. Who'd bother after the spectacular results they'd been celebrating? And now the sun was rising again, a lightshow, red fingers of a fiery dawn on the horizon. Rain later, perhaps, but right now it seemed as if the weather was still joining in their celebration with the sun of a new day and early morning dew sparkling on the road.

The car, delivered to the glinting glass tower of the West London office block only a day earlier, was unfamiliar but a joy to drive, fast and responsive, roaring along the country lanes. Roof down, music blaring, hair ruffling in the wind. A quick detour for breakfast with an old friend then home to sleep off the excesses of the previous night. Hard not to let the eyelids droop, but only half a mile or so to go. Stay awake. Think about the smell of the coffee he'll have ready and turn the music up even louder.

Then an unexpected bend in the road. A change in the angle of the sun, now a glare on the windscreen making it difficult to see. A twist of the steering wheel and the car bumped onto the grass verge. Veering back again onto the road with sickening jolt, it juddered to a halt, the engine still running but the car unable to move. There was something in the way. The driver shivered and pulled on a hoodie before climbing out of the car, running fingers over the dent in the bodywork and gasping at the bundle lying in the road.

What was he doing here? Who goes out for a walk at dawn on their own, not even a dog for company? He hated dogs, anyway, and was not known as an early riser. He should have been at home making coffee. He'd have known how badly it would be needed, used as he was to his own habit of drinking the night away.

Cautiously nudging the body and getting no response, panic set in. A drunk driving charge, licence suspended, a hefty fine, even a prison sentence. No, that mustn't happen. No need to ruin two lives. But what to do? Leave him here and hope the car hadn't been seen? Call an ambulance, drive away and pray that the call wouldn't be traced?

The driver staggered back to the car, pulled the phone off its dashboard charger and called the only person in the world who could be relied on to help.

1

For a town of historic interest and royal connections, the police station was about as boring architecturally as one could get. A three-storey, red brick block with a patch of scrubby grass outside, it had been under threat for several years. But in spite of multiple schemes to move the staff into other buildings and sell the site for development, it was still there.

Charlie Hannington grabbed a parking space as near as she could to the entrance and gazed glumly at the building. The shilly-shallying discussions between council and police authorities meant that little had been done for the upkeep of the place. Bad enough outside, with unfilled potholes in the car park and dingy windows, Charlie imagined the inside would be worse; it would be in need of a lick of paint, new flooring and modern window blinds. She opened the back of her car and lifted out a cardboard box containing a potted plant – a gift from her mother following her promotion – some family photographs, a battery-operated pencil sharpener and a mug with a picture of a dog on it. She signed in at the desk and was directed to her new office on the second floor. The one lift, housed at the far end of the building, was out of order, so she carried her box up two flights of stairs, pushed open the door and looked around. The room contained three desks, some swivel chairs, a whiteboard on wheels and a dying pot plant. On the far side of the room was the door to what would be her own office. She crossed the room, opened the door and put her box down on the desk. The previous occupant, Detective Inspector Lomax, had left a half-used reporter's notepad, a papier-mâché bowl of paperclips and a biscuit tin with a picture of a thatched cottage on the lid, a few stale ginger nuts inside.

Charlie tried not to feel disappointed. Police stations were never exactly homely places and they'd suffered from austerity cutbacks just like every other public building. Given the choice, she would have gone for an office in the flashy new investigation centre on the Oxford ring road. She'd hoped to become part of the major crime team there after passing her exams and her single-handed arrest of a suicidal murderer. But it was not to be. And she'd known what to expect after her interview with Detective Superintendent Archie Groves.

Groves, tall and grey-haired, and wearing a suit and tie that suggested he spent most of his time behind a desk, had peered at her over the top of his spectacles. 'Ah, Charlotte. So sorry to hear about your father. How is your mother coping?'

How did he imagine she was coping, widowed after forty years of marriage? 'She's okay.'

'Good, good. Always had time for your mother, lovely woman. But come in, have a seat.'

Charlie sat down on a leather chair on the far side of his desk while he flicked through some papers, eventually handing her one of them. Glancing at it, the truth began to dawn. This was not where she was going to work. All her ambitions flew out of the window. She wasn't going to be part of the team here in Oxford. She was being sidelined to a backwater, to a heap of a building that looked, from its picture, like it was earmarked for demolition.

Groves beamed at her. 'You'll be running a small team right there,' he told her, jabbing at the picture with his finger. 'A beautiful, historic town in the Royal Borough.'

Yes, she had heard of the place. She had in fact grown up near there.

'Who knows, you could be mixing with royalty.' He beamed at her.

Was he expecting her to thank him? For the chance, a very slim one, of bumping into a minor royal in Waitrose. Senior royals were guarded by the protection branch and rarely poked their noses outside the castle except in armoured cars. She knew what her assignment there meant. She was being kept out of the way of anything interesting. She'd be dealing with drunk tourists, burglaries, possession of drugs, an armed robbery if she was lucky. Major crimes would be handled by the team here at the hub. But it was promotion, she grudgingly admitted. She should thank Groves. But she didn't. She stared back at him with a mutinous expression.

'We thought it would suit you well. Big fish, small pond and all that.'

Well, it was a start. One day she'd be a big fish in a big pond. She should, as her mother was always telling her, be patient. These things took time and a lot of hard work.

'And you live nearby,' Groves added.

Actually, her mother lived nearby. Charlie had yet to step onto the housing ladder and her new posting meant only that she would move out of a rented flat and into a house she didn't own. Well, she'd save the hassle of renting and would not be landed with a mortgage. And it would be much better for her mother to have Charlie and Kai living in rather than twenty miles away, one or other of them having to commute when the childminder was sick. Living in the family home could have an upside.

'Tell me,' Groves asked. 'Do you have childcare problems?'

'No, sir,' she said. 'Do you?'

He laughed. 'A fair question. My lot have all grown up and left home.'

And no doubt they grew up with their mother taking all the strain of organising their lives.

'It's just as a single parent... you have a son, I believe.'

'Kai,' said Charlie. 'He's fifteen. And I would like to point out that in all those fifteen years I have not taken a single day's leave as a result of chicken pox, parents' evenings, nativity plays, dentist appointments or anything else.'

'Fine,' said Groves, holding his hands up in surrender. 'It's not a question I should be asking.'

'No, you shouldn't,' Charlie agreed, although she had to admit she was lucky. Her mother had always been there for her, ready to step in when needed.

CHARLIE LEFT her box to unpack later and walked back into the main office to wait for the rest of her team to turn up. Where the hell were they? Was she about to work with a group of people who had no respect for time? A few ground rules would need to be made and pinned to the wall, with punctuality highlighted.

She looked around for a board to pin them to and saw only blank walls, painted grey, scuffed from countless shifts of furniture, and dotted with the remains of Blu-Tack. In one corner, rain dripped into a yellow plastic bucket.

The door opened and a man came in. In his mid-thirties, he was straight out of central casting's crime drama department – brown bomber jacket, supermarket jeans and trainers.

'Morning, babe,' he said, grabbing one of the chairs and sitting down with his legs sprawled in front of him. 'You one of the new detective constables?'

'No,' she said coldly. 'I'm the new detective inspector, Charlotte Hannington. And you are?'

'DS Gary Trotter.' He appeared unfazed by his mistake. 'Ma'am,' he added with a hint of a sneer.

Great. She'd need to add the proper way to address fellow officers to her list of rules. She could probably report him for his use of *babe*, but that wouldn't be a great start in terms of team building, not on their first day together. Looked like he was another reject from the investigation centre. He'd have a three-bedroom new-build on an out-of-town estate, a couple of kids and a stay-at-home wife who complained that he never spent any time with her.

Charlie was just wondering whether to get Trotter to sort out the furniture or send him out for coffee, when the door flew open and a small, dark-haired woman bounced in followed by a young man with stooped shoulders and a gloomy expression. The woman bounded up to Charlie and held out her hand. 'DC Anya Shafiq,' she said, grinning. 'Most people call me Annie.'

'To blend in?' Trotter asked.

'I don't understand,' said Annie.

'You know, more British.'

'I was born in Solihull,' said Annie. 'Want to see my passport?'

Charlie made a mental note to look up unconscious bias courses and book Trotter onto one ASAP. She turned to the young man and smiled. 'And you are?'

'DS Bateman,' he said.

He was a stringy type, mid-twenties, bony hands with long fingers, and untidy hair that hadn't seen a comb for a while, never mind a pair of scissors. He was wearing jeans and heavy boots and was huddled inside a navy-blue donkey jacket several sizes too big.

Annie glanced at the bucket in the corner and tutted. 'Shall I go and ask for someone to come and fix that?'

'Wouldn't waste your time, love,' said Trotter.

'I know a guy in maintenance,' said Annie. 'He'll do anything for me if I ask nicely. I could pop downstairs now and find him.'

'Worth a try,' said Charlie, who was reminded of the Christopher Robin stories. Annie was definitely Tigger. She was either going to be bright and useful or an over-enthusiastic pain in the backside. Bateman, on the other hand, was a shoo-in for Eeyore. 'Your first name?' she asked him.

'Leslie. You can call me Les,' he said with a gloomy expression.

'Cheer up, Les, mate,' said Trotter. 'It might never happen.'

Les shrank further into his coat, suggesting that whatever it was had already happened.

'Bloody hell,' said Trotter. 'We look like a frigging equality and diversity poster.'

He wasn't wrong, Charlie reflected glumly.

2

Jonny Cardew spent the morning in the office at *Jasmine's*, tidying up the Breakfast Club accounts ready for the auditors. As a charity supported by Cardew Packaging Solutions, a company of which Jonny was still a major shareholder, he couldn't afford to make mistakes. But he didn't need to worry. Jasmine's accounts were always in good order. The Windsor breakfast club had got off to a flying start nearly two years ago and the books had balanced almost immediately. The second club, opened by his wife Belinda in High Wycombe a year later, was less successful. Nothing to worry about; it was just taking a little longer to attract members. High Wycombe was a less affluent town and the demand for free meals outstripped the number of those who could afford to pay the membership fee. They'd need to address this in the next few months, or they'd have to rethink the terms of membership.

Jonny thought about the two venues. The two cafés were similar; both within a short walk of train stations, both situated close to shops and offices. Windsor had the advantage of tourists, but while that attracted customers to *Jasmine's,* it didn't help the breakfast club. If anything it might even discourage it, although there was no evidence of that. Tourism drew in casual coffee drinkers and lunchers. The clientele who came for breakfast were usually long gone by the time the first castle visitors arrived for snacks. The main difference between the two establishments was the publicity that the Breakfast Club Detectives had generated in *Jasmine's*. After solving four murders, people dropped in to see where it had all begun, some even suggesting crimes they might investigate. There were not too many murders in the area. There were burglaries, car thefts and organised shoplifting, but none of these really appealed to any of the four detectives. Jasmine hinted that she didn't want people queueing up to have petty crimes investigated. Serious crime she could make time for. The rest of the time she was busy enough serving people who were genuinely hungry. Retired DS Roscoff, the unelected leader of the group, had rudely refused a request for surveillance from a man who thought his wife was having an affair. 'We don't do those kinds of investigations,' she had said brusquely, possibly losing Jasmine a customer in the process. Ivo, in his role as handyman around the town, had had requests from customers who thought they could use him as a cut-price burglar alarm by giving him jobs to do while they were away on holiday. Requests that Ivo refused, more politely than Katya, by insisting that his clients should remain at home while he was working *for insurance purposes*. Jonny didn't ask if this was an actual request from the insurers or simply a means of discouraging customers from trying to get cut-price surveillance.

Jonny himself missed the cases they'd worked on. He'd always wanted to be a detective, but right now he was worried that there might be no more cases. Their highly supportive detective inspector at the local police station had now retired and been replaced by a someone much younger. They'd lost their direct link to the police. DI Lugs Lomax was a long-term colleague and close friend of Katya, and Jonny failed to see how they'd get the same inside information with this new inspector. Katya had never heard of her and her attempts to find out more had led nowhere. All she'd managed to discover was that the new DI was recently promoted, having been a DS with a major incident team in Hampshire. And to make matters worse, Flora Green, Lugs' sergeant, had also been promoted and had moved to a new force. Katya knew nothing about the DS who was to take over her job, either.

Jonny saved all the documents he'd been working on and, satisfied that all was correct, he attached them to an email and sent it all to the company accountant. The rest of the morning stretched ahead of him. He went down to the café, thinking he might get a coffee and chat to Jasmine about the current dearth of crime in the area. But all the tables were taken and Jasmine was up to her eyes in orders. He decided instead to walk to *Shady Willows*, where Ivo looked after a park of cabins occupied by elderly residents. But arriving there, he found Ivo clad in waders, shoring up the riverbank with sandbags. Heavy rain was forecast, apparently. Ivo's dog, Harold, was pleased to see him though, and Jonny spent a few minutes tossing sticks for him. Was he not going to find any of the detectives with the time for a chat about their future? He could double back into town, where he might find Katya at home. But probably not. She liked to be out and about during the day because her flat was too expensive to heat. She'd be at one of the libraries, or searching for warm clothes in a charity shop. And Katya was moody. She might be happy to chat about how to find new cases, particularly if bribed with the prospect of a hot drink and something to eat. But she was equally likely to tell him that cases would either come along or they wouldn't and there was not a lot they could do about it.

Harold was the only one of the detectives who had greeted him with any shred of enthusiasm, but even he was getting bored with fetching sticks and had settled down for a nap underneath Ivo's wheelbarrow. Jonny was on his own. But it was a nice day. Mild for the time of year. He'd put on a pound or two over Christmas and he needed some exercise. He and Belinda had been going to get a dog, had even visited a litter of labradoodles back in the autumn. But they'd been too late, and all the puppies were spoken for. 'We'll wait until the spring,' Belinda said. 'Better time for house training.'

There was no law that said one had to be accompanied by a dog when out for a walk. At least, Jonny had never heard of one. He'd continue his walk upstream from *Shady Willows,* heading for a pub where he could get a beer and a sandwich. It was a couple of miles away and by the time he got there it would be near enough to lunchtime.

There were few people out and about today, in spite of the weather, but after walking another mile, a very large, brown dog bounded towards him. It was a friendly dog, pausing alongside Jonny and wagging its tail. Jonny fondled its thick, furry head and looked around for its owner. Fifty yards ahead of him on the footpath was a boy of fifteen or sixteen running towards them. 'Meg,' he shouted as he came within earshot. 'Meg, come here.'

The dog failed to respond, seeming more interested in making friends with Jonny. The boy arrived at Jonny's side and pulled a lead from his pocket, attaching it to Meg's collar. 'Sorry,' he said. 'We don't get to meet a lot of people along here, not during the week.'

'No problem,' said Jonny. 'She's a beautiful dog, and very friendly.'

'She's a rescue dog. Mum got her to keep Gran company after Granddad died. She could probably take her back now because we've moved in with Gran. But we kind of like having Meg around.'

He was a strikingly good-looking boy – dark, curly hair, brown eyes and a smile that could probably melt ice. He was wearing an embroidered Afghan coat of the kind that was popular among hippies in the 1970s. One of Jonny's friends had owned one and he recalled a strong aroma of goat. 'Nice coat,' he said.

The boy performed a model-like twirl, opening the coat to show a deep-pile brown lining, not unlike Meg's own coat. As he completed his twirl, Jonny spotted what he was wearing under the coat, a navy-blue blazer with a badge. 'Not at school?' Jonny asked, wondering if he'd met up with a truant and if he had, whether or not he should report him.

'Study morning,' said the boy. 'And I always study better after a good walk.'

Good enough for Jonny. Probably just an excuse of the *dog ate my homework* type. And Meg certainly looked more than capable of swallowing a good deal of homework. But it wasn't his place to argue. 'A levels?' he asked.

'GCSEs,' said the boy, sighing deeply. 'Tough going, to be honest. Me and Mum have just moved up here. It's the same syllabus and all that, but it's a new school to get used to. Mum's promotion came through and if she'd turned it down, she'd be stuck where she was for years. Plus, we got to move in with Gran, which was nice.'

They were now heading towards the village where Jonny was hoping for a pub lunch.

'Do you live in the village?' the boy asked.

Jonny shook his head. 'I live in town,' he said, with a glance over his shoulder. 'I'm trying to walk off some of the overeating I did at Christmas.'

'New Year resolution?'

It wasn't, but it should be. And it wasn't too late for a New Year resolution. He'd walk four miles every day, he decided.

'Lucky you, living in town. I'm dead jealous. It's very isolated where we are. Gran's house is just over there.' He pointed towards a large, red brick farmhouse at the edge of a field.

'Your gran's a farmer?' Jonny asked.

Kai laughed. 'You'd not ask that if you'd met her,' he said. 'She's where I get my elegant dress sense from.' He did another twirl. 'Mum's more into jeans and rugged footwear. At least, she is when she's working.'

'Is she a farmer?' Jonny was getting confused.

'Police. Granddad bought the house when they sold all the land to some massive conglomerate. It's all industrial crop production now. Our nearest neighbour is three quarters of a mile away and I don't know anyone in the village yet, never mind in Windsor. It's okay for Mum and Gran. They have cars, but I have to bike everywhere, even when it's raining. Plays havoc with my hair.' He ran the fingers of one hand through his hair, tucking some stray curls behind his ears. 'Well, I suppose I'd better be getting back and do some studying.'

It must be hard for a kid being uprooted and having to get used to a new place. Even for a confident lad like this one, who had none of the awkwardness of most teenage boys. Perhaps Jasmine could give him some work in the afternoons or weekends. She had a rapid turnover of student help, fitting in waiting tables or washing-up shifts around their college timetables. 'Not looking for a part-time job, are you?'

'Depends,' he said. 'I'm probably working for a few months in the summer, but a bit of pocket money now would come in handy. I could catch some of the great stuff that turns up on Vinted at this time of year.'

Jonny looked at him blankly.

'You know, unwanted Christmas gifts. I got this coat last year. Gran had signed up for a Vinted account. She's into retro stuff at the moment, 1950s mostly. She let me buy the coat on her account. I don't think she let on to Mum how much it cost.'

Jonny pulled a flyer for *Jasmine's* out of his pocket. 'Pop in some time and have a word with Jasmine. I guess you might enjoy waiting at tables. Jasmine and I run a breakfast club together. It's aways busy and Jasmine often needs help.'

'Thanks,' he said, folding the flyer and putting it in his pocket.

'If you're interested, drop in and tell Jasmine I sent you. It's easy to find. Just down the stone steps from the Royal Station.' He held out his hand for the boy to shake. 'I'm Jonny Cardew.'

'Kai Hannington,' he said. 'Lovely to meet you.' He gave Meg's lead a tug and headed across the field to the farmhouse.

3

It was the end of a long day when Charlie sat down at her desk, warming her hands on a mug of pumpkin spiced latte with an extra shot, delivered from Starbucks by her station sergeant. 'Because it's your first day here,' she was told. 'Don't expect it every day.'

But at least they did now have a crime to solve. At first, the call had not been promising. A disturbance at an old house on the borders of the town, a suspected break-in. But the response team had called in the paramedics, so it was obviously more than a simple burglary. She'd dispatched Trotter to investigate. Trotter, she'd concluded, was a self-proclaimed *speak as I find* type, who had managed to insult the three other team members, including Charlie herself, within half an hour of arriving in the office that morning. But in spite of this, DC Annie Shafiq had volunteered to go with him. A brave offer after Trotter's borderline racist comment earlier in the day. Annie struck Charlie as a feisty type. Tiny but brave. There was a hint of Jack Russell terrier about her. Charlie was confident that any more remarks from Trotter and she'd give as good as she got. This left Charlie to deal with the fourth member of the team, DC Les Bateman, who was suffering an identity crisis of some kind that left

Charlie baffled. He'd been a beat copper in Newcastle and was then on leave of absence for three months. After that, he'd gone straight into detective training. That was all the information there was on his file. Nothing about the reason for his leave of absence or why he had moved so far for this post. He was unresponsive to her tentative suggestions about in-house help from HR and failing to reveal any clues about his former life when her phone rang.

It was Trotter. He was still out investigating the suspected burglary. Surely he didn't need her to hold his hand. 'What is it?' she snapped.

'You need to be here.'

He was asking for her help? Really? Or was he just going to gloat because he'd already arrested a burglar. 'You can't handle a burglary?' It didn't take a sergeant. Annie could have managed it single-handed. She was probably champing at the bit to get on with it. Hell, even downtrodden Les could probably detain a burglar.

'It's not a burglary. And I can handle it. But I assumed you'd want to be in on this one.' He texted her the address and ended the call abruptly.

BEEDHAM HOUSE WAS a few miles out of town, at the end of a bumpy lane a mile or two from the Bagshot Road. In its heyday it must have been lovely. A three-storey home for a well-to-do family, a sloping roof with two tall chimneys, an arched front door and at one side, a pillared patio with steps leading to a garden, once a series of gravel paths, lawns bordered by box hedges and a lily pond, but now overgrown with brambles, the lawn turned to moss and the pond full of green sludge.

Charlie came to the end of the lane and drove between two pillars, once gateposts but now lacking a gate, into an overgrown gravel drive. On either side of the entrance were two cottages, behind which she could see some sheds, a greenhouse and a paved area surrounding what might have once been a swimming pool, but which was now a fenced-off pit lined with crumbling concrete. It was an isolated, not to say desolate place that had apparently resisted any attempts by the many local developers to improve it. Charlie wondered why. Land around there was usually snapped up. It was close to London, a major motorway network and four airports. Planning restrictions in green belt were strict, but where there were existing buildings, regulations were usually relaxed. And yet here was Beedham House with its gardens and outbuildings, dilapidated and deserted.

When she and Bateman arrived at the main entrance to the house, they were greeted by a squad car and an unmarked Vauxhall Astra; a pool car, Charlie assumed. As she parked on the gravel drive, a green and yellow paramedic's car passed her, heading back towards the lane and away from the house.

Charlie was surprised to see people pushing and shoving each other at the end of the drive, trying to get a glimpse across the crime tape at the inside of the house. Where had they sprung from? It was amazing how quickly news of a police presence spread, even in an out of the way place like this. 'Get this lot moved,' she said to Bateman as they climbed out of the car. She headed towards the house, where Trotter was standing at the door waiting for her, already fully kitted out in a white suit and blue shoe covers. She should have told him to wait for the crime scene team. He should have known that himself. On the other hand, she had to admit she was keen to see for herself what was going on. Trotter's white suit suggested they were looking at something far more interesting than a burglary. 'A body?' she asked, trying not to sound hopeful.

Trotter nodded. 'The paramedics confirmed absence of life and the scene is now secure.'

'A suspicious death?'

'They couldn't tell how he died so they've called in the pathologist.' He handed her a plastic package, which she tore open. She heaved the white suit it contained over her own clothes, turning up the legs and wondering why the police still hadn't cottoned on to the fact that women officers were, on the whole, not as tall as male ones. 'Where's Annie?' she asked.

'Over there with the woman who called it in.' Trotter pointed towards one of the cottages.

'There are people living there?' she asked.

'Both cottages are occupied, but the house itself is empty. I thought Annie would do a good job of calming down the residents.'

Typical. Women get the comforting tasks, leaving the men to do the exciting stuff. But she couldn't really see Trotter being any use as a sympathetic shoulder, so she supposed he'd made the right decision. 'Okay,' she said, pulling up the hood of her suit and snapping on a pair of gloves. 'Let's take a look before the crime scene lot get here.'

She followed Trotter into the house, which was empty of any furniture but home to many spiders. Scraps of newspaper littered the floor, along with some empty sandwich packets and flattened drink cans. A huge fireplace in the entrance hall still contained ashes but not, Charlie assumed, left by the departing residents. More likely the result of illicit teenage parties, or squatters looking for somewhere dry to sleep.

'It's up in the attic,' said Trotter, heading for a wide staircase.

They climbed to the first floor and Trotter led her to a second flight at the end of a long landing, which in turn led to an attic room with wooden beams and a skylight letting in a shaft of sunlight. Apart from a spectacular display of cobwebs, the room contained only a wooden trunk and a rocking chair, in which sat a man. And Trotter was correct. He was dead.

Taking care not to touch anything, Charlie pulled up a face mask and shuffled towards the chair, bending over it for a closer look. There might be no obvious cause of death, but Charlie didn't imagine the man had settled himself in the chair for a snooze and then died of natural causes. One of the man's arms, she noticed, had fallen from the armrest onto the trunk. The fingers of his left hand dangled claw-like over some words scratched into the lid.

*If You Seek **Revenge You Should Dig Two Graves***

. . .

CHARLIE UNZIPPED ENOUGH of her suit to reach into the pocket of her jeans for her phone. She took a photo of the message, put the phone away and stood back. 'Not much we can do here. We'll wait for the crime scene people outside.' They headed back down two flights of stairs.

A grey-haired man was parking his car in the drive when they reached the front door. He climbed out and frowned at the two of them before opening the back of the car and lifting out a black leather bag. Charlie stepped forward and offered her hand. 'DI Hannington,' she said.

'Yates,' the man grunted, ignoring her outstretched hand.

'I'll go and check on Annie and Les,' said Trotter. 'Leave you two to chat.' He stripped off his suit, bundled it into the back of the Astra and walked briskly towards the cottages.

He obviously didn't remember her, but Charlie had met Edwin Yates once before and had decided he was an arrogant twat. He'd done nothing so far this morning to alter her opinion. His grunted greeting suggested his opinion of her was not much better. He nodded at her patronisingly and disappeared up the stairs. Charlie stood in the doorway and watched a van approaching up the drive. The scene of crime investigators. A remarkably cheery bunch, considering the grimness of most of their work.

Yates reappeared as they were unloading equipment from the van. 'All yours,' he said to the head of the team. 'I'm done here, so get the body moved as soon as you like.' He turned to Charlie. 'You were right,' he said in a manner that suggested this was the last thing he wanted to admit. 'The man is dead.'

'Cause of death?'

'Can't say,' he said, ripping off his protective suit in a manner that suggested it was riddled with lice. 'You'll have to wait for the post-mortem.'

'I don't suppose you can tell me when he died.'

'You expect me to wave a magic wand?' He scowled at her. 'You'll get my report once I've had a chance to do the PM.'

'You'll let me know when that is?'

He nodded curtly and got back into his car, flinging his bag onto the passenger seat.

Charlie watched as he drove away. There was not much more she could do until forensics had done their job. She'd round up her own team and leave the scene to the CSIs.

BACK IN THE OFFICE, she knew she had to phone the case in to the hub. It was something she'd rather not have to do. A Senior Investigating Officer would be appointed, and she and her team would probably be pushed aside and left with the grunt work. As it turned out, however, she'd chosen the right moment. DCI Paddy Philips was on call. Paddy was a laid-back type, counting off the days until his retirement. 'Suspicious death?' he asked.

'We don't know, sir. Not until the PM. There was nothing obvious.'

'It's been manic here today. A major incident in Banbury. Can't you handle it yourself?'

'Of course, sir.'

'Good girl. Just keep me up to date, okay?'

She ended the call with relief. She'd not liked being addressed as *good girl* but if that meant she could run the case herself, she guessed she could put up with it.

She left her office to see what the rest of the team were up to. Annie had reorganised the room. Somehow the leaking roof had been attended to and the yellow bucket removed. She'd watered the pot plant and sprayed the leaves. It now sat in a ceramic dish on the windowsill, looking like an aging film star who'd recently had a facelift. From somewhere Annie had conjured up a set of mugs and a kettle, which sat on a shelf at the side of the room next to a packet of PG Tips, a jar of instant coffee and a coronation biscuit tin containing, or so the label promised, shortbread proudly made in Scotland.

It was getting late and they'd had a long day. There was not much they could do right now; they would have to wait for forensics.

They'd know a lot more when the crime scene report arrived, and the cause of death was established. It was the lull before the storm. But there would be plenty to get on with the next day, so she sent the team home, instructing them to be back at eight sharp the following morning. After they left, she wheeled the whiteboard to where it could easily be seen from all three desks and wrote a list of tasks for the team to start on the next morning.

Confirm the identity of the body and inform the next of kin.
Arrange house to house enquiries.
Collect and collate info on Beedham House.

She printed out the photo of the message on the lid of the trunk, pinned it to the board and stared at it. Was it a suicide note, a message from a murderer or from a victim? Or perhaps it had nothing to do with the body at all.

Then the phone rang.

They'd found another body.

4

It was pure chance that Katya Roscoff turned on her phone just as the newsflash appeared on her screen. She usually ignored them. There'd been enough news recently about destruction around the world, dismal economic forecasts and politicians behaving badly. But this one was different. Her attention was drawn by the first line: BODY FOUND IN HOUSE NEAR WINDSOR. She clicked on the message, hoping to find out more. Was it some poor soul who lived on their own, had perhaps been dead for days, even weeks before anyone noticed? The article didn't say, but it did mention that police were called to a disturbance in the house and discovered the body of a man. Could it be murder? The police had said only that they were exploring all avenues, which in Katya's experience meant they were faffing around waiting for forensic reports before getting off their backsides and doing something about it. Like publishing details and opening case files.

Katya scrolled to her contacts and her finger hovered over Lugs' number before she remembered that would be pointless. He had already set off in his camper van for sunnier climes. Couldn't get away fast enough. New Year's Eve he'd had a grand send-off. New Year's Day he was headed for Dover. By now he'd be halfway down

France. There was no point in trying anyone else at the local nick. She could hardly storm in there demanding that the new DI give her a rundown of the incident. From the little Lugs had told her, DI Hannington didn't sound like the type to chat over a pint in a pub or share a bag of chips on a bench by the river. There wasn't even anyone else in the team she could chat to. A new sergeant, moved in from Staines, a constable who'd come from somewhere miles away. Tyneside, Lugs had thought. Something dodgy about that. Why move so far? Sounded like Tyneside had wanted to get rid of him. The only other detective on the team was a youngster called Annie Shafiq. Katya had met her, but only once and very briefly when she'd called in to see Lugs. Shafiq had been a new uniformed constable then and was now in the detective team, so she was either very bright or very pushy. Either way, Katya didn't think she'd give away any details of what could well turn out to be a murder case.

Breakfast was what Katya needed now, and a meeting of the Breakfast Club Detectives. She pulled on a down coat – a purchase she had made in a charity shop the day after Boxing Day and one she was extremely proud of. The fact that it was a lurid shade of green didn't worry her too much. She'd be less likely to be knocked down by a car, wouldn't she? And the broken zip wasn't a problem. It still worked but the catch at the bottom was stuck and she either had to step into it or pull it on over her head. But that was a minor inconvenience compared to the warmth she enjoyed once inside the coat.

Once rugged up in gloves, scarf and bobble hat in addition to her coat, Katya tucked a map of the area into her pocket and set out.

The cafe was busy. 'It's the cold,' said Jasmine as she took Katya's order. 'Makes people extra hungry.'

Made sense to Katya. She felt the same herself and decided to go for porridge with brown sugar. Jasmine returned to the counter and ladled out a helping of porridge from a copper warming pot. Katya hoped she wasn't too busy to sit around discussing dead bodies. She'd make time if it meant getting involved in a murder case, but until then she probably didn't need the distraction. 'Are Jonny or Ivo around?' Katya asked.

'Jonny's busy filing the tax stuff. He'll be up in the office all morning, but he asked not to be disturbed. Ivo's here. He's fixing our blocked shower drain. Shall I ask him to come and have a word when he's done?'

'Please,' said Katya. 'I'm hoping we can find out more about this body that's been found.'

'I saw that on the news,' said Jasmine. 'Out towards Bagshot, isn't it?'

'Still in this area, though. It'll be handled by the local team.'

'Is it a murder?'

'That's what I want to find out.' Sooner or later there would be a police statement about whether or not this was a suspicious death, but Katya wanted to be ahead of the game – get in there and find out what was going on.

'Pity Lugs left,' said Jasmine, pulling up a chair and sitting down next to Katya. 'Do you know who's taken over?'

Lugs had not been very forthcoming about that. He was retiring and Katya supposed he had little reason to be interested in who would take over. 'No,' she said, answering Jasmine's question. 'A DI Hannington from Brighton or Hastings, somewhere like that. Lugs didn't have any details.'

'And Flora has moved as well. Been promoted, hasn't she?'

Lugs had been pleased about that. Flora had joined his team as a new detective, risen to sergeant after Katya retired and was now a detective inspector. She'd probably be detective superintendent in the blink of an eye. 'Yeah, she's an inspector now.'

'You'd think they'd have promoted her into Lugs' post.'

If there was any sense among those in charge, they would have done, and Katya would still have had an ally in the local force. She frowned. 'They should have done, but top brass like shifting people around when they've just moved up a rank.'

'Perhaps she wanted to move,' Jasmine suggested. 'Get the feel of a new area.'

That was possible, Katya supposed. But why would she want to? She thought Flora was happy here.

Harold trotted in and greeted Katya with a wag of the tail, Ivo following in his wake. 'All done,' he said to Jasmine. 'Shouldn't give you any more trouble.'

'Thanks,' said Jasmine, standing up. 'I'd better get back to work. Usual breakfast?'

Ivo nodded as she started to stack empty coffee cups from nearby tables onto a tray.

'Make him one of those breakfast rolls,' said Katya. 'He can bring it with him.'

'We're going somewhere?' asked Ivo with a look of surprise. Katya didn't usually seek his company unless there was a case for them, and as far as Ivo knew, there was nothing at the moment.

'We're taking Harold for a walk,' said Katya. 'I want you to drive me to this place.' She pulled the map out of her bag, found the section she was looking for and jabbed at it with her finger.

'Why?' Ivo stared at the place Katya was pointing to. 'There's not much there and Harold can go for a walk anywhere.'

'I didn't think you were much into dog walking, Katya,' said Jasmine as she made a note of the order.

'Harold's our cover. We're going to inspect a crime scene, but we need to look like dog walkers, not detectives.'

'What crime scene?' said Ivo. 'Have we got a new case?'

'Didn't you hear about the body they found?'

'Been up to my elbows in mucky water since half-seven,' said Ivo. 'Haven't had time to see the news.'

'A body was found near the town. They didn't give the exact location, but it's clearly not in the town centre or it would have said.' She opened her phone and showed him the news report.

'I'll get your roll,' said Jasmine, picking up the tray and heading for the kitchen.

'Do one for me as well,' Katya called to her as she scraped her porridge bowl clean.

Ivo read the message and handed Katya's phone back. 'It doesn't say very much about where it was found. What makes you think it's this place?'

'I don't know for sure but the body was "in a derelict house".' She made quote marks with her fingers. 'Most of the villages round here are full of commuters who can afford to renovate old places. All the derelict houses have been snapped up by developers.'

'But not this one?' said Jasmine, returning with a brown paper bag. 'I wonder why. And where it is.'

'My money's on this place, Beedham,' said Katya. 'It's just a small area at the end of a lane. An obvious place to build or attract renovators, but it's under the Heathrow flight path, close to the motorway and not very accessible by road. If I was going to dump a body, it's the kind of place I'd choose.'

'It looks like a big house,' said Ivo, opening Google Earth on his phone and studying the area. 'I think you're right about the location.' He squinted at Katya's map and compared it with the image on his phone. 'It could be an old manor house and a couple of smaller cottages.' He ran his finger along the map. 'There's a track from the main road but it doesn't look like it's properly surfaced.'

Jasmine handed Ivo the bag. 'Your roll,' she said. 'I've made one for Katya as requested, and a couple of cups of coffee. It sounds like hungry work. Are you planning to turn up at the house and demand to see the body and inspect the crime scene?'

'They'd tell us to get lost,' said Katya. 'But we can find out a lot about what's going on by watching from a distance. If they've sealed it off, we can be sure it's being taken seriously. And if we can identify the house then we can start doing some research of our own.'

'What kind of research?' said Ivo. 'We don't even know the name of the victim.'

'We can find out who owns the house and if anyone was seen there recently.'

'Won't the police do all that?'

'They will, but this is a new team. They're not local like us. We can keep one step ahead of them.'

'All the way to arresting a suspect?'

'Don't be silly, Ivo. Of course we don't have powers of arrest. But if we can convince this new team that we know what we're doing, they might contract us to do some detecting for them.'

'Like the body in the river case?'

'Exactly.'

'You're assuming this new DI will be up for that?' Jasmine asked.

'Maybe. Maybe not. But we can at least try. Come on, Ivo. Let's get going.' She stood up and climbed back into her coat.

5

Gary Trotter arrived in the office only five minutes late. Annie and Les were both logged onto their computers, working their way through lists of searches that the DI had given them. For God's sake, she must have been up all night preparing those. He hoped she would have something more interesting in mind for him this morning. He started to remove his jacket.

'Don't,' said the DI. 'We're off out.' She picked up a set of car keys and tossed them to him. 'We're taking a pool car. Same place as yesterday. Come on. What are you waiting for? We haven't got all day and I want to be there before the pathologist arrives and starts treating me like a truanting schoolgirl.'

Gary followed her as she charged down the stairs two at a time.

'The pathologist's already been,' he said, panting to keep up with her, noticing that she was waiting by the car not in the least out of breath. He really should get more exercise.

'Perhaps you should join a gym,' said the DI, tapping impatiently on the bonnet of the car.

Gary clicked the key fob to unlock the doors. 'Passed my last physical,' he grunted, unwilling to discuss his lack of stamina with this upstart of a boss, who appeared to have the energy of a small child on speed. 'What's the rush, anyway?'

'They've found another body,' she said. 'It was in that trunk in the attic.'

'Near where they found the first body?' said Gary. 'Can't be a coincidence.'

'I agree. The CSIs called me last night having broken into the trunk. It was their idea to close down the scene and wait until this morning.'

'Man or woman?' Gary asked.

'A man. Been dead a while, they said. They want to bring in a specialist team and do a thorough search of the area.'

'They think there may be more bodies?'

'It's possible. They didn't find any more in the house, but they need to check outside.'

They'd be digging up the garden, using imaging gadgets, maybe even cadaver dogs. What he and the boss were going to do, he wasn't sure. Wouldn't it be more useful to stay in the office and wait for the reports to come in? It would definitely be warmer. He buttoned up his jacket and started the car, turning up the heating to its max, although it was unlikely anyone had driven the pool car yet this morning, so the heating probably wouldn't kick in until they were there. He revved the engine and skidded out of the car park.

'Take it easy,' said Charlie. 'The body won't get any more dead before we get there.'

Wasn't she the one in a hurry? Gary wished he'd been assigned to the kind of boss who sat behind a desk taking it easy. But at least there wasn't much traffic this morning. Too early for the morning rush hour of four-by-fours taking kiddies to school. And what there was, was heading into town, not away from it.

FIFTEEN MINUTES LATER, they were at the end of the lane. The cordon had been moved and the area extended to include the gardens and the drive. Gary waved at the constable who was standing by one of the gateposts. He opened the window and showed his pass, gesturing for him to let them through. He could see Yates' grey Tiguan ahead of them, parked close to the front door of the house. The boss wouldn't be pleased about that. Gary would probably get the blame for not getting her there first. The cordon having been pulled aside, he sped up the drive and skidded to a halt outside the house.

'Who are those people?' the DI asked, pointing through the passenger window at a group of three people, a small child and a dog, who were standing at the gate of one of the cottages. 'I thought we sent all the gawpers home yesterday.'

'We did. The woman with the baby is probably Ruth Richards, who reported the disturbance. She lives in the cottage with her boyfriend. Annie talked to her yesterday and there didn't seem to be any reason for her to move out. Annie said she'd go back and take a statement from her if it was needed. The cordon was only around the big house, so she could come and go as she pleased. I don't know who the other two are. They weren't here yesterday.'

'Well, go and get rid of them. And tell Ms Richards she needs to move out for a day or two. We're extending the crime scene to cover both cottages and the grounds. Do you know who lives in the other cottage?'

Gary stared at the second cottage. 'Doesn't seem to be anyone there at the moment.' Annie had knocked on their door, but no one answered. Peering through the letter box, she'd seen some mail lying on the floor. 'Looks like they might have gone on holiday,' said Gary. They'd not been in at the time of the disturbance, so they probably weren't implicated in the murder.

'Annie didn't think to ask the Richards woman about them?'

'Don't know,' said Gary. 'I didn't ask her.'

The boss sighed loudly. 'Call her now and get her to find out who they are and where they've gone. Hopefully they'll be on holiday for a few more days, but they need to be warned about what's going on here. And we will need to speak to them.'

Gary got out his phone and made the call. Then he set off back down the drive to talk to Ruth Richards and move the two dog walkers on.

6

Ivo had done his best to steer the van around the potholes as the lane narrowed from what had begun as a tarmacked road but was now a muddy track with grass growing in the middle.

'Bingo!' said Katya as Ivo swung the van round a bend in the track. Ahead was a large house with murky windows and a moss-scarred roof with missing tiles and broken guttering. Nearby there were two cottages and some outbuildings. Parked up outside the house was a police car bearing the Thames Valley livery and a plain grey Transit van. 'Pull over,' Katya ordered. 'You can park by that gate.'

'What if something wants to get into the field? Like a tractor.'

'There's plenty of room. Just pull onto the verge.'

Ivo did as he was told, and Harold strained at his lead, sensing a walk. 'What are we going to do?' he asked.

'We'll walk Harold, of course.'

'What if the police question us?'

'Why should they? We're just a couple of dog walkers. We won't breach the cordon.' She pointed at the crime scene tape at the end of the drive. No chance they could get anywhere near the house. They should have brought binoculars.

'Are you sure this is the place?' Ivo asked. 'They might just be checking up on an empty property.'

'Why would they do that?'

'Maybe someone reported squatters.'

'I don't think the police would bother much about that in a deserted place like this. Anyway, see that grey van over there?'

Ivo nodded.

'That's an unmarked ambulance. They use them to transport dead bodies.'

'So you think the body's still inside the house? Wouldn't it have been moved sooner?'

'There's a lot for the crime scene team to do before they authorise the removal of a body.' She looked at her watch. 'The police were called to the scene yesterday afternoon. They'd have called in a paramedic to confirm absence of life and then the team would have got to work. There must have been a lot of evidence if they had to stay overnight.'

Ivo shivered. He really didn't fancy the role of a crime scene investigator if it involved working all night in a spooky building with a dead body in it.

'I imagine they finished and called the ambulance in this morning. Seems like a long time, but we've probably come at exactly the right moment to watch them remove the body.'

'Lucky us,' said Ivo.

'Come on, then. Let's go and take a look.' She pointed to the two cottages, which were outside the cordon, where a woman was standing by her garden gate with a toddler on her hip. 'We'll go and see what she's got to say.'

They climbed out of the van and Ivo attached Harold to his lead. Harold shook restlessly. This was the kind of place where he was usually allowed to run free. But Ivo wasn't risking it. He couldn't have Harold running under the tape and charging all over a crime scene. There were probably dire penalties for a dog owner who allowed that.

Katya walked purposefully over to the woman by the gate. She was wearing a long woollen skirt with a thick jumper that appeared to have been knitted by someone with poor eyesight, using the leftovers from a jumper factory. She was wearing muddy wellingtons and carrying a grimy toddler with a runny nose.

'Morning,' said Katya cheerfully. 'What's going on here?'

'Dunno, really. I heard shouting from the big house yesterday.' She nodded in the direction of the house. 'It's been empty for as long as I've lived here, so I called the police.'

'Do you live here on your own?' Katya asked.

'No, with my boyfriend, Colin. He got home just after I made the call. He said I shouldn't have done that, but a nice police lady – Asian, she was – came and asked us some questions. We couldn't really tell her anything except I'd been frightened by the shouting. She didn't say what had happened, but she left us a card so we could call if we remembered anything. I cooked us an early tea and put the baby to bed. Then we watched telly for a bit and went to bed as normal. It was a bit of a surprise to find them all still here this morning.'

'Is your boyfriend here now?'

'No, he went to work as usual.'

'What about the other cottage?'

'There's an elderly couple lives there, Peg and Reggie Braddock. Worked for the people at the big house before they left. They've gone on holiday. Tenerife. Their family paid for it for their wedding anniversary.'

'Very nice,' said Katya.

Probably not top of the suspects list, Ivo thought.

'They'll be disappointed when they get back and find they've missed all this. Are you police? Do you know what's going on?'

'I'm not working this case,' said Katya, with what Ivo felt was a skilful avoidance of the question. 'But perhaps you could give me some details and I'll pass them on.' She rummaged in her pocket for a notebook and pen.

'What details?'

'Perhaps start with your name.'

'Ruth Richards. And this is Sonny.' She wiped the child's nose and shifted him to her other hip.

'And how long have you lived here, Ruth?'

'Nearly two years. It's a dump but round here, well, we were lucky to get it. Rents are through the roof. Colin, he's my boyfriend, found this place.'

'Who are you renting from?'

'Some company. Colin said he saw it advertised online.'

'So you don't know who owns it?'

'Same as owns the other cottage, I think, and the big house, I suppose. Dunno who it is.'

'Who do you pay rent to?'

'Oh, Colin does all of that. It's some property company. Don't know what they're called.'

Did these two never talk to each other? Ivo wondered. Ruth seemed pretty clueless and he was beginning to dislike the sound of Colin the boyfriend, which was probably unfair since Ivo had not actually met him. Perhaps if this did turn out to be a murder, and it was still a pretty big if, Colin might be the prime suspect. A disgruntled tenant, possibly. A meeting in the house with the landlord. Some shouting and a struggle that went wrong. But as Katya was always telling him, he shouldn't make assumptions.

The door of Beedham House opened and two men came out wheeling a gurney with a black body bag, which they loaded into the van. Katya stopped asking questions and watched them. It shouldn't be long now before there was an announcement from the police about whether or not it was being treated as a suspicious death. If it was, Ivo knew that Katya would get involved, whether officially or not, he wasn't sure. But he knew her well enough to know that she wasn't going to be left out of a murder case.

The van drove away and Ivo expected the CSI team to go as well. He guessed they'd leave the uniform officers to guard the scene. They'd not want people tramping around on it until they knew the cause of death. But to his surprise, rather than anyone leaving, another car arrived. A Vauxhall Astra was allowed through the tape at the end of the drive and Ivo watched as it drove up to the front door, scattering gravel as it went, and parked next to the police car.

Katya nudged him. 'That's a pool car,' she said. 'I remember it from my working days. Must be past its best by now. No funding for new cars, I suppose. It'll be the detective team taking a look.'

A man and a woman climbed out and glanced in their direction. Ivo thought the woman looked stylish, dressed in well-cut jeans with a long blazer and white high-tops, long hair in a plait reaching almost to her waist. The man was far from stylish, but he did look like a typical plain-clothes copper in jeans, a brown bomber jacket and scruffy trainers. As they reached the door, a man in a suit came out and after a short conversation, headed for the VW Tiguan and drove away. He was grey haired and wore dark grey trousers and a sports jacket.

Katya nudged Ivo. 'Pathologist,' she said. 'Dr Yates. Bit full of himself. The woman is probably the new DI.'

Ivo thought Dr Yates looked more like a teacher, and in his experience, teachers could be full of themselves. He'd never met a pathologist, but who was to say they didn't have a lot in common with teachers.

The woman went into the house and bomber jacket man walked towards them. 'Detective Sergeant Trotter,' he said, waving his ID in their direction once he was within shouting distance. 'Which of you is Ruth Richards?'

'That's me.' Ruth hefted the baby from one side to the other. Something she did a lot, and Ivo wondered why she didn't just put him down to run around. He was wearing a pair of wellies and there were plenty of puddles for him to splash in.

'We need you to leave,' said Trotter abruptly. 'We're cordoning off the whole area.'

'Why?' Katya asked.

'Developments,' said Trotter, not bothering to turn in her direction. 'Ruth, do you have someone you can stay with for a day or two?'

Ruth shook her head tearfully. 'Well, I might be able to go to my sister's, but she won't have Colin in the house. He's got a mate he might be able to stay with, but he's at work now and he won't know what's going on. He won't be happy if he comes back here and finds he's not allowed in the house.'

'Can you call him?' Trotter suggested.

Ruth shook her head. 'Not while he's working. He's a delivery driver. They're not allowed to take calls.'

'When will he be back?'

'This evening, probably.'

'Well, we need you out of here. If you don't have a car, we can arrange for someone to take you into town.'

'You can't just turn her and the baby out of her house,' said Katya.

Trotter turned and glared at her. 'And you are?'

'DS Roscoff,' she said, following it with a muttered 'retired'.

'Ruth,' said Trotter, ignoring Katya. 'We can't force you to go, but I'd strongly advise it. We need to search the area and you might find it upsetting.'

'Will you have to come in the house? Colin won't like that.'

'Probably not, and if we do, we'll get a warrant. I'm afraid your Colin won't have a lot of choice in the matter. But right now, we're more interested in the gardens. We'll be bringing in imaging equipment and sniffer dogs. It's probably just for the rest of the day, but if it's longer we can get the council to find you somewhere temporary. And you two,' he said, frowning at Katya and Ivo. 'What are you doing here?'

'Walking the dog,' said Katya, pointing to Harold.

'Then I suggest you go and walk it somewhere else. But give me your names and numbers in case we need to contact you again.'

Katya and Ivo gave him their details. 'And this is Harold,' said Ivo.

'Right,' said Gary, not bothering to write it down. 'Ruth, go and get a few things together and let me know when you're ready. I'll get someone to drive you wherever you want to go.'

He left them and strolled back towards the house.

'Charming,' said Katya. 'As a DS, I hope I had better manners.'

'I don't know what to do,' Ruth sniffed. 'I don't want to stay here on my own.'

'Why don't you give your sister a call?' Ivo asked.

Ruth searched her pockets, hefting the baby from side to side, and eventually pulling out a phone with a cracked screen. She tapped in a number and waited. 'Not answering,' she said after a few moments, tapping the screen and pushing it back into her pocket.

'Why not leave her a message?' said Ivo.

'Dunno, I didn't think of that.'

'Don't worry, love,' said Katya, tearing a page out of her notebook and scribbling *Jasmine's* address and her own phone number on it. 'Get them to drop you off here.' She handed the note to Ruth. 'You can have a hot meal while we try to contact your sister and your boyfriend and let them know what's going on.'

Ivo agreed that was a good idea, although he didn't imagine it was Katya showing her soft side. More that it might give her a toe in the door of the police case.

∼

CHARLIE HAD JUST FINISHED a call to Annie when Gary arrived back at the house. Annie had done her homework when talking to Ruth the day before and Charlie was impressed. She'd not only found the name of the couple living in the other cottage, Peg and Reggie Braddock, but she'd discovered the name of the agent they were renting the cottage from. She was now contacting them for a phone number for the Braddocks, and by the time she and Gary arrived back at the office, Annie would probably have called them and explained the situation.

'How did you get on?' she asked as Gary approached.

'Just need to arrange a lift for Ruth and the kid.' He pulled out his phone.

'Get one of those to do it,' Charlie said, nodding towards the two uniformed constables who were guarding the scene. 'We'll be here for a while, and they'll be back before we need to leave.'

Gary suggested this to one of the PCs, who looked pleased to be relieved of his guard duties, if only for a short time. He walked over to the cottage where Ruth was waiting with a tote bag over one shoulder, Sonny clutched in her other arm. The PC took the bag from her and helped her into the police car.

'Right,' said Charlie, opening the back door of the car they'd arrived in and pulling out two plastic bags. 'Let's get suited up and take a look.'

'Getting to be a habit,' Gary muttered.

'Let's hope they don't find any more bodies,' said Charlie. 'I might just be allowed to lead the case with two victims. Mass murder and it would definitely go to the hub.'

Beedham House was now empty; the CSI team were concentrating on the gardens of the house and the two cottages, scanning them for signs of ground disturbance. Dr Yates had glanced briefly at the second body, watched as it was loaded into the body bag and taken to the ambulance. He'd returned downstairs, muttering something about hoping this was the last body he'd be called out to, before getting into his car and driving away, taking little notice of the potholes in the drive. Charlie was glad to see him leave.

She and Gary climbed up to the attic once more. Charlie tapped her iPad and opened the file that the CSIs had uploaded with a photo of the second body. She passed the iPad to Gary. 'I'll be interested in Yates' report. I'd say this one's been dead for several years. What do you think?'

'No idea,' said Gary. He tapped on the photo of the body in the trunk. 'From the look of that, I'd say it's definitely a historic case. It's just a skeleton wearing the remains of a suit. I'm guessing a male.'

'I agree,' said Charlie. 'Look at the shoes.' The corpse was wearing a pair of dark brown, highly polished brogues.

'Amazing how well expensive leather lasts,' said Gary. 'These shoes are in far better nick than either the body or his clothing.'

'We'll get Les looking into that,' said Charlie. 'I seem to remember from my horse-riding days that if leather is treated correctly when new, it preserves particularly well in difficult conditions. Some academic did research into boots dug up in World War One trenches. And these shoes might just be made to measure, which will make IDing the victim easier.'

There was not much to see in the attic apart from the yellow markers left by the crime scene team, the rocking chair and the now-empty trunk with the lock broken. Charlie was pleased to see that they'd left it open. She peered inside, wondering if there would be another scrawled message. There was nothing, but she assumed it would have been searched for DNA and fingerprints and she'd be able to tell more from the crime scene report. She hoped it would tell her how long the body had been there. It couldn't be a coincidence that two bodies had been found in the same attic room, could it? Their murders must be connected in some way, even if they were years apart.

Gary was staring at the trunk. 'There must have been more than one killer involved. It would take some welly to get a dead weight into the trunk. Unless he was already in it when he was killed.'

He was right, but this guy had been dead for a while. If he'd been killed in the trunk there would be one hell of a mess. But the trunk looked clean. 'Perhaps the killer was helped by victim number two before he killed him as well,' Gary suggested.

'Doesn't work,' said Charlie. 'Not if the two murders were several years apart. Better not to make any guesses until all the reports are in.'

They checked around the rest of the house and Charlie took some more photos, but there was not much to be seen. The rooms were empty and anything useful would have been bagged up and logged as evidence. She and Gary would make more progress back at the office.

They went downstairs and back into the garden, where the CSIs were still busy with their equipment. 'Nothing to report so far,' said the senior officer. 'We should be able to wrap it up early tomorrow. I'll email my updated report then.'

They headed for the car. 'Any trouble with the dog walkers?' Charlie asked as Gary clicked to unlock the doors.

'Not really. They left before the car picked Ruth up.'

'Did you get their names?'

'Yeah.'

'Feel like telling me?'

'Oh, yeah, okay.' He searched his pockets for his notebook. 'Katya Roscoff and Ivo Dean. They gave me contact numbers. Oh, and the dog was called Harold. Didn't get his number.'

That was as close as Gary had come to any kind of humour that didn't insult anyone. 'We'll check back with them later. If they are regular walkers here, one of them might know something about the people who lived in the house. But right now, we'll head back to base for a debrief.'

7

'How old is he?' Jasmine passed Ruth a cup of tea and put a blue plastic mug of milk down on the table in the office. 'Can he manage a regular mug?'

'He's nearly two,' said Ruth, shivering and wrapping her hands around the teacup to warm them. 'He can manage a cup if I hold it for him.' She put the hot tea down on the table and knelt on the floor next to Sonny, who was playing with a yellow wooden tractor and truck, pushing it along the floor and bumping it against the skirting board. She held the mug for him until he'd drained it.

'Bikbik,' he said, stretching out a hand towards the table, where Jasmine had left a plate of digestives. Ruth opened her bag and handed him a rusk.

Katya, sitting as far as she could from the child, finished the call she was making on her phone and reached for her own coffee. 'All sorted,' she said. 'I got through to your boyfriend's employers. They can tell him you're here when he returns from his delivery run. He'll be able to pick you up in about half an hour. They said he could get a taxi. Does he not have a car?'

'No, he gets to work on his bike,' Ruth said, handing Sonny another rusk. 'And thanks ever so much. I don't know what I'd have done if Sonny and me had been on our own.' She picked the child up and sat him on her lap, where he played happily with the coloured beads she was wearing.

'Any luck with your sister?' From what she'd heard about him, Katya wasn't too hopeful about Colin the boyfriend's chances of finding them somewhere decent to stay.

'She's still not there. I've left her a message to call me.'

'Well,' said Jasmine. 'You're welcome to stay here until you contact her, but I should get back to work. Will you be okay up here?'

'She'll be fine,' said Katya, not looking overjoyed by the prospect of Ruth and Sonny for company. 'We can have a nice chat.'

'I'll watch out for your boyfriend and show him up here when he arrives. What does he look like?'

'He's got light brown hair in a ponytail, and a black leather jacket.'

Pretty much as Katya had imagined him. She wondered if he knew anything about the events at Beedham. Where had he been while the shouting was going on?

Jasmine nodded and headed back downstairs. 'I'll pop up later with something to eat.'

'Thanks,' said Katya. She'd certainly need it. Getting sensible information from Ruth was like pulling teeth. And Ruth was still shivering. 'Not warm yet?' she asked. 'I should have asked Jasmine for a rug.'

'I'm okay,' said Ruth. 'It's just the shock of having to leave the house so suddenly. But it's nice and warm in here. I'll be fine when I've drunk my tea.' She picked up her mug and sipped the tea. 'Do you work here as well?'

'Kind of,' said Katya. 'We're a group of detectives.'

Ruth looked puzzled. 'Like the police? Do you catch criminals?'

'I used to be in the police and since I retired, I have worked with them. But mostly the four of us solve the cases they're not interested in.'

'So do you know what happened at Beedham House?'

About as much as you, love. If Katya had been the one with the police on her doorstep, she'd have found out a lot more by now. Did this girl have no sense of curiosity? 'Well, we know someone died there. We saw the body being carried out.'

'On that trolley thing, in a black bag.'

So she had been watching. 'That's right.'

'Well, then there must be two bodies. They left with another one just like it last night. Colin and me thought it might be stolen stuff they'd found in the house.' She shivered again. 'But if there's dead bodies, I'm not sure I want to go back there. Not with little Sonny and all. But where would we go?' She picked up her phone and tried her sister's number again but with no luck.

Katya hoped she'd get a response soon. 'Let's wait and see what Colin says. You say he has a friend living nearby?'

'In Slough. Quite near the depot where he works. But it's only got the one bedroom and I don't really fancy staying there.'

You might not have a lot of choice unless your sister turns up soon. Best to change the subject. 'You were the one that called the police yesterday?'

She nodded. 'Colin was cross about that, but the police lady said I'd done the right thing.'

Why should that have made Colin cross? Unless he had something to do with the incident. 'What did you tell the police lady?'

'Constable Shafiq, she was called. She was very nice. Sonny liked her too.'

Yes, Katya remembered Annie Shafiq as an efficient, sympathetic type. If she'd not become a detective, she'd have made a good family liaison officer. 'What prompted you to call them? Did you see anyone?'

'I told her all that yesterday.'

'I know, but we want to help, don't we? So tell me again what happened.'

'I heard glass smashing, like someone had broken a window. And then a lot of shouting from the house.'

'Had you seen people there before?'

'We sometimes saw lights. We thought there was squatters, but me and Colin didn't want to know. We don't want any trouble and we're proper renters, Colin says, with a contract and everything.'

'You saw lights in the house? Is the electricity still connected?'

'Dunno, but this was more like candles, or a torch, perhaps. And we'd not seen anything for a few weeks so we thought they'd gone.'

'Until yesterday, when you heard someone break in. Did you see anything?'

'Didn't look outside. There was shouting and I was scared. And then just after I'd called 999 Colin got back home. He was all for going to have a look then we could call the police back and say we'd made a mistake. But I tried to stop him. What if he'd been attacked? And it wasn't long after he got home that the police car came, so it was too late from him to go and look.'

'You said there was shouting. Was it just one person? Shouting at someone in the house, perhaps?'

'I don't know. There was a man's voice and someone banging on the door. There might have been more than one, I don't know.'

'Were there any cars outside the house?'

'I don't think so. Oh, I think I might have heard one.'

'Arriving or leaving?'

'There wasn't a car when the police arrived, so I suppose it must have been leaving.'

'Did you tell DC Shafiq you'd heard a car?'

Ruth shook her head miserably. 'I forgot, and Colin kept shaking his head at me when she asked the questions. Like he didn't want me to say anything. I should have told her, shouldn't I?'

'Probably. But I expect they'll want a statement from you, so you can tell them then.'

'Will I be in trouble?'

They'd probably be annoyed. Katya would have been, but witnesses did forget things. It didn't usually mean they had stuff to hide. 'Doubt it,' she said. 'They'll realise you'd been frightened and weren't thinking clearly.'

Ruth looked relieved. 'I'll write down everything I remember, then if they question me again, I won't miss anything out.'

'Good idea,' said Katya. 'And apart from occasional squatters, you've never seen anyone at the house?'

Ruth shook her head.

'Did you ever go inside?'

She looked horrified by the idea. 'I don't go out much, only when Colin is with me. I go to see Reggie and Peg quite a lot.'

'Reggie and Peg?'

'Mr and Mrs Braddock. They live in the other cottage. They're ever so nice. Peg sometimes makes cakes just for Sonny, and Reggie gives us carrots and stuff from his garden. Colin says I should get him to teach me about gardening, but I don't have much time.'

'You said they'd gone to Tenerife?'

'Yes. I don't like it when there's no one there.'

Katya could understand that. It was an isolated bit of land. Hardly the best place for a young woman and a baby.

She thought she'd probably learnt as much as she was going to from Ruth when the door opened and Jonny came in, followed by a young man with a ponytail. Colin, Katya assumed. He took the baby from Ruth and gave her a peck on the cheek. 'What's going on?' he asked. 'You got yourself turned out of the house? I told you we had to sit tight.'

'It was the police said we had to move out, just for a day or two.' Ruth clung to him and burst into tears. 'They say there's dead bodies in the house,' she whimpered.

'Really?' said Jonny. 'How many?'

Colin frowned. 'I'd better take you to Tony's. He says we can stay on his sofa as long as it's only for tonight.'

'I don't want to go there,' said Ruth. 'I don't trust him and there'd be no room for the baby. He might report us to the social and then they'd put Sonny in care.'

'No one's putting Sonny in care. Don't be stupid.' He grabbed Ruth by the arm. 'Come on, let's get going.'

'Leave her alone,' said Katya, suddenly feeling protective.

Colin scowled at her. 'You stay out of this, Mrs er...'

'I'm Katya Roscoff,' she said. 'Detective sergeant, retired.'

'Retired, huh? Then you'd better mind your own business.'

Ruth struggled to free herself from Colin's grip. 'I'm not going with you.'

'We're wating for Ruth's sister to call her back.'

'That's right,' said Ruth defiantly. 'I'll move in with Joanne.'

'Please yourself,' said Colin. 'Just wish you'd told me that a bit sooner. I've just lost half a day's work. And I'll probably get charged for the taxi.' He looked round at all of them. 'I'll be on my way, then. See ya.' He headed for the door and they heard him stamp down the stairs.

Good riddance, Katya thought. Although he'd left them with a problem. What on earth were they going to do with Ruth and Sonny if Joanne failed to return her calls?

8

Charlie stood at the board, pen in hand. Annie had come in early and had done a good job of organising what was pinned up. It gave the impression that they'd made more progress on the case than they actually had, but once bodies had been discovered, there was a lot of sitting around waiting for reports to arrive. Normal for this kind of case, but it wouldn't stop the nagging from above about lack of progress.

Les arrived with a cardboard tray of coffees and a bag of pastries, which he handed round.

'Right,' said Charlie, choosing an apricot Danish and setting it to one side so as not to spit crumbs at the team. 'First, we've had our senior investigating officer confirmed. It's DCI Paddy Philips. Any of you worked with him before?' Les shook his head; not surprising, since SIOs were rarely sent too far from their own patch.

'I think I met him once,' said Annie. 'But not for a case I was working on.'

'I know him,' said Gary. 'Lazy bugger by all accounts.'

Hardly the way to talk about a senior officer, although Charlie was inclined to agree. 'He's laid back,' she said.

'That's one way of describing him,' said Gary between mouthfuls. 'These are good buns.' He grinned at Les.

'From a little place in town where I stop off for my breakfast.'

'Might try it one day. I usually just go to Starbucks.'

'All freshly baked on the premises,' said Les.

'Could we get back to the case?' said Charlie, tapping her pen on the desk. 'We do have a couple of murders to solve.'

'Will DCI Philips be coming in?' Annie asked.

'He's not shown any sign of it yet,' said Charlie. 'But that's good. It means we get to work the case ourselves. So we'd better make a damn good job of it.' She turned to the board and the pictures of the two bodies. She pointed to the younger and better preserved body. 'Not many details yet, but this guy, according to some stuff they found in his pockets, was Stefan Halliwell. We'll need to confirm that. Les, you can pull everything together later and see if there are any records of him on the system, DNA, fingerprints, et cetera. We'll be able to check dental records if we need further confirmation. We must trace his next of kin as a priority before we release his name.'

'What about the other victim?' Annie asked.

'That's more of a problem. He had nothing on him to identify him. No wallet, so no bank cards. Nothing helpful with a name and address. We might get something useful from the PM, but as Gary pointed out, his shoes could be a good place to start.'

'His shoes?' said Annie. 'Why?'

'It's about all that was left of him,' said Gary. 'Plus they look expensive and handmade. Not too many bespoke cobblers around these days. It should be easy to trace who bought them.'

'There could be enough of his clothes left to do the same,' said Charlie. 'And again, we can check dental records.'

'What about witnesses?' Annie asked.

Was Annie the only one with sensible questions? 'We'll talk again to the couple in the cottage. We'll bring them in separately for that.'

'You think one of them did it?' said Gary. 'I don't think it's likely to be skinny little Ruth. Could be the boyfriend, I suppose.'

'I think Colin the boyfriend sounded quite controlling when I talked to Ruth,' said Annie.

'Doesn't make him a murderer,' said Gary.

'No,' said Charlie, 'but at this stage we shouldn't rule anyone out. Check him out anyway. What about all those people who were standing around when we arrived? Les, you moved them on. Where did they go?'

Les unfolded a piece of paper on which he'd drawn a sketchy map. 'The area around Beedham and the cottages seems very isolated, but at the back of the cottages is a housing estate. It's not accessible to Beedham House by road, but there is a footpath running along the back between the estate and the cottages. People had heard the police siren and came to see what was going on.' He turned over the map. 'I took their names and addresses. They all live on the estate.'

'Good work,' said Charlie. 'I had a call from Dr Yates. The PM is at twelve. I said I'd go – anyone want to come with me?'

Annie's hand shot up.

'You'll barf, love,' Gary warned. 'Bound to.'

'Want a bet?' said Annie.

'Go on then. A round of coffee and a bag of buns.'

'You're on,' said Annie, reaching across to shake his hand.

Was this a sign that they were starting to bond as a team? Gary's snarky remarks were water off a duck's back to Annie. Even Les was opening up a bit. 'Right,' she said. 'Annie and I will head off to the PM. Gary, you and Les get back to the scene and do some house-to-house enquiries around the estate.'

It was a six-mile drive to the mortuary on the far side of Slough. A chance to get to know Annie a little better. 'You've always worked in this area?' Charlie asked.

'I was in Slough until I passed my detective exams.'

'That must have been quite recently. You don't look old enough to have been in the force for very long.'

'I'm twenty-four,' she said. 'I started the PC apprenticeship when I left school. Then two years in uniform, but I've always wanted to be in CID.'

'And this is your first case?'

'Yeah. I was lucky.'

Luckier than the two guys they'd found dead, certainly. But there was nothing wrong with being keen. Charlie had been the same when she was Annie's age, although she'd come in through the graduate programme. 'You cope well with Gary. I hope he hasn't upset you.'

'Nah, you work in Slough, you get a lot worse.'

'You'd not met him before?'

'Never had much to do with the Staines lot.'

'What about Les? It was a big move for him all the way from Tyneside. Any idea why?'

'None at all. Do you want me to ask him?'

'Probably best to leave it a while. Maybe he'll tell us himself when he knows us better.'

They arrived at the hospital and Charlie signalled to turn into the car park.

'Don't try to get in here,' said Annie. 'It's almost impossible to find a parking space even if you work here. I'll show you a way round the back. I've got a mate who works in the refuse department. He'll let us park there for nothing and it's not far from the mortuary entrance.'

'You've got some useful mates,' said Charlie, laughing. 'Someone to stop the water dripping into our office, help with hospital parking.'

'I was at school in Slough. Met a load of useful people.'

'I thought you came from Solihull.'

'We moved here when I was twelve. Dad came to Slough to join his cousin, who runs a taxi company.'

Useful to know. 'So why the police?'

Annie shrugged. 'Didn't want to be a taxi driver or move back to Solihull, where the whole family wanted to marry me off.'

9

'That was interesting,' said Annie as she climbed into Charlie's car after the post-mortem.

'Very,' said Charlie. 'We'll go through the report in detail when Yates sends it through, but what did you pick up from it?'

'I was more interested in the DNA result than the actual PM. That the two victims are related.'

Charlie had been struck by that as well. It was a familial DNA match, suggesting that the two victims might have been cousins. The earlier victim, a male of about sixty years of age, had been dead for around five years. A cracked skull and vertebral fractures suggested he'd been beaten to death. He'd been put in the trunk after his death, but Yates was unable to say whether or not the trunk had been in the house for five years or if it had been transported there at a later date. That seemed unlikely to Charlie, but they needed to find out how long the house had been empty.

The second victim had been smothered and had died only two or three hours before his body was discovered. They had not yet confirmed that this was Stefan Halliwell, and they should do this as a priority. They needed to inform the next of kin as soon as possible, and certainly before the media got wind of who he was. Once they had done that, and knowing they were related, identifying the earlier victim would be a lot easier.

They'd watched as Yates removed the first victim's shoes. 'See that?' Yates had said, pointing at the right foot and easing the toes apart with a pair of tweezers. 'He's been shot in the foot.'

'Can you tell when?' Charlie had asked.

'This was a while ago. Nothing to do with his death. There's evidence of bone regrowth so I should think we're looking at several months before he died. It's probably why he was wearing handmade shoes.'

Charlie took photos of the man's bare feet and the shoes, including a label stitched to the inside with the name of the maker, Walter Gibbins. She sent them to Les, suggesting that once he and Gary had finished the house-to-house, he should try to find out more about the shoes and who they'd been made for.

'So,' said Annie, looking thoughtful. 'We've got two victims who were related to each other but who died about five years apart. Both were murdered, but not in the same way, and more than likely not in the same place. Do you think the message on the trunk means anything?'

'A message left by the killer? I really don't know. We should check the CSI notes and see if they've any idea when it was written.'

'It might help to know if it's a quote from somewhere.'

'It should be easy enough to find out. You can Google it after our debrief session.'

The traffic was heavy as they drove back to the station. Once off the relief road, Charlie pulled into a petrol station. She handed Annie two twenty-pound notes. 'Jump out and stock up with sandwiches. It must be way past lunchtime. Get some crisps and chocolate as well.'

ONCE BACK IN THE OFFICE, they found Gary and Les had returned before them and both were staring into computer screens. Annie put her bag of food down on the table. 'Lunch,' she said.

Gary jumped up and tipped out the contents of the bag. 'Anyone mind if I grab the cheese?'

Les looked up from his computer screen. 'What's left?'

Gary studied the packaging. 'Er, cheese. Bit of a boring selection, Annie.'

'It's all that was left.'

'Nothing wrong with cheese,' said Les. 'After that house-to-house I really don't mind what I eat.' He smiled nervously at them. 'I think I've found something. We might have an ID, boss. Thanks to the photos you sent.'

'That was the easy bit,' said Charlie. 'Sounds like you're the one that did the research. Could be the first real breakthrough in the case.' Hoping to boost his confidence, Charlie crossed the room and peered over his shoulder at his computer screen and an email he was reading from Walter Gibbins, maker of bespoke shoes.

'I sent him the photos of the victim's shoes and asked him to check his records. It must be a quiet day for bespoke footwear makers. He replied within half an hour. He made a pair like these five and a half years ago for a Laurence Trubshaw.'

'Wouldn't they have made them for a lot of customers?' Gary asked.

'Probably,' said Les. 'But not many would have been made for a deformed foot. Not like this one.'

Gary joined them and stared at the picture. 'That looks painful,' he said, taking a bite of his sandwich.

'Gunshot wound, according to Yates,' said Annie.

'Shot himself in the foot, did he?' said Gary with a snort of laughter.

'Not really funny,' said Annie. 'And by the way, you owe us a round of coffees. Mine's a double shot caramel latte with extra cream.'

'You managed not to throw up then? She's not lying, is she, boss?'

Charlie shook her head and smiled. 'I'll have an extra-large cappuccino. And don't forget the buns.'

'I did work experience in a mortuary,' said Annie. 'I knew I could handle it.'

'You might have said.'

'And risk a free coffee?'

'Back to work,' said Charlie. 'Well done, Les. Keep going and see what you can find out about Mr Trubshaw. Annie, start a task list.' She threw her a marker pen and Annie caught it and started a bullet point list, adding *Research Laurence Trubshaw* at the top.

'Anything from the house-to-house?' Charlie asked.

'Nothing interesting. We spoke to people who'd come out to watch what was going on. They'd heard the sirens and decided to take a look. Nobody knew anything much about Beedham House. One bloke said he walked his dog there sometimes but had never seen anything, or anyone. One or two of them had spoken to the people in the cottages but only to say good morning now and then. None of them knew them well.'

'Right,' said Charlie. 'We might go round again when we've confirmed the identity of both victims. The names might jog some memories. Gary, see what you can find out about Stefan Halliwell, who according to the DNA is related to the other victim.'

Annie made a note of that. 'What do you want me to do, boss?'

'Keep tabs on Ruth Richards and Colin Sugden. Something doesn't feel right there. You got on well with Richards, so as soon as we know where they're staying, go and have a chat with her, but try to choose a time when Sugden's not around. Find out when the couple in the other cottage are getting back and talk to them as well. And it would be really helpful if you could keep the crime board tidy. The DCI's dropping in this afternoon for an update and he'll be leading a press conference.'

10

Ivo drove the van up a long drive and parked outside a red brick house. Harold, sensing this could mean a walk, started tugging at his harness. 'Better wait here,' Ivo told him. 'There might be a dog.' He was careful when visiting clients with dogs. Most people were glad to see Ivo when they needed something fixing, but their dogs often had other ideas and could be quite unfriendly. Ivo preferred to steer clear of any kind of dog animosity. He climbed out of the van as the front door opened, revealing a woman with white hair and, as he'd feared, a dog. A very large dog. He left the van window open a crack and got out his tools, leaving Harold watching with a downcast expression from the driver's seat.

The woman stepped forward and shook Ivo's hand. 'You're very welcome,' she said. 'I was so relieved to come across your flyer. You've no idea how hard it's been to find anyone to do the work. We used to have a lovely man, Mr Wakefield, do you know him? He retired a few months ago.'

Ivo had heard of Mr Wakefield. He'd picked up a lot of work since his retirement.

'I'm Diana,' she said, handing him a list. *A day's work, possibly two,* Ivo thought as he read it. 'Perhaps you could have a look round and you can give me a quote. It's mostly small stuff, but things mount up, don't they?'

There was a gate catch that needed attention and some gutters to clear, as well as a long list of small repairs inside the house. Ivo reached for a torch. It was nearly five o'clock and getting dark. 'I'll take a look outside first,' he said.

'Lovely,' she said. 'Then come in for a cup of tea to warm you up before you look round the rest of the house. The kitchen's on the left as you come through the door. Oh, and bring your poor dog with you. Meg is very friendly.'

Ivo shone his torch up at the gutters. He'd need a long-handled brush and a ladder. He made a note of that and then looked at the gate between the drive and the garden. A simple matter of a new catch. He added it to his list, then returned to the van to let Harold out, just as a boy on a bicycle skidded into the drive, narrowly missing the open door of the van. He dismounted and dropped the bike onto the gravel. 'Oops,' he said. 'Don't usually get anyone parking here. Are you a burglar casing the joint with your torch? You'd better watch out. My mum's a copper.'

Ivo laughed. 'I'm just the handyman. Doing an estimate for your mum. She's invited me in for a cup of tea, so she'll be able to vouch for me.'

'Elderly lady with a colourful jumper?'

Ivo nodded.

'That's my gran. Mum won't be home for ages. She's got a couple of murders to solve.'

'She really is in the police? You weren't just trying to frighten me away in case I was a burglar?'

'She really is. But come in. Gran's probably made a cake.'

'She said it would be okay to bring Harold in,' said Ivo. 'I was a bit worried about your dog. She's very large.'

'She is, but soppy as anything. Yeah, bring Harold in. We can have a doggy party.'

Ivo opened the van door and put Harold on his lead, still wary about taking him into the house. He needn't have worried though. As they went into the kitchen, Meg opened one eye but stayed where she was, in an enormous dog basket by an Aga. She spotted Harold and lazily wagged her tail. Harold gave her a cautious sniff but then decided a table laden with home-made cakes was a lot more interesting.

'Come and sit down,' said Diana. 'I see you've met Kai.'

'He thought I might be a burglar,' said Ivo, laughing. 'Nearly crashed into the van with his bike.'

Kai was starting to remove his coat. A strange one with embroidery and a thick fur lining. Ivo had never seen one like it before.

'Not so fast, young man,' said his grandmother. 'Go and put your bike away properly or Ivo will probably run it over on his way out.'

'Wish he would,' said Kai. 'I hate the thing. Can't wait until I can drive.' He flounced out, sighing loudly.

Diana handed Ivo a cup of tea and pushed the plate of cakes in his direction. Harold sidled closer and gave him one of his poor starving dog looks. Ivo patted him on the head. 'Not for you,' he said.

'I can give him a Bonio,' Diana offered.

'He's fine. If he ate everywhere I was working, he'd be enormous. Not that I don't like big dogs,' he added, not meaning to offend Meg, who was enormous because that was the kind of dog she was. Not from overeating.

Kai returned and stripped off his coat. He sat down next to Ivo and grabbed a cake.

'How was school, darling?' Diana asked. 'Did you survive another day without being thrown out?'

'They'll let me back tomorrow as long as I don't wear purple socks.'

'Kai doesn't get on with the uniform rules,' Diana explained.

'They don't actually have a rule about sock colours. Well, they do. It says *no white socks*. Doesn't mention purple ones. It doesn't mention green, either. I might try those tomorrow.' He picked up a second cake. 'What time's supper?'

'Eightish? But we won't wait for your mother. She'll probably be working late.'

'The two murders?' Ivo asked.

'You know about those?'

'Kai told me just now.'

'I'm not sure you should be gossiping about her work, Kai. You don't want her to get into trouble, do you?'

'It'll be all over the internet soon. It's not like she tells us any details.'

Ivo picked up the list of jobs Diana had given him. 'I'd better be on my way. I'll email you a quote tonight.'

'Will you be able to do it soon?'

'Probably the end of the week. Do you mind if I come on Saturday?'

'As long as you can put up with the teenage horror here.'

'No problem.' He finished his cake and he and Harold returned to the van. This was going to be interesting. Plenty of work here, and a chance to pick up hints about a double murder case. Katya had thought there were two bodies. He'd be able to tell her she was right. Did detectives work on Saturdays? Probably, if it was a big case, but he might just get to meet one of the detectives on the case and maybe pick up some useful information about it.

11

Charlie walked Detective Chief Inspector Philips to his car with gritted teeth. He'd barely looked at the evidence or the case notes, and he'd swanned into the press conference with a look of having taken charge and an assurance that the whole case would be done and dusted in days, if not hours.

He climbed into his car and pressed a button to open the window. 'Send all those notes through to me at the hub,' he said. 'And your action plans at the start of each day.'

Did he not realise how few admin staff they had? Either Les or Annie would have to collate it all, and she could really do with them following up leads, not typing notes.

'Keep me updated with progress.' He closed the window and drove off.

Charlie stormed up to the office, where she broke the news that Annie and Les were going to have extra paperwork. 'He's not going to be here, where he can see for himself what's going on,' she told them.

'It's not a problem, boss,' said Annie. 'Les and I can get it done before we go home.'

'No, let him wait. You've worked quite hard enough for one day. Get off home, all of you. We'll make an early start tomorrow.'

'Anyone fancy a drink?' Gary asked.

It wasn't a bad idea. A bonding session away from the office. 'A quick one, then. My mum will have cooked a meal and I need to make sure my son has done his homework.'

'We eat late,' said Annie. 'So my dad and brother can stoke up before the evening taxi dash from the pubs.'

'Les?'

'Nowhere special to be,' said Les.

'The Queen Vic at the end of the road suit everyone?' Gary asked.

'I'LL GET THEM,' said Gary as they found an empty table. 'What would you all like?'

Charlie settled for a shandy, Annie for a bitter lemon and Les for a pint of Guinness. She and Annie had to drive home and she assumed Gary had to as well, but to her surprise, when he arrived back at the table with a tray, she saw that he'd ordered himself a pint of best and a double whiskey chaser. She couldn't stop herself from commenting. 'Not driving after that, I hope?' She really didn't want one of her team on a drink drive charge.

'Nah,' said Gary. 'I live here.'

'In the town?' Annie asked.

'No, right here. I've got a room upstairs.'

'You live in a pub?' said Les. 'On your own?'

'Lived here since the wife chucked me out six months ago. That's why I jumped at the chance of a job here. The commute to Staines was a pain in the bum. Miss the kiddies, though. Still,' he added, downing three quarters of his pint in a single gulp, 'it was my own fault.'

'Why?' asked Annie, staring at him wide-eyed.

'Sleeping with the duty solicitor, wasn't I? There was gossip at the nick and a spotty-faced uniform PC decided my wife needed to know.'

'But why move here?' Annie wasn't going to let this go.

'Mate of mine owns the pub, and it got me out of the way of two women doing their best to scratch each other's eyes out.'

'Are you still seeing the duty solicitor?' asked Les.

'No. It all got a bit heavy. Janine seemed to think that Karen throwing me out meant a happy ever after as far as she and I were concerned.'

Gary's personal life was even messier than Charlie's. In fact, living with her mother and son seemed positively respectable in comparison. She decided not to go into details of her relationship with Kai's father right now.

'But you see your kids?' Les asked.

'Every other Sunday, plus a week in school holidays.'

'How old are they?' Charlie asked, with a sudden feeling of sympathy for Gary. There'd never been any question of custody over Kai. She and Solomon had always had a civilised relationship. Kai enjoyed spending time with his father and made his own decisions about when he did it.

'Libby's ten and Josie's eight. One day I'll get a place where they can have their own rooms and we can negotiate better access arrangements.' He drained his pint and took a swig of the chaser. 'Enough about me. Tell me, boss, why did the press conference make you so snarky?'

'I wasn't snarky, I was bloody furious. You realise Philips' appeal for information from the public is going to bring every nutter in a fifty-mile radius out of the woodwork? In my last job we had a nutjob team. I don't see anything like that here.'

'You could refer them to the DCI,' suggested Les.

'I wish,' said Charlie. 'He'd be down on us like a ton of bricks, saying we weren't up to the job and we'd lose the case to a load of suited wankers from Oxford.'

'That's good, isn't it?' said Annie. 'The DCI being so far away, I mean, not the suited wankers. It leaves you in charge, doesn't it? And I'm sure we can handle a few false confessions.'

Annie was right. There were advantages to being out on their own. As long as they didn't mess it up. 'We'll support you all the way,' said Les. 'Annie, how about we get in at six tomorrow and get the paperwork done and off to the DCI?'

'I'd be up for that,' said Annie. 'And we can do the same with these daily plans he wants.'

A six a.m. time stamp should impress DCI Philips. Charlie was warming to her team. 'Okay, strategy meeting at seven tomorrow morning. Shall I bring breakfast?'

'I can do that,' said Les. 'I pass this great café on my way in.'

'Do they do bacon and egg rolls?' Gary asked.

'The size of dinner plates, well, maybe not quite, but they keep you going for a while.'

'Four of those, then,' said Charlie. 'And large coffees all round.' She was unsure of his financial circumstances. A newly appointed DC's salary wasn't huge. Did he have a family to support? She found a couple of twenty-pound notes and handed them to him. 'Will that cover it?'

Les nodded and put the notes in his pocket.

'There'll be an online menu,' said Annie. 'We can work out what we all owe you. Perhaps set up a kitty if we're going to do it regularly. What's the place called? I'll check it out this evening.'

'It's called *Jasmine's,*' said Les. 'A great little place between the station and the shops.'

'Do you live near there?' Charlie asked. Rents in town were steep.

'I rent a bedsit near the arches.'

'You were lucky to find that,' said Annie.

Les shrugged. 'Found it through a... contact,' he said.

Probably best not to pry into his *contacts*. Charlie reached for her coat. 'I'd better get going. Not wanting to sound like a bossy mother hen, I suggest you all get a good night's sleep. We've plenty to do in the morning.' She left and strolled back to the police station car park, wondering what they were saying about her. But she was the boss, and it was their right to discuss her behind her back. She'd done it often enough herself before her promotion. She'd soon know if they were on her side or not.

12

Charlie kicked off her shoes and rubbed her tired feet.

'Half an hour,' her mother called from the kitchen. 'Time for a shower before we eat.'

Her mum was right. Charlie exuded the sweaty rankness of exhaustion. The metallic smell of the mortuary still hung in her nostrils and her hands still carried a whiff of the latex gloves she had peeled off earlier. Add to that the beery smell of the pub and she was probably about as unpleasant as she could get. But now she could take time out for scented shower gel, the caress of freshly laundered towels and a meal of the roast chicken currently sending wafts of deliciousness in her direction. When had she last eaten? Sometime around three that afternoon, when Annie had bought sandwiches at the petrol station after the PM. A miserable selection, all that was left after the lunchtime rush; tired slices of cheese in dried-up white bread that tasted of very little. But the team had worked on, processing the evidence, staring at the photos, endlessly searching online. The press conference was the final straw after a long day of fruitless searching. Twenty-four hours in and the case was going nowhere. They were all exhausted. But time in the pub had helped them unwind and then they all went home to get a good night's sleep. Hopefully they'd return refreshed the next day.

Thank God for home and family. A warm haven after the chill of the murder scene and the less than welcoming building that housed her office. A numbness had overtaken all of them. A necessary lack of emotion as people had calmly set about the tasks that were part of a familiar routine; no time for feelings, it was all too raw for that. Nightmares might come later, but for the last two days it had been the quiet voices of the CSI team, a rustle of white suits, the click of a camera, the sound of footsteps on stepping plates. Each of them with their own job to do, with their own way of coping, respectful of lives taken too soon. Respectful but draining.

HER SHOWER FINISHED, Charlie ambled downstairs, twisting her still-damp hair, fixing it into an untidy knot. She sank into an armchair and hoped the rest of the team were also relaxing. Annie lived with a big family, plenty of noise and laughter. In her imagination Charlie pictured a table groaning with food, cooked, Annie had told them, by her mother and a couple of aunties. Theirs was a traditional family. Stay at home women, the men out at work driving taxis at all hours. So where did Annie fit in? Were they proud of their ambitious daughter? Why wouldn't they be? Charlie really should stop making assumptions about people. She'd been quite wrong about Gary. She'd assumed he had a wife and kids but she'd forgotten the stresses of police life. She wondered if he was lonely. It must be bleak, only seeing his daughters at set times. Everything had to be organised in advance. They couldn't suddenly go out for a romp in the park or takeaway pizza just because they felt like it. She'd never wanted marriage herself. Even with a baby on the way, she'd been determined to manage it her way, ignore convention and throw rulebooks out of the window. But she'd been lucky. Her parents had always supported her decisions. After Charlie had delivered the news of her impending motherhood, Diana took Harrod's by storm and stocked up on baby clothes. Charlie smiled at the recollection. Perhaps that was where Kai got his love of clothes from. Her father had set up a trust fund to pay for the child's education. Neither parent had expressed anything other than excitement at the prospect of being grandparents. There was no question of marrying Kai's father. Solomon Powell was attractive, charismatic even, but settling down had never crossed his mind. Forcing him to do so would have been misery for all of them. But strangely, Sol had turned out to be a good father. Not in a conventional way – he'd never changed a nappy, mopped up puréed carrots or read a bedtime story. But he would arrive like a whirlwind and whisk Kai off for a few days to, as he put it, teach him about the world. By the time he was twelve, Kai had washed an elephant in Thailand, learned to snowboard in the Swiss alps, met well-known TV chefs and been to dinner at St James's Palace. When he was ten, Sol had signed him up for an audition for the annual Christmas TV advert for a well-known department store. An audition at which Kai trumped every other candidate, and for a few short weeks he appeared several times a night on prime-time TV, breaking the nation's hearts as the *little boy that Santa forgot*. No wonder he resented every minute he was forced to spend in school, killing time until he could start his course in performing arts.

Her thoughts turned to Les. She knew a lot about Annie, simply because Annie was the sort who happily babbled on about her home life. No hang-ups and nothing to hide. She was uncomplicated and outgoing. Gary was outspoken and brash, but Charlie was beginning to feel that his heart might be in the right place and in a difficult situation, he'd be a steady presence. And in spite of his tactlessness, he'd reached out to Les. They'd worked well together, bonded over a dull house-to-house and exchanged a couple of tasteless jokes. Gallows humour. A way to cope. She might have misjudged Gary. He was her sergeant and as such she should give him more responsibility. She had a feeling he'd respond well to it. But Les left her puzzled. Tyneside, where he'd worked previously, was a long way away. The police grapevine didn't extend that far. It was too far for even the most avid of the gossip-mongers. Charlie had read his transfer notes, of course she had, but they contained nothing helpful. Les had passed his detective exams a year ago. He'd passed his latest medical and she was not given any information about earlier ones. But something had halted his career. Two years ago he'd been a uniformed Tyneside constable, but since then there was no record of him doing anything. Had he been ill? Cancer, perhaps, or had he been injured in the line of duty? Something had forced him to make a new start three hundred miles away from his previous post, in a town where he lived on his own in a bedsit. Charlie's curiosity was piqued, but HR hadn't flagged anything she should know about and were cagey about personal details. Rightly, she supposed. But it didn't make it any easier to get to know him. She just had to hope that as time went on, he would trust her enough to tell her a little of his past.

The thump of teenage music from the room above, which Charlie had barely noticed until it stopped, was followed by the sound of her son bounding downstairs. Arriving in the lounge, he ruffled the dog's fur and smiled. 'Tough day?'

Charlie nodded. 'Draining,' she said. 'Murder enquiries are never fun.'

'Is it dangerous at a murder scene?' Kai was carefree and confident like his father. It didn't stop his anxiety about what she did for a living.

She gave him a reassuring hug. 'Not for us. By the time we get there, the response team have checked the area and secured it. I'm quite safe,' she promised.

'I suppose you get used to it, seeing dead bodies.'

'Never,' she said. 'You just get better at handling it.'

'But you'll catch the person who did it?'

She would. Of that she was determined. Not only for the bereaved, but for herself and her team who'd been sidelined. This was their chance to get themselves noticed and, dare she hope, even respected by the smarmy, pleased with themselves tribe at the crime hub.

13

Katya was sitting in *Jasmine's* chatting to Jonny, both of them having just finished bowls of porridge. 'Nothing like it for a cold day,' Katya commented.

Jonny agreed with her and, looking round at the busy café, so did quite a few other people.

The door opened, bringing in a blast of cold air and a familiar figure. Someone Katya had not seen for a while. Teddy Strang, charismatic but unscrupulous journalist and friend of the Breakfast Club Detectives. Katya waved to him. 'Come and join us,' she said, borrowing a chair from a neighbouring table whose occupants had finished eating and were heading off to work.

'I was hoping to find you here,' said Teddy, hanging his scarf over the back of the chair and stripping off a full-length tweed overcoat.

'I hope you're not after a story. Not much going on right now, is there, Jonny?'

Jonny nodded. 'Nothing since the poisoned mushrooms. We're feeling a bit out of touch with local criminal activity since Lugs left.'

'It's frustrating,' said Katya. 'We know something's going on. At least two bodies have been found at Beedham. Ivo and I went to take a look at the crime scene and talked to a neighbour who saw the first one being taken away. And we watched while they took the other. There's been no info on whether or not they were murdered. A detective sergeant sent us on our way. A bit abrupt, I thought. He took our names but didn't seem to register the fact that I used to be one of them. That would never have happened with Lugs.'

'I might be able to help,' said Teddy. 'There was a press conference yesterday evening. Short notice and not well attended. I was lucky to hear about it.'

'Late in the day, as well,' said Katya. 'Aren't they usually in the morning?'

'It was led by DCI Philips. He's the senior investigating officer. Do you know him?'

'I think we've met,' said Katya. 'But as I remember, he's more one for sitting behind a desk and getting other people to do the work.'

'That's the impression I got. I gather he was just visiting the operational team here in town. He probably crammed in a quick presser at the end of the day before buggering off back to Oxford.'

'Were the rest of the team there?' Jonny asked. 'I'm interested to meet whoever it is that's taken over from Lugs.'

'That would be DI Hannington,' said Teddy. 'And there was a DS Trotter.'

'That's the sergeant Ivo and I met at the scene. I didn't warm to him.'

'Don't blame you,' said Teddy. 'He gave the impression the whole case was one big yawn.'

'The new DI?' said Jonny. 'What was he like?'

'She,' corrected Teddy. 'Good-looking woman in her thirties. Snappy dresser. Looked like an ambitious type.'

'How can you tell?' Katya asked.

Teddy tapped the side of his nose. 'One gets to recognise them. But I'm joking. I've met her before. DI Hannington now, but she was a sergeant when we met, working a case in Hastings. She was a bit of a hero who stopped a murderer hurling himself off the edge of a cliff.'

'Did you say her name was Hannington?' Jonny asked.

'Charlotte Hannington, known as Charlie.'

'I think I met her son the other day. A lad of fifteen or sixteen. Arty-looking, bit of an extrovert. He did say his mum was in the police.'

'Are you likely to see him again?' Katya asked. 'He could be a useful contact. Extrovert teenagers probably aren't averse to dropping bits of gossip now and then. A bit like journalists,' she added, with a meaningful look in Teddy's direction.

'He told me he was new to the area and hadn't got much of a social life yet. I suggested he might pop in and talk to Jasmine.'

'What about?' Jasmine caught the end of the conversation as she came to refill their coffee cups.

'This young man I met the other day,' said Jonny. 'I thought you might be able to give him some work. He's a cheery, outgoing type and I know your turnover of student waiting staff is rapid.'

'I could probably give him a couple of early mornings, as long as he's better at getting out of bed than most teenagers.'

'Let's hope he turns up, then,' said Katya. 'We might pick up all kinds of interesting stuff about the DI. But that's not why you're here, is it, Teddy?'

'No. I'm here to give you the lowdown on the murder cases.'

Jasmine looked around. The café was emptying as people left for work. She passed Teddy's order to her assistant, who was handling what was left of the customers, and pulled up another chair. 'Sounds interesting,' she said. 'I'll join you.'

'Great,' said Teddy. 'I don't suppose Ivo's around, is he? We'd have the full team then.'

'He'll be here later to fit a draught thingy round the door. I'll make notes and pass it all on to him.'

'Okay,' said Teddy, reaching into his bag for an iPad. 'I recorded the whole conference and typed it up as notes last night.'

'Did I mishear?' asked Katya. 'Or did you say murder cases, plural? So both bodies were murder victims?'

'You don't miss a thing, do you? Yes. There were two bodies found. One was a forty-five-year-old man initially identified by stuff in his pockets. The next of kin has been informed, but there has been no formal identification of the body. They are withholding the name until that happens.'

'Why the wait?' Katya asked.

'They didn't give any details, but it's my guess it's because the next of kin doesn't live locally, someone who has a fair distance to travel. They'd keep quiet about who it is and when they are likely to arrive. I guess that's to stop the likes of myself hounding them for an inside story. There were no details about the other victim except that he was older. But, and this is very interesting, he is believed to have been dead for about five years. The victims were both discovered at Beedham House. The older of the two was hidden in a locked trunk. The house has been unoccupied for a long time. The DCI didn't say how long. He did say that any members of the public with information about the two victims or the house itself should contact DI Hannington and her team. That's where I thought you lot might find a way in. It sounds as if they don't have too much information right now. The police don't hold press conferences for fun. They're usually after information they've failed to find themselves. So...'

Katya was ahead of him. 'There'll be things for us to do.'

Teddy nodded.

'We need a plan,' said Katya, looking at her watch. 'Meeting in half an hour? Okay with you, Jasmine?'

'Fine. I'm well-staffed today. I'll just sort out someone to handle the lunches.'

'Shall I give Ivo a call?' Jonny asked.

Katya nodded. 'We all need to be there.'

'I'll love you and leave you,' said Teddy, gulping down his coffee. 'Let me know if there's any help you need.'

14

'This is exciting,' said Ivo as he settled Harold under the table. 'A new case. Have the police asked us to help again?'

'Not exactly,' said Katya. 'They've asked for the public to come forward with information.'

'But not us specifically,' said Jonny. 'There could be people queueing up to tell them stuff.'

'Most of it useless, take my word for it. I've experienced it first-hand. That and people confessing.'

'Isn't that good? If someone confesses?' Ivo scratched his head.

'Only if they've done it,' said Katya. 'And those that freely offer themselves are rarely the guilty ones.'

'You mean there are people who confess to crimes they've not committed?'

'Always. You're investigating a murder and there will be queues of people saying they did it.'

'Why?' Jonny asked.

'No idea. I suppose it makes them feel important.'

'So,' said Jasmine, handing round a plate of biscuits. 'We're going to look for information and then hand it over to the police.'

'That's right.'

'Won't they just accuse us of interfering?'

'Not if it leads to an arrest. They'll be extremely grateful and might contract us again in the future.'

'Won't that lead to a lot of duplicated enquiries?'

'There is a danger of that. We need to make sure that our searches go deeper than just finding surface evidence. We're well placed to do that. We're all local and the new police team is not. We've got some useful contacts already. Why do you think I was keen for Ruth to come here?'

Ivo and Jonny looked blank.

'So she would start trusting us,' Jasmine said.

'Exactly,' said Katya. 'Now she's made contact with her sister and freed herself from that Colin bloke, she'll chat to us in a way she never would with the police and she's the closest we've got to a witness.' She walked over to the board, picked up a pen and drew an enormous question mark. 'One body identified,' she said. 'That name will be released as soon as the next of kin has formally confirmed it. We need to find out who the John Doe is.'

'John Doe?' Ivo asked. 'I thought they didn't give the name of the second victim.'

'That's what they call an unknown victim,' said Jasmine.

'Teddy picked up a lot from the press conference that we can build on. I've printed up the notes he made.' Katya passed each of them a copy.

Jonny put on his glasses to read the notes. 'One killed recently, the other five years ago. And they were related to each other. Do you suppose the killings are connected?'

'I'm guessing that's what the police are working on. It's unlikely to be a coincidence. They'll be checking missing persons lists and all the other guy's family to see if there's anything that links them. They'll be questioning relatives and business contacts. As soon as they release names we need to go in a different direction. Jonny, you've got business contacts, see if there's any gossip about who they might be. Jasmine, you can check out their online presence. Things never disappear from the internet, so even after five years there might be stuff about a man who suddenly went missing.'

Jasmine made a note of it. 'It might be worth checking out missing people sites. It's possible family members posted there if they think the police haven't taken a missing person report seriously.'

'I think the crime scene itself is interesting,' said Jonny. 'I went to Beedham House once a long time ago. I'll try to remember why and see what I can dig up about it. There must be a reason why both victims were found there.'

'Plenty of repairs needed,' said Katya. 'Ivo, have you done any work around there?'

'I don't think so, but I'll check my records. The two cottages sound like the sort of places that might have needed small repairs.' He read the page of notes again. 'DI Hannington,' he said. 'Lugs' replacement?'

Katya nodded.

'I've just done a quote for a woman called Hannington, who lives a few miles out of town in a big farmhouse. She wanted her gutters cleaned and some stuff inside the house fixed as well. I assume it's the same family. She said her daughter was in the police.'

'Was there a teenage boy at the house?' Jonny asked.

'Kai,' said Ivo. 'I nearly knocked him off his bike. Yes, I remember. They were going to eat late because his mum was working on two murders. And I'm going back there on Saturday to do the work.'

'Excellent,' said Katya. 'I don't suppose the DI will be there. Murder cases usually mean working all hours. But see what you can glean from the mother.'

'Will do,' said Ivo. 'She was the hospitable type, so I'll get tea and biscuits. And it was an old house. There will be plenty more work there.'

'Jonny, did you say Kai Hannington might be dropping in here looking for work?'

'I did suggest it,' said Jonny.

'Jasmine,' said Katya. 'If he does, can you find something for him to do?'

Jasmine nodded. 'When Jonny mentioned it, I'd thought waiting tables, but maybe he'd be better in the kitchen, washing up with Jonny. Probably better for chatting.'

A pleasing meeting. They'd got off to a good start. Put it all together efficiently and quickly and with any luck, Katya would find herself with a police contract in no time.

15

Charlie had slept well and arrived at work refreshed and ready to take the investigation wherever it led them. Annie was on her own in the office. She clicked her mouse and looked up from her computer, grinning at Charlie. 'Paperwork's all done and sent off to the DCI,' she said. 'I told him we'd send the action plan as soon as we've finished our meeting.'

'Good work,' said Charlie, laughing. 'He'll probably read them both at the same time. I don't suppose he's at his desk much before ten o'clock.'

'I didn't know if I should flag it as urgent, but I decided not to. I thought it made us look too anxious.'

'A good decision, I think. We want to impress him but without looking like we're trying too hard.' She looked around at Les' empty desk. 'I thought Les was going to be in early to help you.'

'He was here. He's gone to get breakfast. *Jasmine's* doesn't open until seven.'

'I didn't think of that. I'm sorry he's had to go out again.'

'I don't think he minded. He seems quite anxious to show he's part of the team. You know, willing to do his bit, however humble.'

'Has he talked to you at all about what he was doing before he came here?'

'Not a word. I think he's got a secret past of some kind, but he's not going to let on to me about it. Actually, I think he's more likely to talk to Gary.'

Charlie nodded. 'You could be right. Strange, though. Gary's not exactly the tactful, sympathetic listener type, is he?'

Annie giggled. 'He told me he says it as it is. I'd call it jumping in with both feet, but it takes all sorts, I suppose. And Les does seem quite comfortable with him, in spite of his remarks when they first met.'

'Perhaps it's a bloke thing,' said Charlie.

'What's a bloke thing?' Gary had pushed the door open with his foot and overheard the end of their conversation. He put a cardboard tray of coffee cups down on Annie's desk and held the door open for Les, who was carrying bags of breakfast rolls.

'Foot in mouth syndrome,' said Annie. 'Like implying that I'm some kind of coolie from darkest India.'

'And that offended you?'

'It was highly offensive, but I'm used to it. I can handle remarks like that.'

Gary shrugged and helped himself to a bacon roll, passing the bag to Annie. 'All context, innit?'

This was a minefield. Charlie's first time leading a team and she was having trouble enforcing the boundaries. Where did harmless banter run into political correctness? She decided to park that for the moment. Plenty of time for a discussion once they'd got to know each other better. And right now they had a case to solve. She picked a roll out of the bag and took a bite of it. 'Okay,' she said, moving to the incident board. 'Gather round. We need to plan our day.' She finished her roll and scrunched up the bag, throwing it into the bin that was on the other side of the office.

'Good shot, boss,' said Gary. 'For a girl.'

He was standing closer to the bin, threw his own bag and missed.

'Sun in my eyes,' he said, watching Annie and Les, whose bags both hit their target.

'I was captain of the netball team at school,' said Annie. 'What about you, Les? Do you throw things a lot? Basketball, perhaps?'

Les looked uncomfortable and busied himself finding notebooks and pencils.

Charlie stood by the crime board and admired Annie's work. It looked efficient and businesslike. All it lacked was suspects, along with a motive. 'Right,' she said. 'Let's see what we can add and start putting a scenario together. Annie, you were going to look into the message on the trunk.'

Annie tapped the photo Charlie had taken of the message. *If You Seek Revenge You Should Dig Two Graves.*

'It's a quote generally attributed to Confucius. It should end, *one for yourself.*'

'All a bit airy fairy if you ask me,' said Gary. 'What the hell are we supposed to make of it? Do we even know if it's connected to either murder?'

'Are we looking at a revenge killing?' Les asked.

'More like revenge for revenge,' said Gary. 'Makes my head spin.'

He wasn't wrong. Charlie didn't want them to be sidetracked by something that could turn out to be irrelevant. 'Anything useful in the CSI report?'

'It's recent,' said Annie, scanning the report. 'Scratched with a sharp point. A lino cutting tool or an industrial stitch unpicker. Oh, and they think the writer might have been left-handed.'

'Well, that narrows it down,' said Gary. 'All we need to do is look for a left-handed print maker.'

'Or a leather worker?' Les suggested.

'We'll keep that in mind. It might be relevant once we know a bit more about the victims. Les, remind us what you got from the shoemaker.'

Les opened the notes app on his phone. 'I got them to check their records. They made the shoes for a man called Laurence Trubshaw in 2018.'

'Lasted well,' Gary commented. 'I've never worn a pair of shoes for that long.'

'It's only six years,' said Annie. 'Perhaps you need to buy better quality shoes.'

'Yeah, right. On a DS salary and the Child Support Agency breathing down my neck.'

Charlie reached for a mug of coffee. 'Not much wear and tear for the last five of those,' she said. 'Not if their owner was lying dead in a trunk.'

'They are an old, established family company with a very slow staff turnover,' Les continued. 'There were people there who remembered him. I spoke to the man who measured him for the shoes. He couldn't tell me all that much. Only that Trubshaw had been injured in a shooting accident. He'd been living in Warwickshire at the time. My guess is that this was a game shooting accident rather than street crime.'

'Sounds like our man,' said Gary. 'There can't be that many people who shoot themselves in the foot.'

'Check that out,' said Charlie. 'Contact Warwickshire Police and see if they have a record of the accident. Find out all you can about Trubshaw at the same time. When was he last seen? Did anyone report him missing?'

Les nodded and wrote it down.

'Let's move on to the other victim. Stefan Halliwell. What do we know about him?'

'Boss,' said Annie, putting her hand up.

'Yes, Annie?'

'The PM report says his wrists were bruised, possibly by cable ties. But he wasn't tied up when the body was found.'

'So the killer tied him up to smother him and then removed the ties? Can any of you think why they might have done that?' They all looked blank. 'Make a note of it, Annie. We'll come back to it. Gary, remind us what you got from the house-to-house?'

'Not a lot. Everyone we spoke to said they avoided the area. They didn't like the spooky empty house and the general opinion was that

Ruth and Colin were not much better than travellers. One woman described them as grubby and said she'd thought of reporting them to the social.'

'That seems a bit unfair,' said Annie. 'That child is obviously well cared for.'

'Check them out anyway. See if either of them is on the system. Any luck with the couple in the other cottage?'

'I talked to their daughter,' said Annie. 'They're due back tomorrow. She's going to meet their flight and take them to stay with her.'

'Where does she live?'

'Wexham,' said Annie. 'Not far from the hospital.'

'We'll pay them a visit,' said Charlie. 'Find out if there's been any trouble at the house before. Gary, check the Land Registry and find out who owns Beedham House. We need to talk to them, too.' Her phone rang and she took the call, writing some notes on a slip of paper. 'That was the family liaison adviser,' she said. 'They've been able to contact Kasia Halliwell, the victim's mother. She lives in Krakow and they've managed to get her onto a flight to Heathrow. One of their officers will pick her up and take her to identify her son's body. She's booked into the Copthorne Hotel. I'll go and talk to her there. We don't need to interview her formally at the moment and a room at the hotel will be less intimidating. Les, you can come with me. Gary, find out who owns Beedham House and when it was last lived in. Annie, you keep digging into Trubshaw's past.' She looked at her watch. 'Meet back here at three this afternoon.'

16

Jonny and Ivo were in the office, looking at photos Ivo had taken of Beedham House while Katya had been talking to Ruth. 'I remember it,' said Jonny. 'It looks a mess now, but forty years ago it was very different. I went to a party there. Early eighties, it must have been.' He held out a photo of his own. 'I dug this out. I thought we'd scan it and add it to the file with your pictures. Not sure if it's much use, but it's interesting to see the house as it was.'

He handed Ivo the photo. He'd found it in a trunk in the attic when he woke at four that morning and remembered that he'd not only visited the place years ago but had a photograph of the occasion. This had been before the days when everyone had instant access to a camera on their phone, but he'd been in the habit of carrying a small camera around with him in his pocket. Something he'd begun when on a gap year and continued for several years after his return. He remembered this particular roll of film because he'd started using it just days before he met Belinda for the first time, and snapped the remaining thirty photos because he'd been unable to take his eyes off her. She laughed when he had the film developed and showed them to her. 'Why had he taken so many of her when he'd only taken two at a party that looked a lot more interesting?' Strange how one remembered little details like that. And who'd have thought it would become a murder scene years later.

Ivo studied the photo of a group of people in evening dress, standing in the garden, Beedham House in the background.

'The house belonged to the Beedham family,' said Jonny. 'I think it was a Beedham who built it back in the 1920s. I'd been at school with James Beedham, who I guess was their grandson, and he'd invited me to this party. That's him.' Jonny pointed to a young man in the picture. 'He was killed in a skiing accident about twenty years ago.'

'That's you,' said Ivo, pointing to a picture of a much younger Jonny standing next to a young woman in a red dress, both of them holding wine glasses. 'Who took the photo?'

'I don't remember. I probably asked a waiter. They were very generous about keeping our glasses topped up. I'm amazed you can recognise me, though. I was a lot slimmer in those days. That was just before I met Belinda.'

'Who's the woman you're with in the photo?'

'I don't remember her name. She was friendly with this guy here.' Jonny pointed to a man standing at the back of the picture. 'Larry someone. James' cousin. I remember the parents well. My own parents used to gossip about them quite a bit. My dad didn't approve, said they were flashy. James' father, Cyril Beedham, married a woman called Coralie. She'd modelled for some well-known photographer in the late fifties. Very beautiful, by all accounts. Well, she's still quite striking here, thirty or so years later. She had a twin sister, Claudia, who was Larry's mother. A couple of socialites they were, always getting their pictures in the society pages. There was a much younger brother, Geoffrey, I think he was called, who'd just got engaged to a Polish woman.'

'Do you know what happened to the family?'

'James' death must have been a shock. I think Cyril and Coralie moved to the Bahamas. I assume they sold the house.'

'Do you know who owns it now?'

Jonny shook his head. 'Easy enough to find out, I suppose. The Land Registry will have record. I expect the police will have already checked that.'

17

Charlie received a message to say that Kasia Halliwell had confirmed that the victim was her son, Stefan. She had been driven to the hotel and was prepared to make a statement.

A young man in a suit and wearing a name badge greeted Charlie and Les when they arrived at the reception desk and made themselves known. 'We've reserved a meeting room,' he said. 'Ms Halliwell is waiting for you. She's ordered coffee and sandwiches. Can I get you anything?'

'No, we're fine, thank you,' said Charlie. They were shown to a room where a grey-haired woman sat at a table, reading a newspaper.

'Mrs Halliwell, I'm so sorry for your loss,' said Charlie as she crossed the room to shake her hand. 'I'm Detective Inspector Hannington and this is Detective Constable Bateman. I can assure you we are doing all we can to find your son's killer. If it's all right with you, we'd like to ask you some questions.'

Kasia Halliwell nodded and indicated that they should sit down. 'I will tell you what I can,' she said. 'But I had not seen my son since his father died and I returned to live in Poland.'

'When was that?'

'Geoffrey died four years ago, but even before that we had very little contact with Stefan.'

'You'd quarrelled?' Les asked.

'Stefan had been in trouble, accused of fraud by the people he worked for. He narrowly avoided prison, and it left him feeling... well, ashamed, I suppose. We tried to help, but he turned his back on everyone he knew. Shut himself away with his computers. The last time I saw him face-to-face was at his father's funeral. Geoffrey left him a little money and Stefan started his software business. But he wanted no more to do with me, so when I was offered work in Krakow, I decided to make a new life for myself there.'

'Do you have any idea who might have wanted to hurt your son?'

'If you'd asked me five years ago, I'd have said there were several people. He'd been involved with some unscrupulous types and lost a lot of money. And then there was a woman he was involved with. I don't know what happened there, but something went badly wrong. And just before that there'd been a shooting incident. I don't think anyone was badly hurt, but he was never really the same after that. I'm sorry I can't tell you any more. Stefan was always secretive and even more so after these events.'

Charlie opened a folder and placed a photograph of Beedham House on the table. 'This is where your son's body was found. Do you recognise it?'

Kasia looked at the picture. 'Yes, I do. But it wasn't like this when I went there. It was a beautiful house then. Now it looks as if no one has cared for it for a long time.'

'You went there?'

'A couple of times, yes. My husband's sister was married to the owner, Cyril Beedham. It was Cyril's father who had the house built.'

'And Stefan would have known the house?'

'I'm not sure. We may have taken him there when he was tiny, but I can't imagine why he would have been there when he was older.'

'Can you tell me a little about the family? You say Mrs Beedham was your sister-in-law?'

'Geoffrey didn't know his sisters all that well. He was twelve years their junior, son of his father's second marriage so they were half brother and sisters. He took me there to meet them when we were first engaged, but really, we didn't spend a lot of time with them. Coralie was married to Cyril Beedham. She came to our wedding, but I didn't get to know her well. She had a twin sister, Claudia. They were both very beautiful and expensively dressed. They made Geoffrey and me feel like poor relations. I suppose that's exactly what we were, so we had very little contact with them after we were married.'

'Can you think of any reason why Stefan should have gone back to the house now?'

'None at all, but as I told you, I knew nothing of his life after Geoffrey died.'

Charlie made a note to look into Stefan's finances. Could he have been hoping to buy the house? Perhaps he'd got the poor relation vibe and hoped to somehow get his own back. Show the rich relatives what he'd made of himself. 'Did the Beedhams have children?'

'Cyril and Coralie had a son, James, but we didn't know him well. He would have been born around 1960, when Geoffrey was ten. By the time Stefan came along, James would have been at university. He was killed in an accident several years later. After that we lost contact with the family. The last time Geoffrey saw either of his sisters would have been at James' funeral. That was in 2003.'

'Was Stefan at the funeral?'

'No, he hardly knew them.'

'Was James an only child?'

'He was, yes. There was a cousin he was close to, Claudia's boy. But I don't remember his name.'

'And did James have a family of his own?'

'There was a woman at the funeral. Could have been his widow, but I don't remember hearing that he'd married. Like I said. Geoffrey and I didn't have much to do with them.'

And yet she went to their son's funeral. Stefan would have been in his mid-twenties when James died. He and James were cousins. And the two murder victims were related, possibly cousins. Three men dying violent deaths years apart: James Beedham, Stefan Halliwell and possibly Laurence Trubshaw. Was James Beedham's death really an accident? Where did the mysterious Mr Trubshaw fit in? What was *his* connection to the house his body had been found in?

Charlie gestured to Les that it was time to leave. They'd not get much more information here and she didn't want to upset Kasia Halliwell unnecessarily. She'd lost a husband and a son only a few years apart. She had enough to cope with. And they could call on her again if anything else came to light. 'Thank you so much for talking to us at this difficult time,' said Charlie, putting her notes away and standing up. 'Will you be staying in the area for a while if we need to speak to you again?'

'I'll stay here until after the funeral. The very kind officer who brought me here is going to help me sort out the arrangements.'

'Good,' said Charlie. 'I'll keep in touch with her.'

Charlie and Les returned to the car for the short drive back to Windsor.

'What did you make of her?' Charlie asked Les as she turned onto the relief road.

'It's a connection to the house and it's given us some names to look into.'

'No suspects, though. Or motive.'

'There were obviously some hard feelings. Resentment that Geoffrey didn't have the lifestyle his sisters had.'

'But can we connect that to either killing? Certainly not the recent one. Even the five-year-old death doesn't fit in.'

'She mentioned a shooting incident. And we know Laurence Trubshaw was shot and had to have specially made shoes. Perhaps Stefan had got into a fight with him.'

'And shot him?'

'Not impossible, is it?'

No, Charlie had to admit it wasn't. But Trubshaw had been shot in Warwickshire. Why would he turn up in a trunk at Beedham House a hundred miles or so away? And why was it another five years before his body was discovered? And even if Stefan had killed Laurence Trubshaw, who had killed Stefan? 'We should look into this allegation of fraud. Even if it didn't go to trial, there should be records.'

'I'll get onto that as soon as we're back.'

'And contact the press office. We can now release Stefan Halliwell's identity as the more recent victim.'

18

Jonny opened a text from Katya. The body found in the rocking chair had now been confirmed as that of Stefan Halliwell, a forty-five-year-old freelance software developer from Slough. Software developers were two a penny, although the fact he was from Slough narrowed it down a bit. Jonny logged into his own company records and found nothing, but that didn't mean much. It just made it a bit harder to find anyone who had known him. He sent Jasmine a message suggesting she could research his social media, although once his name was generally known, everyone and his dog would be checking him out on Facebook, Twitter, Instagram and anything else they could think of. But Jasmine was clever. She knew how to use back doors, whatever they were, and might just turn up something no one else had come across.

Jonny returned to the photo he'd taken at the party and stared at it. He scanned and enlarged it and it was now on the desk in front of him. It bothered him that he couldn't remember more about the people at the party, but the picture had been taken more than forty years ago. It was lucky he remembered he'd taken it at all. And now he knew the house was a crime scene, he couldn't rid himself of the feeling that the picture somehow contained clues to the murders. He looked again at the photos of the people whose names he did remember. James Beedham had been his own age but died in 2003. Jonny found a report of his death in the local paper archives. There was no hint that it was anything other than an unfortunate accident. He'd been skiing in the Austrian alps, had veered off piste and hit an outcrop of rocks. His death had been instant and it was witnessed by at least half a dozen people. Samples had been analysed and found neither alcohol nor drugs in his bloodstream and no faults in his equipment. It was just a tragic accident.

After James' death, his parents, Coralie and Cyril Beedham, sold the house and resettled in an expat community in Barbados where, now in their eighties, they still lived. For the next ten years the house had changed hands several times. Plans had been submitted on a number of occasions for its development into flats, use as a school, for its demolition to make way for houses built on the land. All planning applications were turned down. It was now in the possession of a finance company called Baverstock Holdings, who presumably were prepared to wait until planning regulations were relaxed.

Try as he might, Jonny was unable to remember the name of the woman in red who was standing next to him in the photo. She was very attractive, he remembered that, so it was surprising that he didn't also remember what she was called. It was something unusual, he thought. It would come to him sooner or later, and until it did, he decided to take a look at other members of the family. He googled *Coralie and Claudia*, adding *1950s models,* and discovered they'd had a successful career as twin fashion models. He also discovered that they had been Coralie and Claudia *Halliwell* and his heart missed a beat. Stefan Halliwell was the man who'd been murdered only a few days ago. A murder victim who had the same name as a woman who'd once lived in the house where his body was found. She'd left the house twenty years earlier, but there had to be a connection, didn't there? Stefan Halliwell was forty-five when he died. Could he perhaps be Coralie's son? An illegitimate one, obviously, since she had given him her maiden name, and as far as Jonny remembered, James had never mentioned a brother.

But Coralie must now be in her eighties. She'd have been in her late forties when Stefan was born. Not impossible, Jonny supposed, but unusual. She'd hardly have flown back from Barbados after twenty years to murder her son in a derelict house she used to own, even if he had been the result of a shady affair. Could Stefan have been her sister Claudia's son? That was more likely, but not a lot more. Claudia and Coralie were twins, so the age problem was still there. But again it was not impossible. She had a son of her own around James' age, but Claudia could have continued to use her unmarried name. Perhaps because of her modelling career. Jonny googled her but could find no record of her modelling since the early 1960s when she'd married. He found announcements of the twins' double engagements: Coralie to Cyril Beedham and Claudia to a Peter Trubshaw. Then he remembered the woman in red again. Jonny wondered if she had a connection to the twin sisters. Who had invited her to the party? Was she there because she was a friend of James, or his cousin? They would all have been of similar age. She may have been at the party as one of their girlfriends, but she had been flirting with Jonny in a way that suggested she was not in a serious relationship with either of them. He just wished he could remember her name. In his mind he went through the alphabet, trying out unusual girls' names for each letter. He reached the letter O. Olive? Oriana? Then it came to him suddenly out of the blue. Ottilie. It was all coming back to him. Ottilie had been studying singing in London. *Kent,* he thought. She'd been Ottilie Kent. He wondered if she'd kept the name and regardless of whether she'd married James, cousin Larry or anyone else, had continued to use it. He googled the name and found pictures of her. Ottilie Kent had grown from a tall, slender young woman into the kind of Wagnerian, statuesque figure one sees in cartoons about opera. She lacked only a helmet with horns and a spear to complete the stereotype. She had recently retired from the Birmingham Opera Company. Fair enough. She and Jonny must be similar in age. He wasn't sure when opera singers retired, but it must be quite a strenuous way to earn a living, and she was no doubt entitled to put her feet up.

Although, as his continued searches told him, she was still tutoring students.

He was getting off track. Seduced as everyone was by the side alleys of Google. There was no way she could have had anything to do with Stefan Halliwell's death. He should put her out of his mind and try to work out where Stefan fitted into the Beedham family circle.

19

Charlie carried a tray with two mugs of cappuccino and two slices of fruit loaf to a table under the glass roof of Oxford Services. DI Philip Gregson looked up from the folder of notes he'd been reading and grinned at her. 'Interesting case you've got here,' he said. 'I've checked all we have on Stefan Halliwell and the fraud case, but I'm not sure how much use it will be.'

'Anything you can add would help. All we've got is what his mother was able to tell us, and she hadn't seen him since her husband died several years ago and she moved to Krakow.'

Gregson stirred sugar into his coffee and opened his iPad. 'I remember the case well,' he said. 'It was my first as a DS. Halliwell was accused of diverting money from the company he worked for into an account in Jersey. It looked cut and dried, but the case was thrown out days before it was due to come to trial. There'd been a mix up with some of the evidence from the company and the prosecution was halted until this was clarified. However, it was never reopened and after a year or two the case was closed.'

'Was there anything suspicious about that?' Charlie asked.

'A cover up? No, at least nothing we could prove. We suspected some anomalies in the company accounts, but they covered their tracks well. I imagine they paid Halliwell to keep quiet. They probably had more to lose by bringing it all into the open. That's the problem with some of these IT companies. They know how to paper over the cracks, as it were.'

'Do you remember any names? Anyone working for the company apart from Halliwell?'

'The CEO was a woman.' He scrolled through some pages. 'Here we are, Davina Ferdinand. But the company no longer exists.'

'Bankrupt?'

'Nothing so straightforward. These IT businesses are always winding themselves down only to start up again days later using a different name. Sorry, I warned you I didn't have anything useful for you.'

'You've given me a name to check.'

'Good luck with that, if you're hoping to connect it to the murder.'

'It's better than nothing. Baby steps, you know. But Mrs Halliwell also mentioned a shooting incident that Stefan was involved in. Do you know anything about that?'

Gregson checked his notes again. 'Something and nothing,' he said. 'It happened about six months after Halliwell was arrested. He'd got himself mixed up with a group of animal rights protestors. They tried to stop a pheasant shoot. The police were called, and one bloke got shot in the foot with his own gun after a struggle. The ringleaders were charged with trespass, but it was never proved that Halliwell was one of them. Looked like he was just a hanger-on who got caught up in a scuffle, there for a bit of action. No charges were brought against him. The guy who was shot didn't want to take it any further. He claimed it was his own fault, lost concentration for a moment.'

'Our second victim had been shot in the foot. We think we've an ID for him from the company that made his shoes, but we need to confirm it. Do you have the name of the man who was shot? Any link to Halliwell would be a start.'

He flicked through some more pages. 'Yeah, Trubshaw. Laurence Trubshaw. Chairman of the Warwickshire Game Club.'

That confirmed the owner of an expensive pair of handmade

shoes and the reason the shoes had been made. 'That certainly suggests he's our guy. The same shoes appearing on the feet of a dead man in a trunk close to where Stefan Halliwell's body was found would be too much of a coincidence for it not to be a connection between the two victims. Are you sure it really was an accident, or do you think there's a chance that Halliwell intended to harm Trubshaw?'

'You think Halliwell lured him to the house and actually killed him?'

'It's possible.'

'But why?'

A good question. 'Halliwell might have intended to harm Trubshaw, but why wait another five years before returning to the scene and getting himself killed?'

Charlie needed to get back to the office and try to work it all out. 'Thank you so much for meeting me,' she said. 'I hope I didn't bring you too far out of your way.'

'Not at all. I have a meeting in Bicester so I was coming in this direction anyway. And driving into Coventry can be grim. It was sensible for us to meet halfway.'

'Well, you saved me a long drive. And you've filled some gaps in my case.' She stood up and shook his hand.

He handed her the notes she'd given him and closed his iPad. 'Good luck with the case,' he said. 'Let me know if I can be any more use.'

20

Ivo started with the gutters and then fixed the gate catch. He'd arrived early, hoping to get everything on Diana Hannington's list finished in one day, but, not wanting to wake the family, he'd begun with the outside jobs. He was rinsing the bucket he'd used for cleaning the gutters at a tap near the kitchen window when Kai appeared at the door. He was dressed in paisley pyjamas, a thick woollen scarf and sheepskin slippers. 'I've made coffee,' he said. 'Come in and get warm. It's freezing out here.'

Ivo supposed it was. He'd had to scrape the frost off the van windows before he left as well as smash the ice on the birdbath. Residents at *Shady Willows* were keen to nurture the wildlife on the site. They'd be out there by now, topping up bird feeders. Ivo himself wasn't bothered by the cold. He soon warmed up when he got down to work. Harold, though, remembering the Aga, headed for the kitchen door. Ivo squeezed out the cloth he'd been using, hung it on the edge of the bucket and followed him inside. Meg greeted them with a lazy wag of her tail and Harold edged closer to the Aga, where Kai was cooking something in a frying pan. A coffee pot was perched next to one of the hotplates. Kai nodded at it. 'Help yourself,' he said. 'There's milk in the fridge and sugar in that blue jar on the dresser.'

'Great,' said Ivo, pouring himself a coffee and cradling the mug in his hands.

'I'm making eggy bread,' said Kai. 'Do you fancy some?'

Ivo nodded. He was used to being fed by the residents at *Shady Willows* but hadn't expected it here. He had some sandwiches in the van, but eggy bread was a lot more appealing.

'Pass me a couple of plates,' said Kai, pointing to a stack on the draining board.

He dished up two generous portions and passed a plate to Ivo. 'Gran's not up yet,' he said, 'but she'd want me to look after you. I'm a lark. Never could sleep after about six. Drives the rest of the family crazy.'

They were tucking into their breakfast when the door opened and a woman came in. Ivo recognised her. This was the detective inspector he and Katya had seen at Beedham House. A sergeant had asked them what they were doing there and moved them on, but DI Hannington apparently didn't recognise Ivo. She was probably too far away and would have been more preoccupied with the dead bodies.

Kai jumped up and served up another plate of eggy bread. 'There you go, Mum. You can't go hunting for murderers on a cold morning without a good breakfast inside you.'

'You're a treasure,' she said, taking the plate from Kai and pouring herself some coffee. She sat at the kitchen table and stared at Ivo. 'You must be here to do the gutters,' she said.

'All done,' said Ivo, pulling out his list. 'I've a lot more to do inside.'

'You'll be here all day?'

'Probably.'

'Then I hope Kai has lunch plans for you as well.'

'Oh,' said Ivo. 'There's no need. I've got sandwiches.'

'Rubbish. You need something hot in this weather.'

'Gran was planning chicken soup,' said Kai. 'With last night's leftovers.'

Harold, who had already been given some eggy bread by Ivo, sidled up to the DI and nudged her thigh.

Ivo pulled him away. 'Sit, Harold,' he said, nudging the dog towards his own chair. 'Sorry, he's no manners.'

DI Hannington brushed some dog hair from her trousers. 'He's a nice dog,' she said, patting his head. 'He looks intelligent.'

'He's very intelligent,' said Ivo. 'He's caught two murderers, and a burglar.'

'You'd better take him to work with you, Mum. Meg would be useless.'

'I wasn't thinking of taking Meg to work with me. Her job is to keep you and Gran company.'

'Harold would be glad to help,' said Ivo. 'We've worked with DI Lomax.'

'Really?' She looked surprised. 'You and Harold?'

'Not just us. We're part of the Breakfast Club Detectives.'

The DI was looking impatient. Anxious to get on with her murder enquiry, he supposed. 'Right,' she said, showing no further interest in either Harold or the Breakfast Club Detectives. 'I need to get to work.'

21

As Charlie drove to the office, something was ticking over in her brain. Harold. An unusual name for a dog, wasn't it? She wasn't sure – perhaps there were dozens of dogs called Harold – but somehow this one was familiar.

She and Gary arrived at the same time and parked next to each other.

'Morning, boss,' said Gary, looking rather bright-eyed for someone who'd had to give up his Saturday for a murder case.

'Looking chirpy,' she said. 'I hope you didn't have plans for the weekend.'

Gary shook his head. 'The ex has taken the kids to a party. Promised I could have an extra couple of days with them at half-term.'

'So are you two patching things up?'

'Well, we're managing not to yell at each other so much.'

Not in his usual grouchy mood, then. His moods could shift from grumpy to light-hearted in the blink of an eye. 'Sounds like progress,' she commented, as she remembered that half-joking expression from the other day, when he'd mentioned not asking Harold for his contact details. 'I wanted to ask you something.'

'Oh, yeah? About my love life?'

'No, about a dog.'

'Oh, okay.'

'Those dog walkers at Beedham, you asked for the dog's name.'

'Yeah, Harold. Don't tell me he's our latest suspect. He was a big, black, ugly brute. Friendly, though.'

'And one of the dog walkers was called Ivo Dean?'

'I'd need to check my notes, but I think so, yes. Why?'

'Oh, no reason, really. They were at my house this morning. Ivo's doing some work for my mum. He was telling me that his dog was good at catching murderers.'

Gary roared with laughter. 'You're not thinking of recruiting him to the team, are you?'

'Course not. It just seems more than a coincidence that they were at the murder scene almost before we were.'

'Armchair sleuths,' said Gary. 'Bloody nuisance, usually.'

'They must have set out for Beedham the moment they spotted the newsflash.'

'You think this Ivo guy turned up at your mum's, knowing you were working on the case?'

Charlie gave this a moment's thought. 'No, he was recommended by someone in her book group, I think. I know she'd been looking for a handyman. He didn't just turn up on the off chance.'

'No worries, then. This is quite a small town. We're bound to bump into the same people now and then. And dogs,' he added as they swiped their cards at reception and headed up to the office.

They were barely through the door when Les beckoned Charlie over to his desk. 'Boss,' he said. 'I think I've found something.'

'Don't tell me,' said Gary. 'It was that elderly couple in the second cottage. Strangled Stefan and then flitted off to Majorca.'

'Tenerife,' Annie corrected. 'Mr and Mrs Braddock. Reggie and Peg. And Stefan Halliwell was smothered, not strangled.'

'Don't be silly,' said Charlie. 'I know we said not to rule anyone out, but I hardly think they could have done it. But I suppose we'd better check out their alibi, just to rule them out.'

'Are any of you interested in what I found?' Les asked.

'Sorry, Les,' said Charlie. 'Let's hear it.'

'I called the letting agent to ask about the two rented cottages. And it's not a straightforward let for either of them.'

'Told you,' said Gary. 'It's the Braddocks. Had it in for Halliwell and probably the other guy as well.'

Charlie sighed. 'Let's hear what Les has got to say.'

'Actually,' said Les, 'Gary might not be so far off track. When the Beedhams sold the house, they added a covenant to the deeds that allowed the Braddocks to stay on in the cottage at a fixed rent for the rest of their lives, or until they decided to relocate. But if they stayed for twenty-five years after the covenant was set up, the deeds would pass to them and they'd be the freehold owners of the cottage. That's probably why so many of the plans for the place fell through. There's no way to get onto the land to build unless the cottages are demolished to make room for an access road.'

'I don't see how that makes them suspects for either murder,' said Gary.

'I haven't finished,' said Les. 'Beedham knew he was moving abroad so he appointed a trustee to administer the covenant and make sure it all went to plan.'

'A local solicitor?' Charlie asked.

'A solicitor, yes, but not very local.'

'Posh London one, probably,' said Gary.

'You're wrong,' said Les. 'It was Geoffrey Halliwell.'

'Really?' said Charlie, astonished. 'Stefan's father?'

'Not so surprising,' said Annie. 'Geoffrey Halliwell was Cyril Beedham's brother-in-law.'

'What happened after Geoffrey died? Did the law firm he worked for take it over?'

'I called them,' said Les. 'They didn't know anything about it and assumed Geoffrey had taken it on privately as a favour to his brother-in-law. The letting agent didn't know either. Their only job is to collect the rent and pass it on to the owners. Minus their own fee, of course. The Braddocks always pay their rent on time, and no one has shown much interest in developing the land in the four years since Geoffrey died. I assume it passed either to Kasia Halliwell or to Stefan.'

'Check it out,' said Charlie. 'A covenant on the deeds will be recorded on the title register.'

'It's interesting,' said Annie. 'It shows either Stefan or Kasia might have an interest in the house.'

'Kasia Halliwell didn't mention anything about a covenant, so it was more likely Stefan that took it over,' said Charlie.

'I can't see that would be a motive for murder,' said Gary. 'Is there any financial gain from administering a covenant?'

'I doubt it,' said Charlie. 'The only gain would be finding a way to cancel the covenant after a huge bribe from the owner and allowing the land to be developed. Who owns it at the moment?'

'Something called Baverstock Holdings,' Les tapped into the Companies House website. 'It says here that they buy up *speculative investments.*'

'What the hell does that mean?' Gary asked.

'I imagine it means they buy things that are worthless and wait until something changes so they can sell again at a huge profit,' said Annie.

Charlie drummed her fingers on the desk. 'So if Stefan Halliwell was overseeing the covenant and refused to cancel it, then it might be in Baverstock Holdings' interest to get rid of him.'

'That doesn't account for the other victim,' said Annie. 'Or the revenge message.'

'The message could just have been a red herring,' said Gary. 'The covenant doesn't account for Trubshaw's death five years earlier, though.'

'Coincidence?' Les suggested.

Charlie shook her head. 'Unlikely. Murdering someone in a room that already has a dead body in it? I don't think so.'

'You're sure the two deaths are connected, boss?'

Charlie nodded. 'I'm working on that assumption at the moment.

It doesn't mean we don't follow up other leads, though. We'll talk to the Braddocks, who must be home by now. Annie, can you set that up? Les, find out what the position is with the other cottage. We need to know who lived there before Colin and Ruth moved in and if it's still covered by the covenant.'

22

Katya pulled off her coat and scarf and slung them over the back of a chair. The breakfast rush was over and she looked around, hoping to see Jonny. There was no sign of him, and instead she was surprised to see Ruth Richards approaching with two cups of coffee. There was no sign of Sonny. Katya, who was not good with small children, was relieved. 'I didn't expect to see you here,' she said.

'Jasmine's given me a job in the kitchen, a couple of hours, three days a week. I've just finished my shift.'

She looked a lot better than when Katya had last seen her, but of course that was just after she'd been suddenly turned out of her home. 'Where's the little one?' she asked, hoping the child wasn't about to appear. 'Is his father taking care of him?'

'Colin's been switched to the overnight delivery. It's better paid, but he has to sleep during the day. The police have let him move back into the cottage, but I'm staying with my sister. She looks after Sonny for me so I can pay her a bit of rent. It looks like Colin's hoping he can stay in the cottage on his own.'

'They can't turn him out, can they? Not without a reason.'

'He said they might try, because of Mr Halliwell dying.'

Katya couldn't see why that made a difference. Halliwell hadn't owned either the house or the cottages. 'What does the letting agent say?'

Ruth shrugged. 'Dunno. Something to do with the deeds. I didn't understand what he was saying, but Colin says he has a right to be there.' She shrugged. 'I'm leaving him, anyway. I don't really care where he lives as long as he pays me a bit to support Sonny.'

'What about the Braddocks?'

Ruth shrugged again. 'I suppose it's the same for them. They were saying it would be nice to go and live in Spain in a few years. Their daughter wants them to move into a retirement village near where she lives. They're not keen, though. I think that's why the daughter paid for their holiday. Kind of a bribe.'

Katya took a gulp of her coffee. That didn't feel right. Retirement villages were very expensive, weren't they? The Braddocks' cottage was rented and in any case didn't look like it was worth a lot. Perhaps their daughter was loaded. That must be it. She paid for a holiday in Tenerife for her parents, so why not a retirement home as well?

'That was before the bodies were found,' Ruth was still wittering on. 'They'll probably want to move out as soon as possible now. I'd not want to stay there, even if I wasn't leaving Colin.'

Jasmine joined them, handing Ruth an envelope. 'You can get off now,' she said. 'I've paid the full two hours. Not your fault if it's been a quiet morning. I'll see you tomorrow.'

Ruth put the money in her pocket and carried her coffee cup out to the kitchen.

'Good of you to give her a job,' said Katya, once she was out of earshot.

'I was sorry for her,' said Jasmine. 'She's been stuck in that cottage with the baby and a husband who I suspect abuses her. And on top of that, she was being turned out of her home.'

'I don't understand that,' said Katya. 'Something to do with the deeds?'

'I didn't understand either, so I did a bit of research. I think I might have uncovered a motive for the murder.' She removed a piece of paper from her apron pocket and spread it out on the table.

'A family tree?' Katya asked.

'Jonny worked it out from that photo he had of the party at Beedham House. Stefan Halliwell, the guy whose body was found in the attic, was a nephew of Coralie Beedham, wife of the owner. When they sold the house, Cyril Beedham added a covenant. The tenants of the two cottages were given the right to remain in them and after twenty-five years the deeds would be signed over to them. That would be in four years from now. They'd be the legal freehold owners of the cottages and the land surrounding them. Geoffrey Halliwell, Coralie's brother, was made a trustee to oversee that this happened. When he died, the trusteeship passed to his son, Stefan.'

'Which means the Braddocks can't be evicted,' said Katya. No wonder they were not keen to move. Four more years and they could sell up and move without needing the daughter's charity. 'But Ruth and Colin have only been in the cottage for a couple of years,' she said. 'Surely the covenant only applied to tenants who lived there before the house was sold.'

'That's probably why he is being allowed to stay. With the Braddocks still in the other cottage, theirs would be no use to the developers anyway.'

'Who is the trustee now?'

'Unless Stefan appointed someone in his will, no one. Which leaves the whole thing in limbo for four years. But after that, the property suddenly becomes very valuable. If the Braddocks sell up, there'll be nothing to stop the land being cleared and developed. Until then it's not clear what the legal position is, but it's unlikely the Braddocks could raise enough to fight a legal battle should they need to. If the covenant is in place, they're legally entitled to stay there and they could block any access onto the land. But without an administrator, well, it all looks a lot less certain. From what I understood from a guy I spoke to in the planning department, the Braddocks, with

Stefan's support, have refused every attempt to bribe them into moving.'

'But with Halliwell out of the way... well, I can see how that might be a motive for his murder by someone who'd invested money in the land.'

23

Jonny looked out of the window of his car as a young woman in a red coat opened the front door, emerged from the house with a tote bag slung over her shoulder and walked down the path. She turned left along the pavement and headed for a bus stop a few yards down the road where, as if by magic, a bus appeared. The woman climbed aboard and that, Jonny assumed, was the last he'd ever see of her.

It must be the opera training. The ability to open a door, step into a street and immediately take command, turn heads and even conjure up buses from nowhere. The same presence required to enthral a theatre full of opera lovers just by stepping onto a stage. In his mind, he was back at the party he'd been to forty years ago, where a woman in a red dress had captured not only Jonny's attention but that of twenty or so other guests.

Since finding the photograph, Ottilie Kent had been on his mind. She'd intrigued him then as she did now. A few days after the party, he'd met Belinda and any thoughts of other women were knocked out of his head. But if he hadn't met Belinda, Jonny was fairly sure he'd not have hung back. He'd have nagged at it like a terrier with a rat until he'd discovered how serious she was about James or his cousin. And to be frank, anything less than a formal engagement to one of them, and Jonny would have charmed his way into Ottilie's life.

He'd tentatively mentioned to Belinda that Ottilie could probably throw some light onto members of the family in whose house two bodies had turned up forty or so years later. 'Then you'd better go and ask her,' said Belinda.

'She might think I was some weird stalker. She might remember that I'd made a pass at her.'

Belinda studied the photograph. 'A woman who looks like that would have had men chatting her up every day. She probably still does. She's hardly going to worry about a man, a happily married one, that she met at a party more than forty years ago, wanting to talk to her about the house where there was a murder.'

Jonny still wasn't sure how useful it would be to talk to her, and there was no question that he wanted to discuss anything other than her connection to Beedham. Katya, when he mentioned it to her, was of the same opinion. 'The more we know about the house and the family, the more likely this DI Hannington is to take us seriously.'

So there he was. Sitting in his car outside Ottilie Kent's house, somewhere on the outskirts of Warwick. He'd phoned her earlier and asked if he could call on her that afternoon. She'd told him she would be teaching a student and asked him not to call before four o'clock. But it was now ten past four and he'd seen the student leave. He couldn't put it off any longer. He patted his coat pocket to make sure he had his usual moleskin notebook, climbed out of the car, shimmied past a green SUV that was taking up most of the driveway space and walked up to the front door.

The years had been extremely kind to Ottilie Kent. Jonny would have recognised her anywhere. She was probably unlikely to feel the same way about him, but he was wrong. 'We've met before,' she said as she led him into a large music room with a grand piano.

'It was at a party, a long time ago. I'm amazed you remember me.'

'You were the only presentable man there,' she said. 'Of course I remember you. But I'm not sure why you are here now. Did you say you were a detective?'

'A private one,' he said, handing her one of the cards Jasmine had designed for them for occasions such as this one.

Ottilie took it from him. 'I'm not about to be named in some divorce case, am I? Isn't that what private detectives usually spend their time on?'

'Nothing like that,' said Jonny. 'I'm collecting background for an enquiry into a recent incident at this house. Two bodies were found in the attic. Suspicious deaths, probably.' He pulled the picture of the party out of his pocket and tapped the picture of the house that was visible behind the group of people. 'It's possible there's a link to one or more of the people in the photo.'

She took the photo, and suppressing a gasp – at least Jonny thought it was a gasp – she turned away from him. She took a deep breath and turned back, a smile fixed on her face. 'Beedham House, of course, I remember it now. It's where you and I met. But you said this incident you are enquiring about was recent. The party was years ago.'

'We think there may be a connection to the family who owned the house.'

'Is there anyone in particular that you are interested in?'

'Not really. I hoped you could fill me in a bit, add some names to faces.'

'It was a long time ago, but I'll do what I can.'

At that moment her phone rang. 'Excuse me,' she said. 'I need to answer this. It will be one of my students.' She left the room and Jonny could hear what sounded like a heated conversation. He couldn't make out what it was about, but the impatient tone of Ottilie's voice was unmistakable. Not wanting to appear to be eavesdropping, he wandered over to a shelf of books and examined the titles. It seemed opera was not her only interest. There were several books on eastern philosophies: Al-Kindi, Lao Tzu and Confucius among others Jonny hadn't heard of. He pulled out a small book of sayings by Lao Tzu and was reading it when Ottilie returned. 'A long-term interest of mine,' she said, taking the book from him and replacing it on the shelf. 'I always planned to pursue it further one day, travel to China, perhaps.'

'And will you?'

'Possibly, although I was hoping my daughter would come with me, but she's been...' Ottilie waved her arms in the air as if hoping to make a grab for the right phrase. 'Well, let's just say she's had some personal problems recently.'

'I'm sorry to hear that,' said Jonny, not wanting to pry and not sure what else he could say.

'But you're not interested in that, are you? Come into the kitchen and I'll make some tea. Always easier to think with a cup of something and a biscuit, isn't it?'

Jonny followed her out of the room, thinking it might have been interesting to know more about the daughter's personal problems, but he should mind his own business. They were unlikely to be relevant to the case.

Ottilie led him to a spacious kitchen and bustled around making tea while he sat at the table. 'Right,' she said, passing him a cup and a tin of biscuits. 'Let's have a look at that photo again.'

'I know this is James Beedham,' Jonny said, pointing to a young man on the left of the picture. 'He was killed in a skiing accident more than twenty years ago, so he's of no interest to our case. He won't be a suspect.' He pointed to a young man standing in the back row. 'Could this be James' cousin, Larry?'

She sniffed and wiped her glasses. 'Possibly,' she said, vaguely.

'I'm sorry,' said Jonny. 'I thought you were his date at the party. Did I get that wrong?'

Ottilie shook her head. 'I was dating James in those days.'

'But you knew Larry?'

'Of course,' she snapped, but then, changing the subject, she pointed at the picture again. 'See these two gorgeous women standing by the fountain? Twins, and I couldn't tell you which was which. But one of them, Coralie, was married to James' father, Cyril Beedham. The other was Claudia Trubshaw.'

'Larry's mother?'

She nodded. 'Dead now, I assume.'

Jonny couldn't imagine why she assumed that. Claudia would only be in her early eighties now, wouldn't she? 'Did you know the twins before they were married?'

'Can't say I did. But this bloke here was their younger brother, Geoffrey. He married a Polish woman called Kasia and they had a little boy indecently soon after the wedding.'

'Did James marry?'

'He wanted to marry me because I was pregnant at the time. You wouldn't think so to look at the photo, would you? It was early days and I was considering a termination.'

'James was the father?'

'No. He thought he was, but he was wrong.'

'So you turned him down?'

'Of course. I decided to keep the baby and married her father. A singer called Rodrigo Ferdinand. We divorced after a year and I haven't seen him since. I brought Davina up on my own. James was her godfather.'

'Do you and your daughter ever see Larry?'

'Occasionally. Well, Davina saw him quite often. I didn't really care for him. But he left the country five years ago and I haven't seen him since.'

'Do you suppose your daughter kept in touch with him?'

'No,' she said abruptly.

Did she keep tabs on all her daughter's friends? A daughter who would now be in her forties. 'Do you know where Larry went?'

'He'd always talked of moving to somewhere sunny. I imagine that's what he did. I'm sorry, but I'm quite busy. I'm afraid there's not much more I can tell you.'

'Well,' said Jonny, thinking he'd not achieved very much, but accepting her rather abrupt dismissal. 'Thank you for your help.'

He drove away from the house and headed for home. It had been a waste of time. But as he turned his car into his own drive a thought struck him. Ottilie had not asked about the murder. Not a single question about the victims or when it had happened.

24

Les pulled the car up in front of a small bungalow with a paved area in front occupied by a blue Renault Clio. There was no room for another car and, glancing up and down the road, he could see no roadside spaces.

'Pull off the pavement in front of the Clio,' said Annie. 'We can move if anyone needs to get out.'

'We should have come in a marked car,' Les grumbled. 'You can park anywhere in one of those.'

'And be gawped at by the neighbours?'

They were police. They were used to being stared at. Les pulled the car onto the pavement and parked across the drive, effectively blocking the Clio in. He fussed around, making sure the car was as well off the road as possible. Then gave up. There was no way this was anything other than a bit of illegal parking. 'I don't suppose this will take long,' he said, searching the glove compartment for a police sign and resting it on the dashboard. 'The Braddocks were away on holiday the day of the incident. They wouldn't have known about the disturbance, let alone the murder.'

'They might be able to give us some useful background.' Annie climbed out of the car and headed for the door, Les clambering out and following in her wake.

Annie rang the bell and the door was opened a couple of inches by an irritable-looking woman wearing a pink tracksuit and sheepskin slippers. 'I'm not talking to canvassers,' she said. 'Or anyone trying to sell stuff.'

Annie held up her ID. 'I'm DC Annie Shafiq,' she said. 'And this is DC Les Bateman. We'd like to talk to Mr and Mrs Braddock. Are they in?'

'Thank God for that,' said the woman, opening the door an inch or two further. 'Have you come to tell them they can move back home?'

'They can go back very soon, as far as we know, but we'll need to confirm that with the CSIs. In the meantime, we'd like to talk to them.'

'What about?'

Annie ignored the question. 'Could you let them know we're here?'

The woman stared at them and looked set to close the door again.

Annie moved her foot to stop the door from closing completely. 'Can we come in, please?' she said. 'We need to ask them some questions about a recent incident at Beedham House. Are you Ms Braddock junior?'

'No, I'm bloody not. I've been married twelve years. I'm *Mrs* Ellie Jones.'

'Right, Mrs Jones. Are the Braddocks at home?'

'In the lounge,' she said, sighing. 'You'd better come in.'

She led them into an over-furnished room where an elderly couple were sitting at a table, sticking photos into an album.

'Someone to see you,' said Ellie. 'Police.'

The man was wearing a linen suit, a thick woollen scarf around his shoulders. He stood up and shook Annie's hand. 'Reggie Braddock,' he said. 'Have you come to tell us we can go home?'

'We need to get our winter clothes,' said the woman, who was wearing a pair of cotton slacks and a jumper several sizes too small.

'They've got questions,' said Ellie, pulling up a chair and sitting down next to them. 'They've been on holiday,' she told Annie. 'Won't be able to tell you anything.'

'You should be able to go home tomorrow,' said Les, putting his phone back into his pocket, having checked with the CSI team.

'Not sure if I can manage tomorrow,' said Mrs Jones. 'I'll be needing the car. You'll have to call a taxi.'

'We can arrange a car for you, if you like,' said Annie.

'That would be grand,' said Reggie. 'It's nice to go on holiday, but there's nothing like your own bed, is there?'

'They've been to Tenerife,' said Ellie. 'It was our Christmas present. You loved it, didn't you, Mum?'

'It was okay,' said the woman Annie assumed was Peg. 'Didn't think much of the food, though.'

'Well, you'll soon be back in your own kitchen,' said Ellie. 'Perhaps you can get the police car to stop off at Sainsbury's on the way.'

'Mrs Jones,' said Annie, feeling that it would be easier to talk to the Braddocks without their daughter's help. 'I don't suppose you could make us all a cup of tea, could you? Your father looks a bit cold.'

'That I am,' said Reggie. Ellie sighed and headed for the door. 'Too mean to put the heater on,' he muttered as she left the room. 'Me and Peg just back from holiday where it was warm. And us with only our summer clothes.'

'Perhaps you could go and give Mrs Jones a hand,' said Annie, winking at Les and hoping he'd keep her talking in the kitchen for a while.

'Sure,' he said, heading towards the sound of Ellie's muttering and the clinking of teacups.

Annie sat down between Reggie and Peg and took out her notebook. 'How long have you lived in the cottage?' she asked.

'I was born there,' said Reggie. 'My dad was the gardener, and I took over after he died. Then it was just me and Peg for a few years after Dad passed away. Twenty-one years, three months and four days since Mr Beedham moved away.'

'That's very precise,' said Annie, writing it down.

'It's the covenant, see,' said Peg. 'Mr Beedham said when we'd lived there for twenty-five years after he set it up, it would be ours.'

'Mr Halliwell would get our name put on the deeds and we'd pay no more rent,' Reggie agreed.

'We could even sell it if we wanted to,' Peg added.

'So the covenant was set up the year the house was sold?' Annie asked.

'That's right. Just after James Beedham died.'

'Real tragedy,' said Peg. 'Lovely young man, he was.'

'And you paid rent? It wasn't a tied cottage that came free as part of the job?'

'It was while the Beedhams lived there, but after they left we paid rent. Mr Beedham's solicitor said we'd have more security that way.'

'It was very reasonable, though,' Peg added. 'Five pound a week.'

'And it's been the same for twenty-one years?' No wonder they didn't want to move.

'Never went up,' said Reggie. 'Mr Beedham promised it. Don't know how, but Mr Halliwell told us it was fixed until the cottage became ours.'

'That was Mr Stefan Halliwell?'

'We heard he'd died,' said Peg, pulling a tissue from the sleeve of her jumper and dabbing her eyes. 'Poor Mr Stefan. But no, it was his dad, Geoffrey. But nothing changed after he died. Stefan became the legal trustee.'

'What about the other cottage?' Annie asked.

'That was where the Beedhams' housekeeper lived.'

'Did she have the same arrangement?'

'Yes, but she died two years ago. Then young Colin Sugden moved in with his girlfriend, pays rent and all. Looks like they'll be evicted, though. The covenant was only for the lifetime of the original tenant. Young Colin went to Citizens Advice about it, wanted to challenge it but I don't think he had much luck. He was trying to get Mr Halliwell to write a letter for him.'

'And did he write a letter?'

'Dunno.'

'Doubt it,' said Peg. 'He was okay, but not as helpful as his dad. Didn't know us so well, see.'

Les and Ellie returned with a tray of tea, which Ellie passed around.

'No biscuits, love?' Peg asked.

'Not been to the shops, have I?' said Ellie, with a look that suggested feeding biscuits to either her parents or the police was a favour too far.

'Did you ever see anyone at the house?' Annie asked.

'Occasionally. Blokes with tape measures, people from the council.'

'But not recently,' Peg added. 'They're waiting for us to move out so the land will be worth something.'

'And will you move out when the house is yours?'

'Reckon we will,' said Reggie with a chuckle. 'For the right price, if you know what I mean.'

Annie did know what he meant. That cottage was standing in the way of the development of houses, at least twenty, she thought, probably more if they included flats. Reggie could ask pretty much what he liked for the cottage, or more to the point, the access rights that went with it. The Braddocks would be able to buy a villa in Spain with enough change to live in comfort for the rest of their lives. And that was why Colin Sugden was being threatened with eviction. The owner would not want to risk any kind of long term agreement, and with Stefan's death and no one to oversee the covenant, they could probably put a lot of pressure on the Braddocks to move out before the end of the twenty-five years. 'Reggie,' she said. 'Far be it from me to interfere, but make sure you find a really good lawyer, won't you? These developers can be unscrupulous and will do all they can to get you to settle before the four years are up.'

Reggie patted Annie's hand. 'Don't fret yourself, love. I called me solicitor the moment we got back and heard about Stefan Halliwell's death. He worked with Mr Halliwell senior, so he knows what's what. We've got a bit of money put by and he reckons he can find someone to look after our interest. I'm moving out of that house over my dead body.'

An unfortunate remark, considering recent events.

∽

'That was interesting,' said Les as he unlocked the car and they headed back to Windsor. 'But do you think you should have said that to Reggie about getting a lawyer? Not really police business, is it?'

'I don't know,' said Annie. 'But you know what? I'm not going to stand by and see that sweet old couple cheated out of what's rightfully theirs.'

'You going to tell the boss?'

'Only if she asks,' said Annie. 'And if she does, I'll tell her it was just a bit of friendly advice that has nothing to do with the case.'

'But it might have,' said Les. 'If Stefan Halliwell was killed because of something to do with the covenant.'

'Do you think that's what happened?'

'No idea, but we probably shouldn't rule it out.'

'So how do you explain the other death?'

'He may have had a connection to Beedham House as well. We don't know yet.'

'Even if it turns out he did, well, the Braddocks would still need a good lawyer. Nothing wrong with making sure they know that.'

'You're probably right. And I don't think you told old Reggie anything he didn't already know.'

'That's right. All the same, better not say anything to the boss unless she asks. Okay?'

Les nodded.

25

Jasmine decided to spend an evening online, finding out all she could about what had gone on at Beedham House since Cyril and his wife had left. She found a record of the most recent sale to Monty Letward, a developer and CEO of Baverstock Holdings. He'd submitted plans for the demolition of the two cottages, the conversion of Beedham House into eight luxury flats and the construction of twelve executive homes on the adjoining land. Council planning records were excellent and she discovered all the details that had been submitted. At first, all had gone well and the planning application looked as if it would be accepted with little objection. Then the trustee of the two cottages, at the time Geoffrey Halliwell, engaged an expensive colleague and challenged the application as illegal on the grounds that the tenants of both cottages had the right to stay there and while there, they had rights over who came and went across the land. This began a three-way battle lasting several years. Letward did all he could to persuade the residents of the cottages to accept a payment to release them from the covenant. But Geoffrey Halliwell, having calculated the financial implications for the tenants, dug his heels in and persuaded them to refuse all offers. Letward resubmitted his application, dropping plans for the cottages and with revised access arrangements for the flats. This was turned down by the council, who argued that it left the cottages marooned with no access on and off the land. At this point Letward gave in. He fenced off part of the land and resubmitted plans, not for executive homes but for thirty small, affordable starter homes. Beedham House and the two cottages remained the property of Baverstock Holdings and after the death of the tenant in the second cottage, Letward renewed his attempts to get the Braddocks to move out. He contacted the Braddocks' daughter and offered her a sum of money if she could persuade her parents to move into a retirement development he was building north of Slough. He'd made money from the sale of the houses on the new development, but Jasmine thought it likely that Beedham House and the cottages hung around his neck like a millstone. She wondered if Jonny might be able to discover anything about the financial state of Baverstock Holdings. She looked at the council map of the Beedham Estate and noted roads called Braddock Lane and Halliwell Close. There was also a Trubshaw Avenue and Sugden Road. Jasmine found that very interesting. Braddocks and Halliwells had a connection to Beedham House and there was a cousin called Trubshaw. But the name that really leapt out at her was Sugden. Colin Sugden was living in one of the cottages with his girlfriend, Ruth Richards, but they'd only lived there a couple of years, long after the construction of the estate and the naming of the roads. How could one of the roads be named after him? It must just be a coincidence. She'd not trusted Colin Sugden, but that was because he didn't treat Ruth very well. There didn't seem to be any reason to treat him with suspicion about Halliwell's murder. A road with his name could hardly be a motive for murdering anyone. Since Colin Sugden had only lived in the cottage for two years, he had no claim to it under the terms of the covenant. So what possible good would it have done him to kill Halliwell? Unless, of course, he was working for Baverstock Holdings or paid by them to get rid of anything to do with the covenant. But that didn't make sense. They needed to get rid of the Braddocks, not the trustee. And even the most disreputable companies probably drew a line at bumping off tenants. Although they probably had all manner of other horrible ways of persuading people to move out of their homes.

The crime scene tape had been removed and there was no sign of a police presence any longer. But Ruth had flatly refused to move back into the cottage. According to Ruth, Colin claimed he had a right to live there but, as Ruth told Jasmine, she cared very little about what Colin did now. And Jasmine suspected she didn't really know what Colin was up to. Working at the cafe had given Ruth some new confidence, and with Jasmine's help she was applying for social housing for herself and Sonny. The Braddocks would probably be home any day and without the protection of the trustee, they could be in a vulnerable position. Would they know what their rights were? Someone should talk to them, she decided. She called Katya, who suggested getting Ivo to drive them there.

~

'You okay?' Ivo called over his shoulder.

Ivo's van only had two seats, so Jasmine was huddled in the back next to Harold, sitting on the remains of an old car seat Ivo had picked out of a skip. 'I'm fine,' she said. 'And we're not going far.'

'I can sometimes get three in the front,' said Ivo, 'but...' He glanced at Katya, who in her padded coat was taking up every inch of space in the front.

'Pity Jonny was busy,' said Katya. 'Or we could have gone in comfort.'

'It's no problem, really,' said Jasmine. 'Jonny's chasing some lead on someone he remembers from the party.'

The van turned off the main road and bumped along the lane to Beedham House. 'When they do get around to developing the land,' said Katya, 'the first thing they'll need to do is put in a decent road. I don't suppose anyone's filled in so much as a pothole since the house was sold.'

'I can understand why Ruth doesn't want to stay,' said Jasmine, looking around as they approached the cottages. 'It's very isolated out here, even with the estate so close.'

There was a high fence with a line of leylandii at the end of the cottage gardens. The only access between the new estate and the Beedham land was a small cut through at the end of Halliwell Close. Whoever had designed the development clearly didn't want to create any kind of community between the two developments. Whatever the plans were for Beedham House, they were going to be a step up socially from the affordable homes on the estate.

Ivo drove past the first cottage, the one Ruth had recently left, and which might very well still contain Colin Sugden. He parked outside the second one, home to the Braddocks. This one was in way better condition, with freshly painted window frames and a well cared-for garden. A small grey car was parked under a carport. Katya climbed out of the front seat and stretched, while Ivo unclipped Harold from his harness and then helped Jasmine out. They walked up the path and Katya rang the doorbell, which was answered by an elderly woman wearing pale blue slacks and a mohair jumper.

'Mrs Braddock?' Katya asked. The woman nodded. Katya introduced them all. 'We're friends of Ruth Richards. She was wondering if you were home yet and asked us to drop in and check you were both okay. She's working now and you know she doesn't drive. We were coming in this direction to walk Harold, so we said we'd drop in.' Katya was stretching the truth a bit. But Ruth had said she was concerned about the Braddocks and Harold did need walking.

'That's kind,' said Mrs Braddock. 'We're very fond of Ruth and the little one. Won't you come in for a cup of tea? And do call me Peg.'

Katya didn't need to be asked twice and followed Peg's directions to the lounge.

'Is it okay to bring Harold in?' Ivo asked. 'He's not muddy. We've not walked him yet.'

'Course you can, love. The more the merrier.' She smiled at Jasmine and ushered them all inside. 'Make yourselves comfy. I'll put the kettle on. Reggie's out in his shed. I'll tell him you're here.'

It was a cosy little place. Warm and well cared for. The Braddocks had looked after it as if it were already their own. Katya could understand why they wouldn't want to move, even though it was an isolated spot. But they had a car, which must make things easier.

After about ten minutes, the door opened and an elderly man came in carrying a tray, which he put down on a low table near the fireplace, in which there was an imitation coal fire with several bars switched on. Katya envied them being able to afford to run it. The result of a low rent, she supposed.

Peg joined them, carrying a plate with a home-made sponge cake sprinkled with icing sugar and sitting on a doily. 'Fresh out of the oven,' she said. 'It's nice to be back in my own kitchen again. Just as well you're here to help us eat it, or Reggie would have had to finish it.'

'Already put on a bit while we were away,' said Reggie, patting his stomach. 'But she makes a lovely sponge, does our Peg.'

Peg introduced Katya, Ivo and Jasmine. 'The dog's called Harold,' she added. 'Ruth sent them to ask if we're settled in again after our holiday. That was thoughtful, wasn't it?'

'She's a good girl,' said Reggie. 'And I'm fond of that little lad of hers, as well.'

'You'll miss them,' said Jasmine.

'They're definitely not coming back?' Reggie asked. 'Not surprised. I could have told Colin he was flogging a dead horse, but he kept going on about how old Mrs Sugden had mentioned him in her will.'

Katya's cup wobbled dangerously on its saucer as she stared at Peg in surprise. 'I'm sorry,' she said. 'Did you say Mrs Sugden?'

'That's right. The Beedhams' housekeeper. Had her cottage on the same terms as us. Only she died before the twenty-five years was up.'

'So is Colin related to her?'

'Grandson. Not that you'd have known. He never visited her, not until he found out about the covenant. Then he couldn't do enough for her. Hoped to inherit the cottage, but then old Mrs S went and died, and he moved in. Said being her grandson should give him rights and argued the covenant now applied to him. He didn't get much joy from Mr Halliwell, so he went to Citizens Advice. Don't think they were much help either.'

'He wasn't a good neighbour,' said Peg. 'But I feel sorry for little Ruth, being thrown out of her home.'

'I think they've split up,' said Jasmine. 'Ruth's moved in with her sister. She's been working for me while her sister looks after Sonny along with her own two. Ruth's hoping to get a council flat.'

'Well done her,' said Peg. 'She's too good for that Colin Sugden.'

Harold was sitting too close to the heater. Steam was rising from his fur and he started panting. Ivo stood up and moved him closer to the window. He settled the dog down to cool off and noticed a windowsill with an assortment of objects.

'That's Reggie's collection,' said Peg proudly. 'He's got one of them detector things.'

'All that's stuff I've dug up from around here,' said Reggie.

Ivo examined an array of coins, belt buckles, a couple of toy cars, a bracelet, a bent spoon and on the end of the windowsill a piece of metal twisted into the word *Carrera*. Ivo picked it up and examined it.

'One of my first finds,' said Reggie. 'Must be five years ago. I dug it up by the gate to the house.'

'Off a car, isn't it?' Ivo asked.

'One of them posh ones.'

'You found it just after we saw those two women, didn't you?' said Peg.

'That's right. We don't get a lot of visitors out here, 'specially not early in the morning. Although we're not usually awake very early,' Reg added with a chuckle. 'We might miss a few.'

'What?' said Peg. 'Dawn picnickers? Hardly.'

'Anyhow, we remember when people do come.'

'If we're awake. And mostly it's planning people. Those who want to turn us out of the house. Even though our solicitor says they can't do that.'

'I don't think those two were from the council, or the planning,' said Reggie.

'I dunno,' said Peg. 'Why else would they come so early?'

'How early?' Katya asked.

'Just after dawn,' said Reggie. 'Midsummer, it was. Around half-five, I think. I was only up because I'd forgotten to put the bins out and they need to be down by the gate by half-six. It had been bothering me all night and I couldn't sleep so I thought I'd make a cup of tea. When I took Peg her cup, I opened the curtains and saw these two people. They were just leaving. I don't know when they arrived. I hadn't heard anything, even though I was sleeping badly. They were very quiet until one of them drove a back wheel into the ditch by the gate and the other had to stop her car and help push it out.'

'So there were two people in two cars?' Jasmine asked.

'That's right. A posh sporty car and a smaller one. One of them Fiats.'

'A 500?' Ivo asked.

'That's right,' said Reggie. 'Nice little cars, but overpriced.'

'Did you speak to either of them?'

'Didn't even go out,' said Peg. 'They were well down the drive by then, so they wouldn't have known we were watching them.'

'Do you mind if I take a photo of this?' Ivo asked. 'I've a friend who knows all about cars. It might be worth something.'

'Doubt it,' said Reggie. 'But take a photo if you want.'

KATYA WAS UNCHARACTERISTICALLY quiet as they drove back to *Jasmine's*.

'Penny for them,' said Ivo.

'Just joining the dots,' said Katya. 'Colin Sugden was the grandson of the Beedhams' housekeeper, who would have been a very rich woman if she'd survived the twenty-five years. If she'd lived long enough to sell up, I assume Colin stood to inherit.'

'So you think he's a suspect in the murder?'

'I can see why that might make Colin want to stay in the cottage,' said Jasmine, nudging Harold along the improvised bench so that she could stretch her legs out. 'He was obviously making a case about inheriting the covenant. But surely killing the trustee would be the last thing he wanted.'

'Not if Stefan was being obstructive,' said Katya. 'Perhaps he thought he stood a better chance without the trustee blocking his efforts.'

'Perhaps Colin killed the other bloke and Stefan found out, so Colin had to kill him as well.'

Katya shook her head. 'I doubt it. First, Colin had only lived in the cottage for two years and it doesn't sound like he visited his gran very much. And anyway, what motive would he have had for the first killing?'

'We don't even know the name of the other victim, do we?' said Jasmine.

'Hopefully the police will pull their fingers out and get on with identifying him soon. Once they've released his name we can start researching him.'

26

Jonny was keen to find out more about Larry Trubshaw. He couldn't help thinking that both murder victims had something to do with the house. Jonny felt there was a clue in the photo that would connect them and if he could do that, he might discover a motive as well. He made a list of everyone he could remember from the party and how they connected to each other. The party was long before the first murder, but even though the house had been empty for years, he was sure there was a link. They knew that Stefan Halliwell was the name of the later victim and that the glamorous twins had been Halliwells before their marriages. It was a fairly uncommon name, so Jonny doubted it was a coincidence that Stefan had the same last name as one of the sisters who had lived in the house. There was mention of a younger brother, Geoffrey. Stefan's father, perhaps?

The name Trubshaw kept coming up as well. James' cousin Larry, son of Peter Trubshaw, who had married Claudia. Larry might or might not have been Ottilie's date at the party. She was vague about that, but she had known that Larry moved abroad, so in spite of what she'd told him about disliking Larry, they'd kept in touch. Or at least her daughter had, and mothers and daughters usually talked to each other. They had been planning to visit China together, which suggested they were close.

Looking at the list he'd made, Jonny realised that Larry Trubshaw and Stefan Halliwell were cousins. Would Larry be able to cast any light on Stefan's killing? Jonny would find him and ask. Ottilie claimed to have lost touch with him since he was living abroad, but that shouldn't mean he was impossible to find. Most people didn't just disappear. He wished he had an email for the Beedhams. It would be simple enough to contact them and say he'd known James and now wanted to make contact with his cousin Larry, who he'd known a while back. Larry was their nephew, so they would most likely know where he was. But after a lot of searching, he concluded that Cyril and Coralie had nothing to do with the world wide web. He tried Claudia, searching for both Claudia Trubshaw and Claudia Halliwell, but found only accounts of the sisters' modelling careers.

Jonny had come up against a brick wall, but reluctant to give up, he signed into a newspaper archive he'd used before and searched for Larry Trubshaw. He found a short article in a Warwickshire newspaper from a few years back. An account of an incident involving a protest at a pheasant shoot. Laurence Trubshaw had been shot. Laurence/Larry. Same name wasn't it? So was that the end of Jonny's search? Another unfortunate demise. Apparently not. A link took him to a short piece, which told him that a number of animal rights protesters had been arrested and charged with disorderly behaviour, and also mentioned that although injured, Laurence Trubshaw hadn't pressed charges. Had he been magnanimous to the protesters or worried about gun licence violations? The article didn't say. But it did prove that Laurence Trubshaw was alive. Or at least, he was five and a half years ago. Jonny could find no trace of him since then, so perhaps Ottilie's theory that he was now living abroad was the correct one. And then a thought struck him. If no one had seen or heard from Laurence for five years, could he be the second, as yet unnamed victim? It seemed far-fetched, but when Jonny looked deeper, he discovered that Laurence had lived alone. He'd taken early retirement and was living on a pension, which had been stopped when he failed to confirm to the annuity company that he was still alive. He'd sold his house shortly after he'd been shot, and then disappeared, apparently as Ottilie claimed, to live somewhere in the sun. Had he made it to his new home or had he been killed, his body left at Beedham House? Somewhere, Jonny suspected, there was a bank account containing a large amount of money from the sale of his house. He couldn't do anything about that, but the police should know. They would be able to look into it. If the money was still sitting there, Mr Trubshaw might not be sunning himself in an expat community in Spain. He might have spent the last five years trussed up in a trunk in the attic of Beedham House. Jonny wondered if the police had discovered any of this. Teddy had suggested that the appeal for the public to come forward with information meant that they knew very little about the victims. But would they take his ideas seriously? Would they even listen to him? Lugs would have done, but this new DI? He had no idea. He needed to consult Katya.

27

Charlie drained the last of her coffee and scowled at the team. She'd just had a message from Paddy Philips asking how the case was developing. Reading between the lines, it was more *why the hell haven't you arrested anyone yet?*

'You got anything to report?' she asked, picking up a pen and walking towards the board in the hope of being able to add something. 'Any of you?'

'The Braddocks were helpful,' said Annie. 'They don't like Colin Sugden much.'

Charlie circled Colin's name on the board.

'We can't say he's a suspect just because the Braddocks don't like him,' said Gary.

'I thought he was manipulative,' said Annie. 'Possibly violent. And he's probably being turned out of the cottage.'

'Les, did you check his background?'

'No criminal record,' said Les. 'But he'd come close. Brought in on suspicion of inciting violence after a fight outside the council offices. Something to do with people jumping the housing list.'

'Hardly a motive for killing Halliwell,' said Charlie.

'We don't know much about Halliwell, do we?' said Gary. 'Or the other bloke, Trubshaw.'

Annie checked her notes. 'We know Halliwell had been accused of fraud, but the case was dropped. He was also involved with the scuffle that caused Trubshaw to shoot himself. He was local, lived alone in an upmarket flat in a converted warehouse in Slough. Never married, as far as I can find out. He seemed to live mostly for his work. I traced a couple of companies that he'd had contracts with. People I spoke to said he was an efficient contractor. Got on with the job, kept within budget and completed the work on time. I couldn't find anyone who'd socialised with him.'

'Gary, you checked out his flat. Anything of interest there?'

'Not really. It was all rather impersonal. He bought a show flat complete with furniture. Hard to find any clues about what kind of person he was.'

'How long had he lived there?'

'A couple of years. He bought it with money his dad had left him. Before that he was in a flat share. I checked that with the agent but he wasn't able to tell me much.'

'Then nag him,' said Charlie. 'There must be a record of people he lived with somewhere. Did you talk to his current neighbours?'

'The place was deserted when we searched his flat. I knocked on a couple of doors but it's not the sort of building where people are very friendly. They mostly commute into London and work long hours. Those I did talk to said Halliwell was no problem. They'd seen very few visitors to his flat, no loud music or any other noise. There is CCTV covering the main entrance and parking area. Should we ask to see it?'

Charlie nodded. 'Yes, contact the management and ask for all they've got.'

'They probably wipe it after four weeks,' said Annie. 'But that's still an awful lot to check.'

'Go and chat to your mates downstairs,' said Charlie. 'See if they can spare anyone to help.' If anyone could entice a couple of uniforms to spend a day sitting in front of a computer screen, it was

Annie. 'Les, dig a bit further. Look at his online presence and see if there's anything outside his work.'

Annie was checking back through her notes. 'He did have a girlfriend before that trouble with the fraud case. A woman who worked for the same company.'

There was something not right about that fraud case, and Charlie was wondering if it could have anything to do with the murder – both murders, since it was a few years ago. 'Name?'

'Davina Ferdinand. For the last six years she's been working for a big investment company in west London. Flashy lifestyle, big annual bonuses, holiday home in the south of France.'

'How did you discover all that?' asked Gary.

'I talked to someone Stefan had done some contract work for shortly after the fraud case was dropped. She told me she'd been asked by a friend to give him some work because he'd fallen on hard times. She'd been reluctant at first, but she gave him a few hours work and was pleased with what he did. She started to recommend him to other people. He grew his business out of that.'

'And it was this Davina Ferdinand who asked her to find work for him?'

'So she said.'

'Any reason she'd want Halliwell dead?'

'Can't find one. Should we bring her in?'

'Not yet,' said Charlie. 'I'll go and see her at work. Annie, you can come with me.'

Charlie added her name to the list of suspects, if only because two suspects looked better than one in her updates to DCI Philips.

'Apart from both being found in Beedham House, have we found anything that connects the two victims?'

'The DNA match?' asked Les.

'Must be a factor,' said Charlie. 'Les, work out how they were related. Dig into the records and come up with a family tree. Anything found on Stefan's computer?'

'His whole life was tied up in computers,' said Les. 'So it's a lot more complicated than just going through his personal laptop. It's all still with IT.'

'Then we'll move on to Laurence Trubshaw. What do we know about him?'

'He shot himself in the foot,' said Gary with a snigger.

'What about his lifestyle?'

'He was chairman of the Warwickshire Game Club,' said Annie. 'That's shooting animals rather than the video kind. Until he shot himself, he worked at an estate agent, Hatchwards, a family business in Warwick. His wife left him nearly ten years ago and moved to New Zealand.'

'So she's not a suspect,' said Gary. 'People who do for ex-husbands don't hang about for years to get their revenge.'

'And Gary should know all about that,' Annie muttered.

'Check her out,' said Charlie. 'Make sure she didn't slip back into the country five years ago.'

'She'd probably not have beaten him to death even if she had,' said Gary. 'Unless she's a very large lady and had a friend to help heave him into the trunk,' he added with a laugh.

'Good point,' said Charlie. 'But check anyway. Why did no one report him missing?'

'Shortly after he shot himself, he resigned from his job and sold his house,' said Annie. 'He'd bought a villa on the Costa del Sol so everyone he knew would have assumed that's where he went. I checked that out. He never turned up there. He'd not transferred the final payment so the developers served various notices and then reclaimed the property because he didn't respond to any of them.'

'When and where was he last seen?'

'He lived just outside a village off the M40, north of Oxford. A neighbour had popped in to help him with his final packing the day before the completion of his sale.' She checked her notes. 'Mrs Marcia Jones.'

'That fits in with Dr Yates' time of death,' said Charlie. 'Although, given the length of time before the body was found, he gave us a wide margin.'

28

'Hot chocolate with marshmallows and extra cream,' said Ivo, handing Rosa a cardboard mug he'd picked up from *Jasmine's*. He fished the van keys out of his pocket and put them down next to the mug of hot chocolate.

'Yum,' said Rosa, writing Ivo's name on a luggage label, which she tied to the keys before hanging them on a hook over her desk. 'Although I have to point out that bribery won't work with the MOT people.'

It was an annual dread of Ivo's that something expensive would be wrong with his van and he'd not be able to work while it was being fixed, which meant that he'd not earn enough to get it fixed. When he first moved into *Shady Willows,* the van had been on loan from the site owner, but when Ivo discovered that the insurance didn't cover him for leisure use or work away from the site, he'd bought it and registered himself as the owner. But there was always the worry at the back of his mind that the extra cash he earned wouldn't be enough to cover the running costs of the van.

Rosa had been his salvation, checking the van regularly, sourcing spare parts at scrapyards and assuring Ivo that she could keep him on the road. 'It'll be fine,' she said, spooning cream and marshmallows into her mouth and grinning at him. 'I've looked after this little van as if it was my own. It's going to pass, no problem. Should be all ready for you to pick up later this afternoon. I'll give you a call when it's done.'

Ivo fished into his pocket for his phone. 'I wanted to ask you about something,' he said, scrolling to the photo he'd taken at the Braddocks' cottage. 'Do you know what this is? It's off a car, isn't it?'

Rosa took the phone and studied the picture. 'It's off a Porsche,' she said. 'Carrera model. Very swish. Where did you find it?'

'I met this bloke with a metal detector. He found it in a ditch near where he lives. I don't suppose you've had a Porsche in for repair with this bit missing?'

Rosa laughed. 'Believe me, people who own cars like that don't use garages like mine. They'd go to some flashy main dealer.'

'Even if it was just to replace a bit of decoration?'

'If you can fork out a hundred K for a car, you'd just phone up Porsche for a new decal. They'd hardly need someone to go scrabbling around car breakers looking for one. Is it an important bit of detection?'

'Well,' said Ivo. 'There were a couple of bodies found in a house near to where this was dug up. One of them had been there for around five years, and that was more or less when the bloke I was talking to found this. Most likely it was not connected, but I had a hunch I should follow it up. Around the same time, the bloke and his wife saw a couple of cars very early one morning. One was a Fiat and the other they said was a posh car. Perhaps there was some other damage when the decal was pulled off.'

'I suppose if the driver was doing something they shouldn't and damaged the car, they might have taken it to my mate three doors down, who does body repairs for people who don't want to bother their insurance companies. He's not there this morning, but Airdrop the photo to me and I'll ask him.'

. . .

Ivo and Harold walked back to *Shady Willows*. Ivo spent the rest of the day on jobs around the site and was just about to make himself a cup of tea when Rosa called him. He took the call nervously.

'All fine,' she said. 'I did a couple of small adjustments, tweaked the brakes and replaced a rear light bulb. It passed with flying colours, so you're fine for another year.'

Ivo breathed a sigh of relief. 'Can I come and pick it up?'

'Sure. I'll be here for another couple of hours. I'll be ready to eat by then – can you pick up fish and chips for three? There's someone I want you to meet.'

'Okay,' said Ivo. 'Are you going to give me any clues about who it is?'

'Nope. You'll have to wait and see.'

The timing worked well. Tidy up the site, stroll back into town and drop into *Jasmine's* to see if there was any news. Jonny was researching people who'd been at the party at Beedham House. Too long ago to have anything to do with the murders, but he may have dug up some interesting background. Katya and Jasmine were concentrating on Colin and Ruth. Ivo couldn't imagine that Ruth had anything to do with it, but she might have witnessed something, and Colin certainly seemed like an untrustworthy, even violent type.

Ivo arrived at Rosa's with a plastic carrier bag full of fish and chips, Harold following keenly in his wake. Rosa was just locking up when he arrived.

'We're not eating here?' he asked.

'No, but we're not going far.'

He followed her along the row of workshops under the arches, stopping at a door marked *Phil's Body Shop*. She tapped on the door, which was opened by a middle-aged man dressed in overalls. 'Ivo,' she said, 'this is Phil.'

Ivo shook his hand and passed around bags of fish and chips, which they ate sitting on disused car seats.

'Rosa tells me you are interested in Porsche repairs,' said Phil.

'Have you done any?'

'Just the one. Highly unusual, which is why I remembered it. After Rosa mentioned that you'd found a decal, I checked my records. Just over five years ago, I had a Carrera in with a badly dented offside wing. Brand new, it was.'

'Did the owner say what had happened?'

'Ran into a deer in the Great Park, apparently. Didn't want to go through official channels because the park authorities take a dim view of people crashing into their animals.'

'Did they kill it?'

'Didn't say. I guess there'd be a record somewhere if a deer had been found dead, or even just stunned.'

'Would the missing decal have been like this?' Ivo asked, finding the photo.

'Yes, it would. But it would have been on the back of the car. More likely to have been torn off if the driver backed into a hedge or something. There was no other damage to the back. I said I'd probably have to order one from Porsche or maybe pick one up on eBay. The owner said not to bother replacing it.'

'Do you remember the owner's name?'

Phil shook his head. 'I don't keep detailed records after three years. The repair was recorded in my logbook for that year, but I don't have any other info. As far as I remember she paid cash.'

'She?'

'Yes, didn't I say? It was a woman who brought the car in.'

'Do you remember what she looked like?'

'She was a big woman. The driver's seat was pushed well back. But interestingly not as far as the passenger seat, which was pushed back to its limit and reclined. She must have had a tall passenger, or one who wanted to sleep. She was obviously well off. Well, she'd have to be to own a car like that. But she was also expensively dressed. Looked like she might have been at a party – gold sandals and a flimsy dress with a hoodie pulled over the top. She was wearing dark glasses, but the weather had been hot, so most people were wearing sunglasses. My guess was that she'd hit the deer after drinking too much at a party and didn't want anyone to find out.'

Finishing his fish and chips, Ivo thanked Phil and walked home, thinking over what he'd been told. The police hadn't released details about how the victims died. Nor had they said for sure that they'd died at Beedham House, only that the bodies were found there. There had been very little information from the police. If only Lugs was still there, he'd have been able to tell so much more about the case.

Ivo had a theory. The dead man couldn't have been very large or he wouldn't have fitted in the trunk. Could he have been killed by the large, Porsche-driving woman and loaded into her car, with the help of the Fiat driver, and driven to Beedham House?

It was the kind of theory that Katya would laugh at. But Katya had been wrong before and if this was a workable idea, it told them two things. First, at least one of them must have known that Beedham House was empty. And one of them must have had a key to the trunk in the attic. On second thoughts, he realised, the key could have just been left in the trunk. But even if that was the case, they still knew about the attic and the fact that no one was likely to go there for a long time. So these people had a connection to the house, maybe business or maybe personal. Either way, it would be recorded somewhere. All the detectives had to do was find two people. One, or more likely both of them, big enough to carry a dead man up two flights of stairs and load him into a trunk. Someone who also had a connection to Beedham House.

29

'Do you know what the meeting's about?' Jonny asked, wiping the final plate and hanging the tea towel carefully on the heated rail.

'No idea,' said Jasmine, putting some plates away in a cupboard. She laughed. 'Perhaps Katya's persuaded the police team to let us join in with their murder case.'

'I can't see that happening. Ivo was at the new DI's home, fixing gutters and stuff. He told her about Harold's record of catching murderers, but he didn't think she took it seriously and didn't tell him anything about the case. Why would Katya have had better luck?'

'Did Ivo tell her about the rest of us?'

'Not sure.'

They could hear Katya thumping up the stairs to the office. 'We'd better go and join her,' said Jasmine.

Ivo was already in the office with Katya when the two of them arrived. He looked excited and was showing Katya the photo he'd enlarged of the Porsche decal, and some pages he'd printed from eBay. Jonny and Jasmine both had folders of notes, which they put down on the table.

'Looks like you've all been busy,' said Katya. 'I thought it was time for a catch-up about the Beedham House murders. You all seem to be going in different directions, so I thought we'd try to pull it together and look for connections. Any of you have a suspect yet?'

'Do you?' Jasmine asked. 'My money's still on Colin Sugden. Ruth has been telling me a bit more about him. He's got a violent streak and a grudge against the Beedham family.'

'Ever been in trouble with the police?'

'He once had a police caution after a tussle with someone at a protest outside the town hall about rent rises.'

'Hmm,' said Katya. 'I'm inclined to agree that he's a likely candidate, but a tussle at a demo doesn't make him a murderer. I suppose his grudge is to do with the covenant.'

'Like the Braddocks said, he thought he should be entitled to inherit the cottage after his gran died. According to Ruth, he'd been going on about how the covenant wasn't administered properly.'

'Does she know why he thought that?'

'Only something about his family's devoted service to the Beedhams over the years. It doesn't sound like he had any actual evidence to support it.'

'It could have given him a motive for getting rid of Stefan but not the other murder. He'd only have been a teenager when that happened.'

Ivo opened a packet of chocolate fingers and passed them round. 'Any thoughts about who the other victim was? The police are being a bit slow to release the name, aren't they?'

Jonny shuffled through his notes. 'I have an idea about that,' he said. 'I think it was a man called Laurence Trubshaw.' He talked them through his theory about Trubshaw's apparent move abroad and the fact that he was now untraceable. 'And,' Jonny added, 'he had a connection to both the Beedhams and the Halliwells.'

'You could be right,' said Katya, drumming on the table with her fingers. 'But people do move abroad, never to be heard of again. We'd need a bit more than that. Any idea of a motive?'

'Just a feeling,' he said. 'But I went to visit this woman.' He pointed to Ottilie Kent in the party photo. 'Something wasn't quite right. Can't put my finger on it, but she was evasive about Trubshaw and how well she knew him. She also claimed not to know the name of this man, Geoffrey Halliwell. I thought she was lying about that. And if she was, it means she's covering up the connection between the two victims. And another thing, I mentioned the murders, but she didn't ask me anything at all about them. You'd think she'd want to know who the victims were, particularly as there is a connection to a house and family that by all accounts she knew quite well.'

'You think she's a suspect?'

'She was definitely not telling me all she knew, but I'm not sure if that makes her a suspect. She was an odd type. Into Eastern philosophies.'

'That doesn't make her a murderer,' said Katya. 'But it does sound like a lead worth following up on.'

'We should find out more about her daughter as well. That was another thing she didn't want to talk about. She'd cancelled a visit to China with her but was very evasive about why.'

'Perhaps she murdered the daughter as well,' said Ivo, suddenly taking an interest in what Jonny was saying.

Katya sighed. 'You think this woman bludgeoned a man to death and hid him in a trunk, smothered another man five years later and did away with her own daughter? I think you've excelled yourself this time, Ivo.'

'But we should try to find out about the daughter,' said Jasmine, coming to Ivo's defence. 'She might be involved in some way, even if Ivo's idea is a bit over dramatic.'

'Her name is Davina Ferdinand,' said Jonny. 'Her father was an opera singer called Rodrigo Ferdinand. Ottilie and he were divorced quite soon after Davina was born.'

'Any reason to treat the daughter as a suspect?' Katya asked.

Jasmine typed the name into Google. 'If this is the same woman, she could be a person of interest. She's on the board of a very high-powered property management company in west London. Perhaps she was trying to get her claws into Beedham House to develop it.'

She turned the screen towards Jonny. 'Does she look anything like Ottilie? She's about the right age to be her daughter.'

'Hard to say,' said Jonny. 'Print it out and I'll take a closer look.'

'Does it tell you what kind of car she drives?' said Ivo.

'Why is that relevant?' Katya asked.

'Because posh business people drive expensive cars and Rosa's mate repaired one five and a half years ago. It was missing a decal like the one Reggie Braddock found.'

'That could be interesting,' said Katya. 'What kind of repair was it?'

'Badly dented wing. She said she'd hit a deer in the Great Park.'

'Do we know how the victims died?'

'There's been no information from the police about that,' said Katya. 'It's extremely frustrating. But if one of them had been killed by a car, you'd think they would have asked for witnesses.'

Jasmine picked up a pen and wrote names on the board: Colin Sugden, Ottilie Kent and Davina Ferdinand on one side, Stefan Halliwell and Laurence Trubshaw on the other. Trubshaw was unconfirmed so she put a question mark next to his name. Then she drew a picture of a house between the two columns. 'They all have a connection to the house, don't they?'

'That has to be at the back of it,' said Jonny. 'It's all about ownership and rights over the land.'

'Oh, we should add this guy,' said Jasmine, writing Monty Letward's name alongside the other suspects.

'Who is he?' asked Ivo.

'The man who wants to develop the land,' said Jasmine. 'If we could connect him to any of these people, we'd be onto something.'

'He might have killed both of them,' Jonny suggested.

'I can't imagine why,' said Katya. 'Getting Trubshaw, if it was him, and Stefan out of the way wouldn't really help him get his hands on the house. The only one with any claim to it is Colin Sugden, and that's pretty tenuous.'

'The Braddocks have a valid claim, but they've not been murdered,' said Ivo.

'The house is owned by this speculative company,' said Jonny. 'Baverstock Holdings. Monty Letward is CEO. Is it possible it's one that rivals Davina Ferdinand's?'

'It might give either of them a motive for killing each other or the Braddocks,' said Ivo. 'But not the victims.'

'We can't start investigating big property companies,' said Katya. 'But I do think we've got enough to go to the police.'

'And hand over all we know?' said Ivo. 'They'll take over and we won't get a look in.'

'Or they might be extremely grateful and let us carry on with our enquiries,' Jonny suggested.

'It's a risk we're going to have to take,' said Katya. 'Much as I'd like us to solve the case, we can't withhold information and as I've said before, justice is more important. Get all your notes together and we'll go and see DI Hannington.'

'What, now?' Ivo asked.

'No time like the present,' said Katya, standing up and climbing into her coat.

30

'Some people to see you, boss,' said Les, clearing away empty coffee mugs and sandwich wrappings and squashing them into the already over-full bin.

Charlie had just signed out of an online meeting with the DCI. It hadn't gone well and his words still rang in her ears. They had two suspects – why hadn't they arrested at least one of them? Just collating some final evidence, Charlie had replied. *If only.* Any more stalling and she'd have to pass the case on to the hub. 'No chance it's someone come to confess to murder, I suppose?' she asked.

Les slipped a card across her desk. Charlie picked it up, read it and sighed. 'Who the hell are the Breakfast Club Detectives?'

Annie's ears pricked up. 'They're local private investigators,' she said. 'DI Lomax really rated them.'

'Bloody amateurs,' Charlie muttered.

'No, their boss is Katya Roscoff. She's a retired DS, used to work here.'

'*Used to* being the operative phrase,' said Charlie. 'What do they want?'

'They say they've got information about the Beedham murders.'

'Of course they have,' said Charlie. Everyone within shouting distance of the town had ideas about who was responsible for two murders. Everyone except the team actually in charge of the investigation. 'Go and get rid of them, Gary,' said Charlie wearily.

'They're very insistent,' said Les. 'They'll only talk to the DI.'

'They might know something useful,' said Annie. 'They've been involved in investigations before. There's not much they miss around here.'

'Oh, very well,' said Charlie. It had to be more interesting than a Zoom session with the DCI. 'Les and Gary, you come with me.'

'They're in one of the interview rooms,' said Annie. 'The nice one with the comfy chairs. PC Smithers has made them tea.'

Charlie checked her hair in the mirror, picked up her iPad and they made their way downstairs to the interview room.

There were four of them. A stout woman with wispy grey hair and a bright green coat. The woman who had been outside Ruth's cottage the day she and Gary had heard about the second body. Katya Roscoff, she remembered now. Gary had made a note of her name. Standing next to her was a tall, good-looking man in his sixties, who stood up as Charlie entered the room; a young woman with long, dark hair and a young man holding a dog on a lead. An extremely ugly dog, that looked as if it had been in the wars. Charlie recognised it, and the young man who was holding its lead. She couldn't remember their names. They'd met in her mother's kitchen, where her son was giving them breakfast. How was it Kai was getting to know the locals so much faster than she was? She considered asking Les to fetch some more chairs, but that would look as if she had time for these people, whereas she just wanted to get rid of them as soon as possible. Better if they all stayed standing. 'I'm DI Hannington,' she said. 'And these two are DS Trotter and DC Bateman. I gather you have some information for us.'

The plump woman stood up and shook her hand. 'I'm DS Roscoff,' she said. 'I'm very pleased to meet you at last. These are my colleagues, Jonny Cardew, Jasmine Javadi and Ivo Dean.'

'And Harold,' said Ivo.

Ivo, and Harold. She remembered now. 'We've met,' she said. 'You were working for my mother at the weekend.'

'Kai made me a very delicious breakfast,' said Ivo.

He was the handyman who'd come to clean the gutters. And who, she remembered, had volunteered his dog as a seeker out of murderers. She turned to face Ivo. 'You took over from my mother's old handyman.'

'That's right,' said Ivo. 'You were just leaving for work. I expect you had to get in early, what with murders to solve.'

He was a likeable lad. Charlie almost found herself smiling at him. 'You said your dog had caught murderers,' she said, holding back a laugh and trying not to catch Gary's eye. She just hoped Ivo wasn't there to offer Harold's services again. Although, with the progress her own team were making, even a dog might be able to move things along a bit.

'I've met DC Bateman,' said Jasmine, shaking his hand. 'He pops into my café for breakfast.'

'Best breakfast in town,' said Les.

'Jasmine and I run the breakfast club there,' said Jonny.

'All very nice,' said Charlie. She was obviously missing out on the local social life. Did they really know anything about the case, or had they just come to check her out and have a chat? 'Perhaps if you have information for me, we should get down to discussing it.'

Jonny sat down at the table and opened a briefcase. 'We've made a number of discoveries,' he said, spreading out some papers. 'Of course, I'm sure you know most of this already so forgive us if we're wasting your time.'

They almost certainly were, but she'd better hear them out. She couldn't afford to be in trouble for missing vital evidence.

'First,' said Jonny, 'I have some background on the victims. I've a long-term connection to Beedham House and the family that lived there. I've drawn up a family tree.'

Charlie glared at Les. Wasn't he supposed to have done that? 'Not got around to it yet, boss,' he muttered.

'The two victims,' Jonny continued, 'as you no doubt know, were related – cousins. Laurence Trubshaw's mother, Claudia, was Stefan Halliwell's aunt. Her younger brother was Geoffrey Halliwell.'

'But we've not released Trub—' said Gary, before Charlie put a hand on his arm to silence him.

'What makes you think Laurence Trubshaw was one of the victims?' she asked.

'I deduced it,' said Jonny, handing her his notes. 'I'm right, am I not?'

'I'm not at liberty to confirm that at present. Perhaps you could email a copy of these notes to DC Bateman, so that we can collate them with what we have already.'

Les passed Jonny a card with his email.

'Well,' said Charlie, heading for the door. 'Thank you for coming in.'

'We've not finished,' said Katya. 'You didn't imagine all four of us have the time to drop in if we didn't each have info of our own, did you?'

Charlie was afraid of that. Was she going to be tied up with this lot all day?

'I've a suggestion, boss,' said Les.

31

This was more like it. Jonny had obviously made an impression with his family tree. Katya had hoped that DI Hannington would hear the rest of what they had to tell her, but on reflection, perhaps this was better. Four of them and four of the police team, the young constable had suggested. A nice symmetry there. The DI had left them to sort out the details, and after a short discussion they paired Jasmine with Les. Les was already a regular at *Jasmine's*, calling in most days to pick up breakfast for the team. And breakfast was not the only reason he was there so often. He seemed very taken with Jasmine herself. And both of them knew their way around the internet. They would work well together. She was less certain about pairing Gary with Ivo. They seemed poles apart and she'd be interested to see how that worked out. Ivo always had far-fetched theories about their cases and Gary seemed more like a straight-talking, go-for-the-obvious type and was possibly, like Katya herself, inclined to be impatient. But they'd both shown an interest in the cars that had been spotted at Beedham, so it could work out. Jonny, Katya was sure, would get on well with Annie. With any luck he'd charm her into giving away bits of inside information.

That left Katya herself with the detective inspector, which was right and proper given her status. Now that Ruth was working for Jasmine, Katya had been able to chat to her and slip pertinent questions into the conversation. Katya didn't get on well with small children, but Ruth's sister was happy to look after Sonny while she worked, and staying behind for a coffee and a chat at the end of her shift was no problem. In a roundabout way, Katya had discovered a great deal about Colin Sugden. He was known to be violent. He was also bitter about the possibility of losing the cottage, or rather the money his grandmother could have realised by selling it. She'd not worked out a motive yet but was considering the idea that Colin had been responsible for the earlier death and Stefan had somehow discovered it. Perhaps Trubshaw had his eye on the cottage for himself and had found a loophole in the covenant. Colin had only lived in the cottage for a couple of years, but he would have known about the covenant long before that and any thought that old Mrs Sugden might be persuaded to leave would give Colin a motive for getting rid of whoever it was trying to persuade her.

Katya would pass on all of that to the police team and was considering whether she should call on DI Hannington again or persuade her to come to a meeting in the breakfast club office. She decided on the latter, where she had all the information she needed within easy grasp. Katya called her, suggesting they might make it a working lunch, since the police station didn't even have its own canteen. The lunches Katya recalled from her working days consisted of tasteless coffee from a machine, and if she'd remembered to buy them, sandwiches that had sat on her desk since early morning.

It seemed nothing had changed. DI Hannington jumped at the chance of what Katya described as a plate of Karim's lunchtime specials.

THE DI ARRIVED PUNCTUALLY, and Katya led her up to the office, where Jasmine had set out plates of filled rolls. Charlie looked around her while Katya fired up the coffee machine. She sniffed the freshly ground coffee appreciatively and selected a smoked salmon roll from the plate Katya passed her. 'It seems you are quite experienced as amateur sleuths,' she said, looking round at the board, Jonny's folders of case records and the upmarket coffee machine and computer he'd requisitioned from Cardew Packaging Solutions.

'We think of ourselves as rather more than that. I was, as you know, a detective sergeant before my retirement. DI Lomax contracted me to help out with cases a number of times after I retired.' Contracts that didn't actually mention crime-solving as such. Katya failed to mention that, feeling it was unnecessary since most of the cases had led to the uncovering of crimes.

'And what led to your interest in this case?' Charlie asked. 'I assume your dog walking visit to the crime scene was no coincidence.'

Katya shrugged. 'Dogs need walking. I'd read about the discovery of a body and decided to take a look. Two birds with one stone, you might say. I had no intention of compromising the scene, as I'm sure you noticed. We kept our distance until your sergeant moved us on and interrupted our discussion with Ruth.'

'He was just doing his job.'

'A little abruptly, if I may say so.'

There was a hint of a smile on the DI's lips. 'Sergeant Trotter gets on with the job. And no doubt you have been able to follow through your questioning of Ruth since she now seems to be working here.'

'We took pity on the poor girl after Sergeant Trotter turfed her out of her home.'

'She couldn't stay there. It might have been part of the crime scene. We would have made sure she wasn't left homeless.'

'You would?'

'Did you ever ask anyone to leave their home without making alternative arrangements? Before you retired?' Charlie added with an emphasis on *before*.

'Of course not. But the team I worked with had local knowledge and fewer budget constraints.'

'In any case,' Charlie continued, 'Ruth seems to have fallen on her feet. New job and a new home with childminding thrown in.'

'And she's given us some insights into that boyfriend of hers. Ex-boyfriend, I should say, but she will have told you about him when you interviewed her yourselves.' Katya knew that Ruth had not been interviewed. The only time the police had spoken to her, apart from DS Trotter's abrupt demand that she should leave the cottage, was when Annie Safiq had reassured her after she phoned in the disturbance at Beedham. She was not sure if they'd spoken to Colin Sugden at all. And they definitely should. In Katya's view, he was a prime suspect. A motive, plenty of opportunity and a convenient deposition site right on his own doorstep.

'You will, of course, be updating my team on anything Ruth has told you. An email will do nicely.'

Katya turned to the computer, opened a document and pressed print. The printer having completed its job, Katya lifted out the three pages of notes Jasmine had typed and put them in a plastic wallet, which she placed on the table in front of the inspector. *She'd not have been expecting that.* Katya felt more than a little smug. Amateur sleuth, indeed. They'd show her who were the amateurs around here, and it was not going to be her Breakfast Club Detectives.

The inspector stood up, picked up the notes and headed for the door. 'One of my constables can take a look at these,' she said. 'To see if there is anything we need to add to our own records.'

Katya watched her go. She turned to look at the spotless whiteboard. Time to move the case up a notch or two now they had a toe in the door of the local police team. She'd call a meeting to plan their next steps.

∼

CHARLIE MADE her way down the stairs, feeling she'd been outsmarted by a group of local busybodies. Why the hell hadn't her team formally interviewed Ruth, or more to the point, why hadn't they interviewed Colin Sugden? She pulled out her phone to call Gary when, not looking where she was going, she bumped into someone. She looked up, ready to apologise, but was lost for words. She was staring into the face of her own son.

'Hi, Mum,' he said, looking pleased with himself.

'Kai? What the hell are you doing here? You should be at school.'

'Study period,' he said. 'Dropped in for an interview and Jasmine's just given me a job.'

'What do you mean, a job? You've got your GCSEs coming up.'

'Calm down, mother dearest, it's only a few hours serving at tables on Saturday and Sunday mornings. Maybe a bit of washing-up when it's needed.'

For God's sake, were these breakfast club people taking over her entire life? They were set on solving her case for her, repairing her mother's house and now they were taking over her son as well. Not to mention providing her team with breakfast rolls and coffee. 'If you feel like washing-up, I'm sure your grandmother could do with some help.'

'Gran thinks it's a great idea for me to get a job.'

She probably wanted him out from under her feet at weekends. 'Did she suggest asking for a job here?'

'No, it was Jonny Cardew who suggested it.'

'You know Jonny Cardew?'

'Yeah, I met him when I was out walking Meg.'

Bloody people. Who did they think they were, interfering with her case, muscling in on her family? 'We'll discuss it when I get home.'

'You mean I have to wait up for you? Until midnight?'

It wasn't that bad. Was it? 'I'll be home early tonight, I promise.'

'Dad's picking me up this evening. We're going bowling.'

'What time?'

'About eight. I'll have finished my homework by then.'

'I'll pick you up from school.' Gary could take the strain for the rest of the afternoon. He'd asked for time off to go his daughters' parents evening the next day, so he owed her. He could call her if there was anything urgent. And she could hardly be angry with Kai for spending time with his father. She was going out herself that evening.

32

Charlie slipped on a pair of glitter-encrusted high heels and looked at herself approvingly in the mirror. She cleaned up nicely, even after a couple of hours in the mortuary in scrubs, followed by a session sorting evidence bags in what passed for a storeroom in the dusty basement of the police station. And then there was the meeting with the people who called themselves the Breakfast Club Detectives. Interfering amateurs, she'd thought at first, but she had to admit they had some useful information. In some ways they'd made more progress on the case than her own team.

After all of that she definitely deserved a night out and she hoped nothing urgent would come up at the last minute. But in the middle of a murder case one never knew if that *drop everything immediately* moment would happen. But luck was on her side that evening. She'd been home in time for a shower and a glam-up session – short black dress, black tights, hair fastened with a silver clip and artfully draped over one shoulder, and model grade make-up. And then she remembered she'd need shoes. A search in the bottom of her wardrobe revealed multiple pairs of high-tops – her favoured work footwear – Ugg boots, some shabby trainers and a pair of red sandals she'd bought for a holiday in Majorca eight years ago. Just showed how long it had been since she'd last dressed up for a night out. She'd have to borrow some shoes from her mother. For God's sake, who does that at her age? She was thirty-six, not sixteen. But luckily she and her mother wore the same shoe size, and Diana Hannington was nothing if not a snappy and fashionable dresser. The sparkly heels had been bought for a dinner dance in the days when Charlie's father still attended them in his role of senior civil servant for the Home Office. Charlie doubted her mother had worn them again, and definitely not since her father had died last year. It had been a tough time for her mother, but she was coming through it with the kind of stiff upper lip, keep calm and carry on attitude that was second nature to women of her generation. Her mother, Charlie was certain, would soon be back dressing up and going to parties. Egged on by Kai who, for a fifteen-year-old boy, took an unusual interest in what his grandmother was wearing. She'd probably be on Silver Singles or Ourtime any day now, scrolling furiously in search of a dashing silver fox.

Charlie had almost refused Teddy Strang's invitation. She'd spotted him at the press conference and suspected he was hoping for a few inside details over dinner. 'I'm in the middle of a murder case,' she'd protested.

'Oh, go on,' said Teddy. 'You can't work all the time. How many invitations do you get for slap up dinners?'

Not many recently, but she was not going to let Teddy know that. 'I'm not allowed to consort with journalists,' she told him.

'Rubbish,' he said. 'I promise not to ask about your work. You're allowed a social life, I assume.'

'Well...' She could feel herself coming round to the idea. She deserved a bit of fun now and then, didn't she? 'Okay, but not around here. I don't want to be recognised.'

'I know just the place. A quiet little out-of-town restaurant followed by a club in Basingstoke.'

'Really? There's a night life in Basingstoke?'

'If you know where to look.'

And Teddy, of course, would know where to look. Looking was his modus operandi, a precursor to the searing revelations he wrote –

most often concerning politicians – and sold to the highest bidder. He was an unscrupulous, untrustworthy, devious charmer. In other words, a total rat. And Charlie rather liked him. 'Only if we go Dutch.' She couldn't risk her name appearing on Teddy's expenses claim and he was well known for wining and dining people and chalking it up to the newspaper if he thought he could extract a story from them.

It was a good choice of restaurant, Charlie had to admit as she finished the first two courses and perused the dessert menu. There were no printed prices, which meant it would be eye-wateringly expensive, but what the hell. She was on an inspector's salary now, wasn't she?

What to eat after a crab salad followed by duck breast with passion fruit? 'I'll have the gooseberry, elderflower and sauvignon sorbet,' she said, glancing across the table at Teddy, who was still studying the menu. She took a sip of her wine and looked around the restaurant at the other diners. At the nearest table were two well-dressed men, alpha males eyeing each other like peacocks. One of them knew the staff by their first names and had the kind of knowledge of the wine list that suggested he'd boned up on it in advance. A businessman trying to impress a client, Charlie decided. Although his companion looked bored rather than impressed.

At another table she spotted a young couple simpering at each other, little fingers linked as they raised their glasses in a toast. Charlie found them slightly nauseating. *Wait until you're the one left holding the baby.* She directed that thought towards the young woman, whose little-girl smock suggested that if they weren't talking about moving into their forever home, they certainly should be.

And then Charlie spotted an older couple. The woman in a tasteful, navy-blue cocktail dress and pearls. The man in a pinstriped suit and tie. A tie that was familiar, as was its wearer. *Oh my God*, Charlie thought, grabbing the menu and burying her face in it as if her life depended on it.

'Thought you'd chosen your dessert,' said Teddy, looking at her in surprise.

'We've got to get out of here,' she hissed at him.

'Why?'

'See that couple over there? No, don't stare at them.'

'How can I see them if I don't look?'

'Just a quick glance then, and don't let them see you. Do you know that man?'

'Yeah, Detective Superintendent Archie Groves, isn't it?'

'Does he know you?'

'Dunno. I asked him a question at a press conference a week or two ago.'

Probably an embarrassing one. Teddy didn't do nice easy questions. The superintendent would definitely remember him. 'He can't see me here with you. We've got to get out.'

'You think he'll recognise you all dolled up like that? Not your usual workwear, is it?'

'I can't chance it,' she said, releasing her hair from its clip and pulling as much of it over her face as she could.

'Okay,' said Teddy, handing her his car keys. 'Make a run for it while I cause a diversion.'

They headed in different directions, Charlie towards the door while Teddy lurched past tables, bumping into one close to where DS Groves and his wife were sitting, and knocking a full glass of wine onto the floor.

∽

THE CLUB WAS FUN. Charlie let her hair down, literally, and danced until the small hours, when she remembered she had a team meeting at eight the next morning. Teddy drove her home and she made strong coffee, which they drank sitting in front of the embers of an open fire. Charlie threw on a log and poked at the fire to get it going again. She'd wondered if her mother would still be up when they got back. She'd be a good match for Teddy. She'd had a way with journalists when she was the wife of a high-ranking Home Office official. Charmed the coats off their backs while revealing absolutely nothing. But there was no sign of either her mother or Kai. She could hear the dull thump of music from Kai's room and was relieved that he was safely home. She saw enough of what happened to teenagers allowed to roam the streets late at night. It was after midnight and he should be asleep by now. But there was no school tomorrow and one late night couldn't hurt. He'd probably been sitting up with his grandmother browsing vintage clothing sites.

'So,' said Teddy. 'I know you can't talk about the case, but how do you like your new posting?'

'I was disappointed at first. I thought I would be joining one of the major crime teams.'

'Two murders on your patch sounds like a fairly major crime.'

'Yeah, it's turning out better than I thought it would. I've got a very hands-off DCI so I'm more or less in charge of the investigation.'

'And a good team?'

'I thought they were a load of misfits initially, but they seem to be coming together quite well.'

'All new to the area?'

'All but one. A rather over-enthusiastic DC who worked in the old team.'

'That was with Lugs Lomax?'

'That's right. Did you know him?'

'He was a good bloke. Popular with his team and a bit at odds with the suits.'

'I met a woman yesterday who had been his DS.'

'Katya Roscoff?'

'You know her?'

'Very well. She's a good sort, if a bit of a loose cannon. Where did you meet her?'

'She came to see me with a group she said were called the Breakfast Club Detectives.'

Teddy laughed. 'Didn't take them long to get a foot in your door. What did you make of them?'

'I expected them to be a load of nutters, but I'm afraid to admit they seem to know rather more about my case than my own team. They're each teaming up with one of my lot to hand over the info they've got.'

'And then you plan to say a polite thank you and tell them to push off?'

Charlie nodded.

'Big mistake,' said Teddy. 'They'll likely detain the perpetrator while your lot are still faffing around with forensic reports.'

'Just what I need with the DCI breathing down my neck and a possible carpeting from the D-Sup.'

'You should use them,' said Teddy. 'Lugs did.'

'How?'

'Well, Katya's a retired DS so she's accredited. Also very experienced and perceptive. Lugs had a budget for civilian investigators. Do you?'

'Not as far as I know, but I've not asked, and the DCI is piling on the paperwork so I could claim we need extra support.'

'Best to keep Katya where you can see her. Like I said, she's a loose cannon. Lugs had to rescue her on a couple of occasions, but she's a way of rooting out the bad guys.'

'What about the rest of her team? I can't see anyone allocating funding for a group of amateurs.'

'They won't need it. They're dead keen to help and Katya will keep them under control.'

33

Jasmine's was quiet when Les arrived. Not surprising really, it was only seven a.m. and they'd not been open long. As he had hoped, Jasmine and her assistant, Stevie, he thought it was, were chatting behind the counter. His suggestion at yesterday's meeting with the Breakfast Club Detectives was that each of the team should talk to one of the detectives, make a note of what they knew and then collate everything at their own meeting later that day. He was pleased when the boss asked him to follow up on what Jasmine had to offer. He assumed it was because Jasmine had told them her findings had been online ones, Les being known as the nerdy member of the team. If the choice had been left to him, Les would have chosen Jasmine, not because of her IT skills but because he couldn't imagine anything he'd like more than spending some time in her company. Not a very professional attitude, and he had to assure himself that he had no intention of this being anything other than a formal meeting with a member of the public who might have some useful information.

He chose a table and Jasmine came across to take his order. He could feel himself blushing as she smiled at him. 'The usual bacon rolls to go?' she asked. 'Or have you come to question me about my discoveries?'

'Yes, I mean no...' *Get a grip. Call yourself a detective?* He took a deep breath. 'Yes, I'd like breakfast but I think I'll go for the porridge this morning and I'll have it here. I'm not taking breakfast to work today.' The office would be empty that morning as the boss was out at a finance meeting. Annie was checking up on local council planning records and Gary was off to Warwick to try to trace Trubshaw's movements the days before he left home.

'A good choice, porridge. Very warming. And coffee to go with that?'

'Black, please.' That might steady his nerves. 'And I need to arrange a time to talk about the information you have on the Beedham case.'

'Sure. I'm not busy right now, if you don't mind eating and talking. Or do you want me to come to the police station? I could call in this afternoon.'

Talk here in the warm with a decent coffee, or in a bleak interview room with Gary hovering in the doorway smirking at him? It was a no-brainer. 'Here will be fine, if you're sure you can spare the time.'

'Absolutely. I've got Stevie to see to customers. I'll just get my laptop.'

Les watched as she left the room after a quick word to Stevie. She returned a moment later with his bowl of porridge and a laptop tucked under her arm. 'Coffee won't be a mo,' she said. 'Stevie's just got the machine going.'

Les felt awkward eating while she had nothing. But then he usually felt awkward with young women, so nothing new there. He ate a steadying spoonful of porridge. 'So what have you got for me?' Stupid question. And open to misunderstanding.

But he needn't have worried. Jasmine opened several windows on her laptop. 'Katya suggested I should take a look at the victims' social media. But I expect you've already done that.'

'Stefan Halliwell had this massive set-up. Mostly work. He seems to have had very little social life. We've handed everything over to our IT specialists. It'll be a day or two before they get back to us. I did a quick check around the usual social sites but didn't find anything.'

'No, he has practically no social footprint of his own. I had to do some back-door snooping.'

'Nothing unethical, I hope.' He was joking and had a sudden moment of panic in case she thought he was accusing her of something. People could be like that with the police.

She grinned at him. 'Of course not. What I did was go through all the people in that photo Jonny took. I think there was a copy in the notes Katya handed over to your boss. But it's here if you've forgotten it.' She clicked on one of the small windows that was open on her desktop and the photo sprang to life. 'It's a very old photo and I was quite surprised how many of the people in it had Facebook pages or similar. Most are not very interesting, but I followed up a few tags. I was looking for a link between Trubshaw and Halliwell. Jonny's already discovered that Halliwell senior was at the same party as Trubshaw, but that was years ago, and that Trubshaw's mum was a Halliwell before she married. So they were cousins, but that's hardly a motive for murder, is it?'

'We knew the victims were related from DNA results, but how did you know that Trubshaw was the victim? We've not released it yet.'

'We didn't actually know it. Jonny worked out that it could have been Laurence Trubshaw and your sergeant fell right into his clever trap by saying that his name hadn't been released yet. If it wasn't him, he'd have been more likely to say something like *our enquiries are still ongoing.*'

Very clever. There was a lot more to these people than merely amateur busybodying. And one in the eye for Gary. The boss would no doubt be having words with him about it. 'Gary's the jump-in-with-both-feet type,' he said. 'But tell me more about these tags.'

'Well, first I found this.' She opened a Facebook page belonging to a woman called Ottilie Kent and clicked on her gallery.

'Actors?'

'Close. They're opera singers.' She scrolled down away from the groups of people onstage to a photo of a tall young woman.

Les stared at it. 'Is that her when she was younger?'

'No, it's her daughter, Davina. I took a look at her page as well. I had to scroll back several years, but then I found this.' She clicked another photo of Davina and an older man who was not named.

One of their victims. 'Do you know who he is?' Les asked.

Jasmine looked pleased with herself. 'Look at the photo of the party. This is Laurence Trubshaw. He would have been in his early twenties when this was taken, and maybe early sixties in the later one.' She arranged the two pictures side by side. 'What do you think?'

Les stared at them. 'You're right. It does look like a younger version of the victim, but I don't see how it's relevant to our case.'

'It tells us that the Kents and Trubshaw knew each other for a long time and that they must have kept in touch. Laurence Trubshaw and Ottilie's daughter were quite close, by the look of things. Jonny wondered if he could be Davina's father. He thought he remembered that Ottilie had been seeing Laurence around the time of the party. He went to talk to her, hoping for an update on the people in the photo and asked her, but she denied it and told him she'd married Davina's father, an opera singer called Ferdinand. But it seems Davina and Trubshaw were seeing each other quite often until about five years ago. Whatever sort of relationship it was, Jonny got the impression that Ottilie didn't approve of it.'

'But again, how is that relevant?'

'Don't you think it's interesting that both Davina and Ottilie seem to have lost touch with Laurence about five years ago?'

'And according to the pathologist, he died about five years ago. Food for thought, but hardly enough to treat them as suspects.'

'Yet,' said Jasmine. 'But I did some more research on Davina. Her parents divorced very soon after she was born and Ottilie reverted to the name of Kent, but her daughter kept her father's name. Davina Ferdinand was easy to find. She's been working for a finance company in London for the last six years and pulls in a massive salary plus bonuses.'

'Okay for some,' he said. 'There's not much in the way of bonuses for the police.' They knew about Davina's current situation already, of course. The boss and Annie were off to see her and interview her at work. They also knew that Stefan Halliwell had once been her boyfriend, assuming the woman Annie had talked to was correct. He decided not to tell Jasmine that, not yet.

'Not for café owners either,' said Jasmine, laughing. 'But me and Dad do okay here. We're our own bosses and I'm not sure we'd really like city life, even if it did bring in a six-figure salary. But we were talking about Davina Ferdinand. Before her swish job in London she worked for the same company that accused Stefan Halliwell of fraud. Shortly after losing his job with them, he was involved in a scuffle in which Laurence Trubshaw was injured. So she's connected to both victims.'

'Are you suggesting she wanted both of them dead?'

'No. Well, not yet, but you've got to admit it's interesting. Well, you've probably discovered most of it yourselves.'

'Some,' said Les. 'It certainly suggests some leads we could follow up. But I need to report back to the boss. Can you send me all this stuff so we can collate it with what we've got?'

'Sure. Got your phone?'

Les nodded and took it out of his pocket and gave Jasmine the number.

'It's all in an online folder. I've sent you a link.'

'Got it,' he said. 'And you'll let me know if you make any more discoveries?'

'Of course. I'll keep in touch.'

Les finished his breakfast and stood up. He needed to get back to check through all this stuff before the boss returned for a briefing.

'Um,' said Jasmine as he headed for the door. 'Are you going to pay for your breakfast?'

'Oh my God, of course. I'm so sorry.' He pulled a bank card out of his pocket.

'It's no problem,' said Jasmine, laughing. 'I can set up a tab for you if you like. Or you could join the breakfast club.' She handed him a leaflet, which he stuffed into his pocket. His mind had wandered, and he'd been wondering how ethical it would be to ask an informant out for a drink. Well, he'd blown that one. And anyway, he was carrying way too much baggage to contemplate anything other than a working relationship. He sighed, wondering if he was ever going to be able to let go of the past.

34

'Getting a new car?' Les put a mug of coffee down on Gary's desk and leant over his shoulder to look at his computer screen.

'I wish,' said Gary. 'And even if I could stretch to a new motor, I could never afford one of these. And,' he added, noticing that Charlie had just come into office, 'I'd be doing it on my own time.'

'Doing what?' asked Charlie.

'He's looking at posh cars,' said Les.

'I'm looking for a Porsche Carrera registered as new about five and a half years ago. All in the line of duty.'

'A new line of enquiry?'

'Yeah. Thanks to Les here, and our teaming up with the Breakfast Club Detectives – bloody amateurs, to use your own words.'

'We have to consider all information from the public, even if they do seem a bit like...' She paused.

'A bunch of weirdos?' Gary suggested.

'I didn't say that,' said Charlie. 'I'm sure they are all very thorough and they seem well respected locally.'

'You mean by your predecessor, and Annie?'

'And others.' There was no way she was going to bring Teddy

Strang into the conversation, but he seemed to have some respect for them and that was unusual in his line of work. 'Why the interest in cars?'

'I went out to that place, *Shady Willows,* where the young bloke with the dog lives and works.'

'Ivo Dean,' said Charlie.

'That's the fellow.'

'Did he have anything useful?'

'Possibly. I thought he was a bit of a fantasist at first. An off-the-wall idea about Trubshaw's killing. But then I started to wonder if he wasn't making some sense after all. Les, did you or Annie notice Reggie's collection of stuff when you went to talk to them?'

Les shook his head and looked across the room at Annie. 'What sort of collection?'

'On his windowsill, apparently. He's one of those detector people.'

'They're called detectorists,' said Annie. 'We talked to the Braddocks at the daughter's house, so we didn't get to look at his windowsill.'

Gary clicked open a photo on his screen. 'Reggie Braddock found this.'

'That's off a Porsche, isn't it?' said Annie.

'You have friends with Porsches?'

'Why wouldn't I?'

Gary shrugged.

'Anyway, I don't, as it happens. But I do have a cousin who's mad about posh cars. He's got a load of magazines with pictures of them on the covers.'

'So Reggie dug up a bit of Porsche,' said Charlie. 'I don't see how it relates to our case.'

'Could be a total red herring,' said Gary. 'But Reggie and Peg told Ivo they saw two people at Beedham very early one morning about five and a half years ago. Midsummer Day, Peg said. Reggie hadn't been sleeping well, something to do with taking the bins out. Anyway, he was awake early and decided to make them both a cup of tea. Peg was still asleep, so he pulled back the bedroom curtains to wake her and that's when he saw them.'

'Saw who?' Charlie asked.

'I told you, two people – one was definitely a woman, he wasn't sure about the other. They had a car each, a Fiat 500 and a Porsche. The Porsche driver had backed her car into a ditch by the gate. Typical woman driver, if you ask me. Shouldn't be allowed behind the wheel of an expensive car. She'd have been better off in the Fiat. I've never understood why a bloke would drive one of those.'

Annie clipped him round the ear with a laminated copy of some updated fire regulations that should have been pinned to the wall.

'Anyway,' Gary hurried on before she could remind him that she had passed the police TPAC driving course while he'd only managed the shorter IRV. 'The other driver had to get out and help her push it back onto the road. Reggie watched them drive away.'

'I don't suppose the Braddocks did anything helpful like take down the registration numbers?' Charlie asked.

'Why would they? They had no reason to think these two had done anything other than take a wrong turning from the main road and landed up at the dead-end drive to Beedham House.'

'I suppose that's not unusual. People see a quiet lane and drive up it to walk a dog.'

'Or do a bit of dogging?' Gary suggested.

'At five in the morning?'

'Who knows?'

'What does it have to do with our case?' Charlie asked.

'I'm coming to that,' said Gary. 'Reggie went out a few days later with his shiny new metal detector and found the decal in the long grass by the fence. He cleaned it up and started his finder's collection on the windowsill of their living room.'

'So Ivo's theory is that Trubshaw was beaten to death by a couple of people who drove to the house in separate cars to do it.' Charlie looked at Gary scathingly. 'Did he have any thoughts about what Trubshaw was doing at the house? Did he suggest lending us his dog to sniff them out?'

'No, what he did was quite sensible. His van was due for its MOT. He goes to a woman called Rosa who has a workshop under the arches, where she does car repairs, including Ivo's van.'

'Don't tell me,' said Charlie. 'Ivo interviewed her and she just happened to remember servicing a Porsche five and a half years ago and thinking that the woman who owned it looked like the type to bludgeon a man to death.'

'A Porsche owner wouldn't use a garage under the arches,' said Annie. 'They'd go to a specialist.'

Gary sighed. 'Hear me out,' he said. 'Ivo was there with his van for its MOT. He showed Rosa the photo of the decal and asked if she'd ever worked on a Porsche. Of course she hadn't. She said much the same as Annie. That owners of upmarket cars go to the big main dealers. But she has a mate a few arches down who does bodywork repairs. The sort people don't want to bother their insurance companies with.'

'Bet he doesn't repair Porsches,' said Annie. 'I don't suppose Porsche owners are too bothered about losing their no claims bonuses.'

'Well, that's where you're wrong, Miss Smartypants,' said Gary. 'After talking to Ivo I went to see him. He was a bit shirty with me at first. Said he'd already told Ivo and Rosa everything he knew. But once I reassured him he wasn't in any trouble, at least he wouldn't be if he gave me a glance at his records, he got quite talkative. He *had* only ever repaired one Porsche so he remembered it well. And what's more, the repair was done five and a half years ago. For a woman in dark glasses who paid cash.'

'Very Audrey Hepburn,' said Les.

'Did he have any details?' asked Charlie, looking more interested.

''Fraid not. Most of his work is knocking out small dents for cash, no questions asked.'

'So did he remember anything useful? Like the woman's name?'

'He didn't remember her name. He wasn't sure if she'd even told him. She didn't give him any contact details. Just turned up two days later to collect the car and paid him in cash. As Annie pointed out, posh car owners are not his usual customers so this one kind of stands out for him. The car had a badly damaged off-side wing and a dented bonnet. The woman told him she'd hit a deer in the park.'

'That's not very likely,' said Annie. 'There are surprisingly few deer-related incidents in the park.'

'There are warning signs on the road through the park, so it's not impossible. A deer might wander into the road when there's not much traffic.'

'I didn't say it was impossible. Just unlikely.'

'It's worth checking, though,' said Charlie. 'Annie, see if there's anything on file here and if there isn't, can you get on to the park wardens and see if they have any record of an incident in June five and a half years ago?'

'There was one other thing he told me, boss. He said the car was missing its decal but the owner said not to bother replacing it.'

'So it's possible this *was* the car the Braddocks saw. Any way of tracing the owner?'

'I'm onto it now, boss. Like the repair bloke said, it was brand new. Very few miles on the clock and still with what he described as a showroom whiff. So I'm checking new registrations by women for the first three weeks of June of that year. There were 6,000 registrations on those dates but only around fifteen percent were women.'

'That's still nearly a thousand,' said Les.

'Nine hundred,' Annie corrected.

'I've been on to DVLA. They'll get back to me.'

'It might be worth calling Porsche dealers,' said Charlie. 'It could be quicker.'

Les was gazing out of the window. 'I wonder why she didn't want the decal replaced,' he said. 'Not having it would draw attention to the car, wouldn't it? People might ask awkward questions.'

'If a new one had to come from Porsche, I suppose it could be traced,' said Annie. 'She wouldn't have wanted that. Not if she'd been at Beedham involved in a murder.'

'Perhaps she found one on eBay,' Les suggested. He sat down at his own desk and ran a search. 'You can get one for around eighty quid. Most seem to be sold by the same dealer.'

'Contact him,' said Charlie. 'Find out who he sold one to in late June or July of that year. If he doesn't cooperate, I'll apply for a warrant and get eBay to release sales details.'

'You think we might be onto something, boss?' Gary asked.

Charlie nodded. 'It's definitely a lead. Let's look at what Trubshaw was up to at the time. We know he was supposed to leave for Malaga on the morning of June 22nd but failed to turn up there. Where was he the night before that? Could he have been at Beedham to meet someone?'

'How would he have got there?' Annie asked. 'There was no car left at Beedham as far as we know.'

'What kind of car did he drive?' Les asked.

'It was a VW Polo,' said Annie, checking the notes. 'Not taxed or insured for the last four years.'

'So it wasn't one of the people the Braddocks saw driving off in Trubshaw's car,' said Les. 'Reggie told us one was a Fiat and no one could describe a Polo as posh car.'

'It still might be,' said Annie. 'He might have hired the Fiat planning to leave it at the airport when he checked in for his flight.'

'Then the car hire company would have reported it missing.' Charlie tapped her pen on the desk. 'Unless the woman returned it to them herself. Les, get on to car hire firms with offices at Heathrow and see if they have anything in their records.'

'Isn't it more likely that someone drove him to Beedham? Hiring a car is expensive. It's hardly worth it just for an airport run. It would be cheaper to get a taxi.'

'So now we're looking for a woman who drives a Fiat 500, possibly as a hire car, or a taxi,' said Gary. 'That's even worse than trying to find one who owns a Porsche.'

'So do you want me to check car hire or not?' said Les. 'Or taxi firms?'

'Do both,' said Charlie. 'But begin with taxis that operate near Trubshaw's home in Warwick.'

'Any good checking ANPR records?' Les asked.

'They're only kept for two years,' said Gary.

'I'll get on to DI Gregson and see if there were any incidents reported for that night. We might just spot the Fiat on a traffic cam. Oh, and call the friend who helped Trubshaw with his packing. He might have told her how he was getting to the airport.'

A video file pinged onto Annie's desktop and she clicked to open it. She watched the footage for a few moments then called the others over and ran it again. 'It's from the CCTV outside Halliwell's flat. That's him, isn't it?'

They stared at the blurred image. 'Looks like it,' said Charlie. She checked the time stamp. 'How long would it take him to get from there to Beedham House?'

Annie checked Google Maps. 'About half an hour if he was walking. Ten minutes by car.' She ran the next video, which showed the entrance to the car park for the flats. They could see Halliwell standing by the kerb.

'Could be waiting for a taxi,' said Gary as they watched Halliwell step out of range.

'Or picked up by a friend,' said Charlie. 'But either way, the timing suggests he was making his way to Beedham House. See if there are any ANPR cameras along that stretch of road.'

'It won't help much,' said Annie. 'Unless the driver was speeding or jumping a light.'

'Check it out anyway. You never know, the driver might have been in a hurry to get him to Beedham and broke the speed limit.'

35

'What do you want?' Ruth edged nervously behind Jonny, who was emptying the dishwasher, and stared crossly at Colin Sugden, who had wandered into the kitchen from the back entrance.

'Don't flatter yourself, love. Got a present for the boy, ain't I?'

'I'm working,' said Ruth. 'You should leave.'

'Been promoted?' Jonny asked, looking through the open door at the black car that Sugden had parked untidily against the kerb.

'Nah, picked up some extra work for a business gent. Mostly private deliveries or chauffeuring. But one of my mates works at that Toy Warehouse place on the industrial estate. Got me that.' He pointed to a cardboard box that he'd left at the top of the steps. He used his foot to push it in Ruth's direction. 'For the boy,' he said.

It all sounded dodgy to Jonny. Businessmen with smart cars, mates' rates from Toy Warehouse. But Colin had struck him as a dodgy type from the moment Jonny first clapped eyes on him. Was he being too judgemental?

Ruth looked at the picture on the box and gasped. 'It's one of those ride-on tractors,' she said. 'Like Sonny saw in the park. They cost a fortune, don't they?'

Colin smirked at her. 'Earning good money now. Bet you're sorry you left me, aren't you? You can always come back.'

Ruth shook her head. 'I'm never going back to that place,' she said. 'So just push off.'

'Please yourself,' said Colin. 'You might regret it, though. Going to get a nice little place of my own soon.'

'Yeah?' said Ruth. 'I'll believe that when I see it.'

'Just you wait,' he said menacingly. 'Anyway, duty calls. See ya.'

They watched as he headed down the steps to the car, muttering something that sounded like *plenty more fish in the sea*.

'You okay?' Jonny asked.

Ruth nodded.

'Well done for standing up to him like that,' he said. 'You were very brave.'

'He's all mouth,' said Ruth. 'At least, he is when there's other people around. He was more fists when we were on our own.'

'Well, at least he still cares about Sonny,' said Jonny.

'He'd better not think he's going to buy us back with expensive presents.' She looked suspiciously at the tractor in its box. 'He probably stole that,' she said, giving it a nudge with her foot. 'He's not asked about Sonny once since we left.'

'What are you going to do with it?' Jonny asked. 'You could be in trouble if it was stolen.'

'Oh,' said Ruth. 'I don't know. Sonny would love it, but if we're going to be in trouble…'

'Why don't I have a word with Annie?' said Jonny. 'She could ask if anything like it has been reported stolen.' And if it had, it would give them an excuse to question Sugden about any other suspicious activities, like assisting with a murder.

36

Gary pressed three painkillers from a blister pack and washed them down with a slurp of water from a bottle that had been sitting on Annie's desk for the last week. It had a stale taste, but that was the least of Gary's problems. He slumped into a chair at his desk and wished he could do something about the bitter taste in his mouth, the feeling that someone had fed him a dose of sand and was now hammering nails into his head.

He winced at the sound of the boss crashing into the office, letting the door slam behind her and thumping a pile of papers onto his desk.

'What are you sitting in the dark for?' she asked, switching on the lights and making him blink in protest. Was she trying to blind him?

'Bit of a headache,' he muttered.

'Fun at the parents' evening?' she asked. 'I've been to quite a few myself, but they don't usually give me a hangover.'

'Bit of a barny with the ex. Wanted me to have the girls this weekend so she can go out with the latest boyfriend. I had to say no. Not that I wouldn't love to have them with me, but not in the middle of a murder case. She didn't take it well.'

'And that caused a hangover? Or is that the result of drowning your sorrows in the pub later?'

'Not exactly. Libby's class has got this nice little teaching assistant, Jodie. She gets to the school by bus but lives near here, so I gave her a lift back. She offered to buy me a drink, which seemed fair.'

'And I suppose one thing led to another...'

'You could say that, yes.'

'I assume you were drinking in the Queen Vic.'

'We were, yes.'

'Handy,' said Charlie. 'When you have a room upstairs.'

Before Gary could comment, Les arrived with a bag of breakfast rolls followed by Annie with mugs of coffee.

'Hope one of those is black,' said Charlie. 'Gary's suffering.'

'Out on the tiles yourself the other night, weren't you?' said Gary. Perhaps they should compare dates, and hangovers. But no doubt that would be inappropriate and she'd start going on about politically correct language in the workplace. Luckily her phone rang before she was able to comment. Maybe not so lucky, he thought as he glanced across and noticed Detective Superintendent Groves' name flashing up on her screen.

She scowled at her phone. 'Better get it over with,' she said. 'I'll take it in my own office.'

HE MUST HAVE SPOTTED her and Teddy at the restaurant. She headed for the door and closed it behind her. No way was she going to let Gary eavesdrop on the earful she was about to receive. She took a deep breath and tapped to take the call.

'Morning, Charlotte.' Groves sounded surprisingly cheerful for one about to deliver a rocket. 'Nice to see you out the other night.'

He sounded cheerful about that as well. Was it a trap? 'Just having dinner with a friend,' she said.

'Young journalist chappie, wasn't it? Hope you didn't let anything slip about the case.'

'Of course not, sir. Teddy and I have been friends for a long time. He knows the boundaries.'

'Pleased to hear it. And I'm glad you're taking the occasional break. Your father would be pleased to know that.' Did he have to drop her father into the conversation at every opportunity? 'I hope you are ensuring the same for the rest of the team.'

'Of course, sir. DS Trotter was out with a friend only last night.'

'Good, good. I'm just calling because it sounds as if DCI Philips is tied up with all this bother in Banbury, or is it Bicester? No matter. He's not able to give you the support you need.'

Oh, God. Was he about to foist a different DCI on them? One who'd sit in the office here issuing orders? 'We're managing well, sir. My two DCs are brilliant at keeping on top of all DCI Philips' paperwork.'

'I'm sure they are. But they'll want to be out working on the case. And it so happens that I've found a pot of cash. A small one, but if I don't use it by the end of the tax year it will disappear. I thought perhaps you might like to contract a bit of civilian help.'

Wow, that was unexpected. 'Thank you very much, sir.'

'It's the least I can do. Your father would want me to make sure you are not overworking.'

She doubted it. Her father was pretty keen on the benefits of hard work, and she thought it unlikely he would have discussed it with the DSup, who seemed to have an over-inflated idea of the closeness of his friendship with her father. But then he wouldn't have heard some of the comments her father had made about him. *Fussbucket,* she recalled, and on one occasion *henpecked.* 'Do you have anyone in mind?'

'I believe DI Lomax had a list of reliable people. Probably left it in a computer file somewhere. I suggest you take your pick from that.'

Charlie thanked him again, ended the call and returned to the main office, where the team were downing steaming cups of coffee and Gary had started to look a bit less haggard. 'Les,' she said. 'Did DI Lomax leave any files on the computer?'

Les sat at his desk and hovered his mouse over a folder labelled

Old stuff – Lomax. 'There's a folder with his name on it.' He clicked on it and revealed a list of documents. 'Nothing very interesting. Personal stuff that didn't need to be filed anywhere official. Just useful contacts, I think.'

Charlie looked over his shoulder. 'Can you open that one?' She pointed to a document labelled *Civilian contracts*. 'The DSup is giving us some extra support.'

'There you go,' said Les, clicking on it.

Charlie read it. No surprise that Katya Roscoff's name appeared at the top of the list. *Best to keep Katya where you can see her,* Teddy had said. *She's a loose cannon.* Much as Charlie's instinct was to tell Katya Roscoff to get lost, Teddy probably had a point. Contracting her meant they could keep an eye on what she was up to. And DCI Philips' paperwork should keep her busy.

'Civilian support?' Gary asked. 'Someone to make the tea and do the filing? Don't really fancy that. They might interfere with what we're doing.'

'DI Lomax liked using civilians,' said Annie. 'He said it was good to be part of the community.'

'Don't tell me we're going to work with that breakfast club lot,' said Gary.

'Why not? Katya Roscoff is ex police and you said yourself that Ivo was useful.'

'And Jasmine's been great,' said Les.

'Oh, yeah?' said Gary, winking at him.

'We can only afford one contract,' said Charlie, 'but give Katya Roscoff a few hours and we get four for the price of one. And we get help with the paperwork, which means Les and Annie can spend more of their time on the case.' She turned and smiled at the team. 'Gary and I have both had fun nights out. Annie and Les, you should do the same. Finish work at five-thirty today and go and enjoy ourselves. Gary and I will stay and do whatever needs doing. Unless, of course, another body turns up.'

37

Annie didn't need telling twice. She shut down her computer the moment the minute hand on the wall clock clicked to the half-hour point, grabbed her coat and left. Her cousin was getting married at the weekend and that evening she was having a henna party. Les had no idea what that was but guessed it was a girly sort of occasion. While he'd finished the work he was doing by five-thirty, he wanted to leave everything tidy and in place for when he started work the following day. So by the time he'd closed down his computer, pulled on his coat, said goodbye to Charlie and Gary and left the building, it was nearly six o'clock.

It was a cold evening and as he walked briskly towards the town centre, Les wondered what he would do for the rest of the day. Sitting in his bedsit in front of a tiny TV didn't appeal. He actually enjoyed the long hours that kept him in the office until late. It was warm there and he had company. But here in this strange town, where he'd only lived for a few weeks, he had no idea where to look for companionship of any kind. After the incident, he'd been in hospital before he was transferred to a police rehab centre in Scotland. Then he took a short holiday hiking in the Highlands with Sandy, an old friend of his mother's. After that it was a twelve-week residential detective training course followed by the offer of a posting to Windsor. Moving south, away from where everyone knew about what had happened seemed like a good idea. And work was good. He was getting to like his boss, who at first had seemed cold and impatient. His fellow team members were okay as well. Annie particularly, because she was lively and didn't pry into his personal life. But Gary was okay once you got to know him and were used to his loudmouth lack of tact. It was really quite refreshing. Les was used to people pussyfooting around him, too scared to ask about his past. Gary knew he had a past, although he was clueless about what it was. He hadn't even asked, which made a change. Most people, at least those who knew him before his world fell apart, were exhaustingly solicitous. Was he okay? Not sure. Did he want to talk about it? No, not any more. How could they help him? Just leave him alone to get on with life. Nice, of course, that they cared, but it left him feeling drained and, well, different. But Gary wasn't like that. He treated Les as another mate, an equal – well, not quite an equal, since his rank was higher. But Gary's lack of tact was not aimed at Les himself; it was just a part of who he was. Les liked that. He wanted to fit in, have a few mates and be part of a team.

Les looked at his watch. Should he stop at a pub for a drink? No, it was too early to start drinking. He could find a pub that did meals, but he wasn't really that hungry. Not yet. He walked on past shops that were closed for the day, to the stone steps that led down to the gardens, a five-minute walk away from the Victorian villa where he had an attic bedsit. He'd not made friends with the other residents. It was a place where people kept themselves to themselves. He was lucky. He was one of the few there who had a proper career. But it set him apart. He'd not much in common with his neighbours, who were struggling to find work and many of whom had history with the police, so it was better to keep quiet about what he did.

Halfway down the steps, he reached a walkway and the entrance to *Jasmine's*. Usually he was there for breakfast, but right now the cafe was probably closing, if not closed for the day. But there was still a light in the window and as he passed, he glanced inside. Jasmine and her father, Karim, were tidying up. There were no customers. He was too late for a hot drink, so he turned and headed towards the next flight of steps, turning when he heard the door open behind him. 'Want to come in for a cuppa?' Karim's voice called. 'We've still a few buns need eating up.'

Les turned to face him. 'Sorry,' he mumbled. 'I don't want to disturb you when you're closed.'

'Not at all,' said Karim. 'Come in and get warm.'

Jasmine joined her father in the doorway. 'Yes, do,' she said. 'Unless you're in a hurry, of course. We don't get time to talk properly when you're here for breakfast.'

'No, I'm not in a hurry,' said Les. Quite the opposite. He had nowhere he needed to be until work tomorrow morning.

'You look frozen,' said Karim, as Les entered the café. 'Come and get warm by the fire.'

It was an offer he couldn't refuse. When was the last time anyone had cared about whether or not he was cold? He settled into one of the chairs by an electric log fire, and a cat jumped into his lap.

'Push Omar off if he's a nuisance,' said Jasmine.

'He's not at all,' said Les. It was a long time since he'd last sat in the warm with a cat on his lap. Another thing he hadn't realised he'd missed.

Karim arrived with a tray of food that was left from the day in the café. 'Jasmine and I usually have a natter over the remains,' he said. 'Dig in.'

Les bit into a sausage roll. One that was way more delicious than any he'd bought in the supermarket.

'It was Mum's special recipe,' Jasmine told him. 'Dad's always been the cook, but this was one thing Mum knew how to do really well.'

'It's something I do to help keep her memory alive,' said Karim. 'Not that we'd ever forget her, but when I make these, I can feel her watching over my shoulder.'

'I'm so sorry,' said Les. 'I didn't know.'

'Don't beat yourself up, lad. How could you have known?'

'How long?' Les asked.

'Mum died when I was fifteen,' said Jasmine. 'She and Dad opened the café before I was born.'

'And now Jasmine and I are partners,' said Karim.

'I'm new to the area,' said Les, seeing that Karim was on the verge of tears and thinking he should change the subject.

'How do you like it?' Jasmine asked.

'I've not seen much of the town. We were plunged into the murder case the day I started work and it's taken over.'

'Then as soon as you've solved the case you must let me show you around,' said Jasmine. 'Residents get a free pass to the castle. It's fascinating, but probably more fun if you are with someone. Or are you with someone? Sorry, I shouldn't assume you live alone. It's just that you are always here for breakfast on your own.'

'It's fine,' said Les. 'I am on my own. And I'd love you to show me the castle. If we ever find the murderer and close the case.'

'Are you going to let us carry on helping?'

'I believe we are. The boss was talking about contracting extra help. Her superintendent has found some money, apparently.'

'Great,' said Jasmine. 'We've got a good track record and I've got lots of ideas about the case.'

'Do you want to talk them through now?' Les asked, thinking that his boss wouldn't take kindly to a barrage of ideas from an amateur, however successful. But if he knew the way Jasmine's mind was working, he could check her ideas first. He had access to police databases that Jasmine didn't, and could smooth the way to the DI.

'It's your evening off,' said Jasmine. 'I can't keep you working.'

'I don't mind. And it's not really work if we're just mulling over some ideas.'

'Come up to our lounge,' said Jasmine, once they'd finished the sausage rolls. 'It's cosier in the flat and my laptop's there. I'll make a pot of tea. The sausage rolls can make you thirsty.'

Les followed her up the stairs to the living room. 'Have you lived here long?' he asked.

'All my life,' said Jasmine. 'Why do you ask? Is it very cluttered?'

'No, not at all. It's just, well, it looks lived in.' He wandered around the room, pausing to look at some photos. He picked up one of a woman and a small girl throwing pieces of bread to a crowd of ducks.

Jasmine smiled as she looked over his shoulder. 'Me and my mum. Dad took the photo. He says I used to love going to feed the ducks, but I don't remember it. I was only about three then.'

'It must have been tough for you. Your dad as well.' Les put the photo back. 'I'm so sorry,' he said. 'That was clumsy of me. I should have thought...'

'Don't worry about it. It's why we keep the photos of her where everyone can see them.'

'But...'

Jasmine looked at him. She was used to people not knowing what to say to her, avoiding talking about her mother. She put her hand on Les' arm. 'Please don't be afraid to ask about her. It was tough losing her, but me and Dad got through it and we love to talk about her.'

'It's just... this is such a happy room.'

'Of course it is. It's full of lovely memories.' Now she was the one to feel awkward. Les didn't look as if there were too many lovely memories in his own life. 'You've got a room in one of those big houses at the end of the arches, haven't you?' She was puzzled by Les. He lived in a bedsit in a house run by some trust, a charity that helped people resettle in the community. She'd always assumed that meant those recently released from custody of some kind, but how did that apply to Les? He'd hardly be in the police if he'd committed a crime. She liked him. He was gentle and obviously vulnerable. Not what she'd associated with police officers. Gary fitted her image more closely, as did Annie, and it was easy to imagine Katya in full police mode. Well, she'd not really left that. But Les was harder to place.

She boiled a kettle and made a pot of tea. Everyone felt better after a nice cup of tea, didn't they? Jasmine set out a teapot and some cups on a coffee table. It was a tea set that Karim had picked up at a car boot sale. It was dark red with a decoration of swirling gold leaves, in the centre of which was a portrait.

'That's a fascinating teapot,' said Les. 'Who is the chap with the moustache?'

'No idea. Dad said it reminded him of home, so I guess it's some Persian military bloke.'

'High ranking, I'd imagine, with all those medals.' He watched as Jasmine poured two cups of tea.

'Good old English breakfast, I'm afraid. But I do have a box of Iranian baklava.'

'From an exotic market somewhere?' he asked, smiling. It was the first time she'd seen him smile.

'Waitrose,' she said, laughing. 'But we should be discussing the case. Your boss won't want me wasting your time talking about foreign food.' She opened her laptop. 'I've got a folder of more stuff you might be interested in.'

'We can compare notes. Well, most of mine are still at the office, but I can remember what's there. To be honest it's all going a bit slowly.'

'Are you allowed to share police information?'

He smiled at her. 'Up to a point. There's nothing so far that's particularly confidential, nothing I couldn't disclose to a witness.'

'But I'm not a witness.'

'No, but you have come forward with information. It's not that different.' He scrolled through the pages Jasmine had saved, pausing at a photograph of a group of people dressed to the nines and holding glasses of champagne.

'Ascot races,' said Jasmine.

'That's interesting,' he said. 'Does it have anything to do with the case?'

Jasmine wasn't sure, but all the people she'd identified in the photo had been mentioned in connection to Beedham House and may have had something to do with the murders. 'Do you recognise any of those people?'

He pulled his chair closer to the screen and stared at it. 'Stefan Halliwell,' he said, pointing to the man in the centre of the picture. 'And there's Davina Ferdinand. She's come up in our own enquiries.

She used to go out with Stefan Halliwell when they worked for the same company.'

'Looks like they don't like each other now,' said Jasmine. 'Look at the body language, the way they are turned away from each other like they don't want to admit each other's presence.'

Les tapped his fingers on the table, looking puzzled. 'He was accused of nicking their funds. I suppose Davina Ferdinand wouldn't want to be seen in public with him. And yet, according to our enquiries, it was Davina Ferdinand who canvassed people she knew to get work for him as a freelancer after he was sacked.'

'This photo was taken at last year's Ascot races,' said Jasmine, tapping the screen. 'About four years after Stefan was sacked. They could have fallen out since then.'

'Are you saying she had a motive for killing him?'

'Possibly, but I can't imagine what it could have been.'

'Perhaps one of them wanted to rekindle their relationship.'

'And the other one didn't? Hardly a motive for murder.'

'It can happen,' said Les, his face darkening, but then putting aside whatever had flashed into his head, he asked, 'Do you suppose Stefan Halliwell was interested in horse racing?'

'Not necessarily. Events like Ascot are an excuse for a bit of corporate schmoozing. Horses barely figure for some of the people who go.'

Les looked more closely at the photo. 'We got a report back from our IT people. We'd asked them to check any connections between Stefan Halliwell and the various names that have come up as part of the case.'

'Did they find anything?'

'Nothing out of the ordinary. Business connections, but nothing to raise a red flag about.'

Jasmine looked at the photo again. 'Were any of the connections people in this photo?'

'Hard to say when I can't connect names to photos.'

'Do you know any of the other people?'

He shook his head. 'Send me a copy and I'll see if anyone else in the team recognises them. They're more local than I am. And it's helpful because it tells us that Halliwell and Ferdinand were still in touch even several years after the fraud case.'

'They look as if they know each other quite well. They just don't want to let on to anyone else that they do,' said Jasmine. 'I don't think this was a chance meeting after a five-year gap.'

'No, you're right. I think they were still close but covering it up.'

'I wonder if Davina was involved with someone else in the photo.' She studied the other men in the picture for a possible suspect. None of them were looking in Davina's direction or looking particularly possessive, but camera pictures were very fleeting. It just meant that at that second no one was looking in her direction.

'Look over here.' Les pointed to a figure at the edge of the picture who was partly obscured by the crowd of champagne drinkers. He was wearing a white jacket and carrying a tray of drinks.

'A waiter,' said Jasmine. 'You wouldn't expect posh businesspeople to pour their own champagne, would you?'

'Of course not, but take a closer look. Who do we know with a ponytail like that?'

She couldn't see the man's face, but there was something about his build, and the ponytail. 'Colin Sugden?'

'I'm fairly sure it is, and it can't be a coincidence that the three of them were in the same place at the same time and a few months later one of them turns up dead at a place they were all connected to.'

'I'll send you a link to the whole site,' said Jasmine. 'There could be more photos of people that your team recognise.'

Les nodded. 'I'd also like to know about this man here.' He pointed to another man standing to the left of the group. 'We asked IT to check out the contacts they found on Stefan's computer. They've all been traced but are not of much interest to us. They had been clients of his and all have alibis for the time of his death. And in any case, they are scattered all over the country and their only contact with Stefan was through the work he did for them, which was all completed apparently to their satisfaction. But if this man is who I think he is, he should almost certainly have been one of Halliwell's contacts.'

'You want me to find out who he is?' Jasmine asked, wondering how she could do that if police IT hadn't flagged him up as a person of interest.

'Just to confirm that I'm right. My boss doesn't think it's relevant. Not worth taking time over, apparently.'

'But you think he could be important?'

'If he was here with these people, yes, I think he could be.'

Jasmine stared at the man in the picture. Where was she going to start? 'You said you think you know who he is?'

Les pulled out a couple more pictures. 'I found these on a website. This is Monty Letward, works for Baverstock Holdings.'

'The property developer who owns Beedham House? And you think he's this man at Ascot?' She put the pictures side by side. The Ascot photo was not very clear, and the man was standing at an angle so that part of his face was obscured. But they certainly could be the same person. 'Why would it be relevant if they were all there together?'

'Because when Annie talked to Colin the day Halliwell's body was found, he denied that he'd ever met the owner of the house, and yet here they are within a couple of feet of each other.'

'You should ask Colin Sugden about Ascot.'

'He's not been interviewed yet. We've not taken him seriously as a suspect up to now. But hopefully we'll have reason to pull him in soon and I'd like to see his reaction to the photo.'

'He was here yesterday with a present for Sonny. He was driving quite an upmarket car – said he'd taken on extra work. It must pay well because it was a very expensive present.'

'I don't suppose you saw the registration for the car?'

'No, sorry. It was Jonny that told me about it. I wasn't there. He might know what make of car it was, though. I'll ask him.'

'And could you check out all those Facebook pages again? See if Letward appears on any of them?'

'This Davina Ferdinand, does she work for Baverstock as well?'

'No. According the research your friend Jonny did, she's with some high-flying financial management company.'

Jasmine clicked open the file that held Jonny's notes. 'Ah,' she said. 'I thought I'd remembered correctly. Davina Ferdinand is also the daughter of the woman Jonny took a fancy to at a party at Beedham. Ottilie Kent.'

'Got a sheet of paper?' Les asked.

Jasmine pulled a sheet of plain paper from her printer. 'Going to make a mind map?'

'Kind of,' said Les, pulling a pen from his pocket. 'It's like putting links in a chain. We start with Cyril Beedham, his son's death and the covenant he set up. That connects Trubshaw to the Halliwells and also to the Sugdens – Granny Sugden and Colin. Monty Letward's company owns Beedham house. They wanted to develop the property but were prevented by the covenant. Davina Ferdinand might well have the resources to finance him.' He wrote it all down and passed it to Jasmine.

'Impressive,' she said. 'But it doesn't tell us how either of them came to be murdered. Or who among all these people might have had a motive.'

38

Katya arrived in Charlie's office bearing two cups of cappuccino with extra shots. A bit of bribery rarely went amiss, particularly when it meant nosing into police business. The outer office was empty, the team presumably out and about searching for evidence. Katya crossed the room and peered through the glass door of the inspector's office. Charlie was sitting at her desk, tapping on a computer keyboard. Katya, unable to find anywhere to put the coffee cups down, pushed the door open with her foot and went in without knocking.

Charlie looked up from the computer screen. 'Ah,' she said. 'On the dot of ten. I appreciate punctuality. Come in and have a seat.'

Katya sat down and pushed a coffee mug in Charlie's direction. 'Cappuccino,' she said. 'Extra shot.'

'Great,' said Charlie. 'Thank you very much.' She eased off the lid and took a sip.

Katya glanced down at the bin below the desk, which was already well supplied with *Jasmine's* coffee cups. Charlie noticed the direction of her gaze. 'Excellent coffee,' she said. 'One of my PCs drops in most days and keeps us supplied.' She sighed audibly. 'My son's got a job there washing up and now we appear to be working with the

Breakfast Club Detectives. Can't seem to get away from the place, can I?'

'Can't imagine why you'd want to,' said Katya huffily. 'It's *the* place to be seen. Good food, good company and a bit of crime solving thrown in. What more could anyone want?'

'I'd rather hope that people would come here for crime solving,' said Charlie. 'But it seems my superintendent begs to differ, since he suggested we work together.'

'Still Archie Groves, is it? Always had time for him.'

'Of course, you might have worked under him before you retired.'

'Didn't see a lot of him, but he was always supportive.' Lugs used to whinge about him from time to time, so that might not have been entirely true, but Katya was not going to bring that up when it seemed Archie Groves had stepped in to authorise her working as a civilian PI.

'He and my father were buddies,' said Charlie. 'Archie still keeps a fatherly eye on me. I usually resent it, but in this case, I think he's doing me a favour.' She pushed a piece of paper across the desk in Katya's direction. 'Usual contract, I believe. DC Bateman found it in a folder DI Lomax left for us. Perhaps you would sign it and keep the top copy.'

Katya skimmed through it and signed on the dotted line. Charlie was right. It was exactly the same as one she signed for Lugs a few months ago. She folded up a copy, put it in her bag and passed the other sheet across the desk. 'So where do I start?' she asked.

'We'll go through the case files together and see if you have anything to add.' She clicked open a folder on her computer but was interrupted by a call to her phone.

Katya tried to look as if she was not eavesdropping. Not that she'd learn much from one side of the conversation, which seemed to mostly involve Charlie looking cross and sighing.

After a few moments the call ended. 'That was DC Shafiq,' said Charlie. 'She and Sergeant Trotter are following up a car that was spotted near Halliwell's flat on the day he was killed and it's taking longer than they expected. Annie and I were off to talk to Davina

Ferdinand, who is expecting us in about half an hour, but that car could be important. You'd better come with me instead.'

That was fine with Katya. She'd rather be out and about than trawling through case files.

∼

A SHORT DRIVE UP the M4 and swinging off at Hammersmith Flyover, they pulled up outside a glitzy glass office block, at the top of which was a neon sign with a logo in sage green and citrus yellow lettering. Charlie flashed her pass at a uniformed man who was standing in a kind of sentry box, not unlike those outside St George's Chapel in Windsor. 'Park over there,' he said, raising a barrier and pointing to a row of parking spaces marked for visitors.

Having parked, they made their way through automatic glass doors into a reception area filled with ten-foot-high potted ferns, sofas and coffee tables. As far as Katya could see there was no sign of coffee, which seemed like a waste of tables that had been designed with coffee drinkers in mind.

Charlie marched up to a reception desk, behind which sat two young men – very young men, barely out of school, or so it seemed to Katya. They were immaculately dressed in navy blue pinstriped suits and ties with sage green and yellow stripes. They were wearing name badges that carried the same logo as the roof outside, and announced their names, Barnaby Crouch and Frederick Hollowby. Ex-Etonian interns supported by trust funds and destined for six-figure-salaried jobs in finance companies. Or possibly property companies, Katya thought, remembering why they were there. Barnaby checked their ID and issued them with visitors' lanyards. 'If you just take a seat over there,' he said, 'I'll let Ms Ferdinand know you are here.'

They'd barely had time to lower themselves onto a sage green sofa when Barnaby waved them over. He pointed to a bank of lifts. 'Tenth floor,' he said. 'Ms Ferdinand's PA will meet you there.'

. . .

THE LIFT WAS SO quiet and smooth Katya was surprised when the doors slid open and they found themselves in a carpeted corridor, where huge glass windows gave them an impressive view across London. They were met by a woman dressed in a similar suit to the two men at reception, but this one was a skirt suit and the tie was replaced with a Thatcher-style pussycat bow. Navy blue silk with the now-inevitable sage green and bright yellow stripes. 'This way, please,' she said, having examined both their passes. She headed down a corridor to the far corner of the building and led them into an office where a woman sat behind a shiny black desk, swallowing pills from a white plastic tub and washing them down with water – at least, Katya hoped it was water – from a cut glass decanter.

'I'll do the talking,' Charlie hissed at her. 'You keep quiet and listen.' She headed purposefully towards the desk, holding out her ID. 'DI Hannington and DS Roscoff,' she said, reaching across the desk to shake Davina Ferdinand's hand. A gesture that Ferdinand ignored, placing both hands firmly in her lap, out of reach.

'Take a seat,' she said. 'I must warn you that I don't have long.'

'We're conducting enquiries into an incident at Beedham House recently,' said Charlie.

Davina Ferdinand frowned at them. 'I can't see how I can help you with that,' she said. 'Beedham House is nothing to do with me.'

'But you know the house I'm talking about?'

'I've heard of it, of course. I have a friend who is hoping to develop it.'

'Hoping to?'

'There are some legal problems, I believe.'

'When did you last visit the house yourself?'

'I've never... Well, possibly with my mother when I was a child. She was acquainted with the family who owned it.'

'You will know that we are carrying out a murder investigation at the house?'

'I think I read something about it.'

'We have reason to believe you knew the victims.'

Ferdinand reached for the glass of water and took a swig. 'Victims?'

'Laurence Trubshaw and Stefan Halliwell. When did you last see them?'

She was slow to answer, turning her head to look at the view through the window. 'Let me think. Laurence moved abroad. I have not heard from him for more than five years.'

'Would you have described him as a close friend?'

She shrugged. 'I suppose so.'

'And yet you didn't keep in touch after he moved abroad?'

'I work long hours.'

'So,' said Charlie. 'Stefan Halliwell. When did you last see him?'

'We used to work together, but I've seen very little of him since I left that company. Stefan was accused of fraud. An unfounded accusation, it turned out, but I moved to London myself quite soon after that and we lost touch.'

'But people we've spoken to told us that at that time you and Stefan were close. In fact, you asked friends of yours to give him some contract work.'

She shifted uncomfortably in her seat. 'I may have done. I don't remember.'

'You know Stefan Halliwell took over the trusteeship of the cottages after his father died?'

'Yes, of course. It's the covenant that caused so much trouble to the developers.'

'Strange, then, that Stefan's body was discovered at Beedham House, don't you think?'

Ferdinand tossed down another couple of pills. 'I can assure you, it's many years since I've had anything to do with the house. And I've never been in the attic. And if that's all, I've a meeting to attend.'

'I think that's all for now,' said Charlie, with an emphasis on *for now*. She stood up and indicated for Katya to follow her. Katya, who had been taking notes, tapped her pen on her notebook. 'I have a question,' she said. The DI had headed for the door and Katya was careful not to look in her direction. She had promised not to speak, but a grain of an idea was forming in her head. She looked up from the page. 'What kind of a car do you drive?'

'I don't drive,' Ferdinand snapped.

Katya gave her what she hoped was a piercing look. 'Never?'

'Not for many years.'

Katya would have liked to ask more, but Charlie was clearing her throat impatiently, so she put the notebook and pen into her bag and followed the DI out of the room.

Neither of them spoke until they reached the car. Charlie clicked to unlock it and they climbed in.

'What the hell was that about?' said Charlie testily. 'I told you to keep quiet.'

'Just an idea the team might want to follow up.'

Charlie sighed and pulled the car out of the car park, heading back to the M4. Katya hadn't specified which team might want to follow up her idea and she hoped Charlie hadn't noticed.

At that moment a white van pulled across the lanes of traffic without warning. Charlie pressed her hand to the horn and swerved into the inside lane to avoid hitting it. 'Bloody van drivers. Caught him on the dashcam, though. He'll be hearing from us in the next day or two,' she said, with a look of satisfaction.

She drove up the slip road to the motorway and settled into the middle lane at a steady seventy miles an hour, overtaking a line of lorries in the inside lane. 'What do you think of our Ms Ferdinand?' she asked.

Katya was surprised to be asked. She suspected the DI had only invited her along so that she wasn't left on her own in the office to poke into their records. 'Lying,' she said flatly. 'You need a warrant to check her company accounts. Bet you'll find substantial sums either to or from Baverstock Holdings. Something's going on there. Palms getting greased in all directions.'

'We've already asked for Halliwell's bank records. It won't be so easy with these big finance companies. They're experts in keeping things hidden.'

Katya flicked back through the pages of her notebook until she found two folded sheets of A4 paper. She scanned through them. They were just as she remembered. The press conference had said only that two bodies had been found at Beedham House. There had been no mention of the attic. 'You've now released the names of both victims,' she said, turning to the DI. 'Did you release any details of where they were found?'

'Beedham House,' she said, in a tone of voice that suggested this was an extremely stupid question. 'That was made clear at the press conference.'

Katya waved the pages of notes in her direction. 'I had a friend at the press conference. He recorded the whole thing and transcribed it for me. No mention of an attic.'

'And that's not all,' said Charlie. 'PC Bateman found a magazine photo of Ferdinand and Halliwell attending Ascot races last summer, so we know she was lying about not having seen him for years.'

'You going to bring her in?'

'Soon, I think. We've enough to get an interview plan together.'

39

'Bloody cheek,' said Diana Hannington, tearing the letter in half and hurling it into the kitchen bin. She slammed a frying pan down onto the Aga, poured in some olive oil and started beating a bowl of eggs with what Ivo thought was an unnecessary amount of force. She chucked them into the pan, which hissed loudly, objecting, it seemed to Ivo, to her violence, but more likely because she'd let the oil overheat.

Kai stared at his grandmother open-mouthed. 'Calm down, Gran. It's really not worth losing your temper over a pan full of eggs. I can just have toast if you've burnt them.'

'Sorry,' said Diana as she scooped out the omelette, placing it carefully on a plate. She sliced it in half, slid one half onto another plate and passed them both across the table to Ivo and Kai. 'It wasn't the eggs. And they're not burnt.'

'So why did you lose it?' asked Kai. 'I've hardly ever seen you cross.'

Diana poured herself a cup of coffee and sat down between the two of them. 'It's that bloody man.'

'Boyfriend?' asked Kai.

'Don't be silly, dear. I've had another letter from that Monty

Letward. He's trying to persuade me to sell the house to him so he can use the land to build tacky four-bedroom executive homes. Probably complete with en suite bathrooms.'

Ivo pricked up his ears at the mention of Monty Letward. Wasn't he the bloke who'd wanted to buy up the cottages at Beedham House? Probably for the same reason, to develop the land for new houses. New houses were good, Ivo thought. But not if it meant turning people out of their homes. 'That name came up at our meeting the other day. He sounded a bit threatening.'

'He's not threatening you, is he, Gran?'

'Not at the moment. He's trying bribery first. He's offered me a brand-new retirement flat in a luxury development near Sunningdale. All moving expenses paid, plus a substantial cash sum.'

'So where would me and Mum live?'

'Mum and I, dear,' she corrected. 'And you are going to stay here. I'm not selling.'

Kai fished the letter out of the bin and put the torn pieces together. He read it and then turned to a glossy brochure with a picture of some happy-looking wrinklies sitting at an open-air bar. 'You don't fancy luxury living with like-minded people?' he quoted from the brochure.

'I'd sooner be dead,' she muttered.

'He can't force you to sell, can he?'

'No. I own the house outright. It's a freehold property with no debts. Your grandfather paid off the mortgage years ago and it's in trust for your mother after I've gone. But I'm going to get my solicitor to send him a strongly worded letter to tell him my decision is final and to stop harassing me. More toast, Ivo, dear?'

Ivo shook his head. 'I should be going. I've finished washing the patio and cleaned the conservatory windows.'

'No need to rush off,' she said. 'I'd be interested to know about this meeting of yours and why the subject of Monty Letward came up.'

'Ivo's one of the Breakfast Club Detectives,' said Kai. 'It's really cool. They meet at *Jasmine's* and solve murders and stuff.'

Diana laughed. 'Perhaps they could help your mother out.'

'Actually,' said Ivo, 'we have been helping the police. We've been getting information about the murders. I had a meeting with Sergeant Trotter. We may have found the car that took one of the bodies there.'

'Really? That is interesting. I didn't know private investigators worked with the police.'

'They do, Gran. That's what my next acting gig is. I'm going to be the son of a rich film star who gets kidnapped. I get rescued by a PI called Pippa Strong. It's going to be on Netflix,' Kai explained to Ivo. 'We start filming at the end of June. Luckily it's after my exams finish or Mum wouldn't have let me do it.'

'Wow,' said Ivo. 'When can I watch it?'

'It won't be out until sometime next year. I'll let you know.'

'Wasn't there a series of Pippa Strong novels?' Diana asked.

'By Ellery Anders,' said Kai. 'She's doing the screenplay.'

'I must get them on my Kindle,' said Diana.

'I must let Jonny know,' said Ivo. 'He's always reading crime novels. I think he might be writing one as well.'

'So Monty Letward was involved in Beedham House?' Diana asked. 'He's not one of your suspects, is he? Murdered the owner to get his hands on the land?'

'I don't think so,' said Ivo. 'We don't know much about him yet.'

'Pity,' said Diana. 'If he was banged up for murder, he'd have to stop trying to get me out of my house.'

'Hey,' said Kai, mopping up the remains of his omelette. 'What are you doing this afternoon, Ivo?'

'I'm going to give Harold a good long walk. I might drive over to the Great Park and look for places where the deer are in danger of being knocked down by cars.'

'You want to run over a deer?' said Diana. 'I'm not sure that's allowed.'

'It's part of our case. We think the deer accident may have been a false alibi. I just want to check if it could happen.'

'What I was thinking,' said Kai, 'was that we could go and have a look at Beedham House. My character, the one who gets kidnapped, is held captive in a deserted house. In a cellar, and if Beedham House has a cellar it would help me get into the role, if I can pick up a bit of the atmosphere.'

'Won't it all be closed off by the police?' Diana asked.

'No,' said Ivo. 'They've released the crime scene. The people in the cottages have been allowed to move back.'

'That's settled, then,' said Kai. 'I'll bring Meg, shall I?'

Ivo laughed. 'I think we can get both dogs in the back of the van.'

∽

IVO DROVE up the lane with the dogs panting down the back of his neck, both sensing a walk and anxious to get out and run about. He parked where he had parked before. They put the dogs on their leads and walked towards the house.

Reggie was in his garden, digging. He looked up and waved as they approached his cottage. 'Ivo, isn't it?' he said. 'You were here with your detective friends. Took a picture of my detector finds.'

'That was very useful,' said Ivo. 'I passed it on to the police and they think it's a real lead in the murder case.'

'Well I never,' said Reggie. He reached out an arm and stroked the top of Meg's head. Then he looked up and grinned at Kai. 'Do I know you from somewhere?' he asked.

Peg, having heard voices, came out to join them. 'I know you,' she said to Kai. 'You were that poor wee boy that Santa forgot.'

'What?' said Ivo.

'It was a TV advert a year or two back,' said Reggie. 'Peg couldn't take her eyes off it.'

'Guilty as charged,' said Kai. 'It was four years ago. I've changed a bit since then.'

'No,' said Peg. 'I'd recognise those brown eyes anywhere. But the two of you must come in and have a cup of tea. I've made a chocolate cake, and you can give me your autograph.'

'Kai wanted to look round the house,' said Ivo. 'He's going to be in a crime series on Netflix and wants to see what a creepy house feels like.'

'It's all locked up,' said Reggie. 'But tell you what I'll do. Have your tea and cake or I'll never hear the end of it. Then I can let you in through the garden door into the basement. I've still got a key from when I worked there.'

'You'll need a torch,' said Peg. 'And it would probably be best if you left the dogs with us. There's a lot of rubbish in the house, broken glass, nails, tin cans and the like, which could hurt their paws.'

'Not to mention a few dead rats and trapped birds. Peg's right. I should leave them with us. We'll be happy to look after them.'

'Okay,' said Ivo, deciding that Peg was just after an excuse to spoil the dogs. 'But don't let Harold eat too much cake. Don't believe that half-starved act he puts on.'

40

Jonny was making one of his rare visits to his office at CPS, the cardboard and packaging company he'd run for many years before his retirement, for a board meeting, a dull affair during which Jonny had found it hard to stay awake. Once it had ended, it seemed impolite just to push off home when everyone else was still working. He decided he had better go and spend some time in his office. His role in the company was now a minor one, managing CPS' charitable sponsorships. He'd delivered a report on the progress of two breakfast clubs and his suggestion that they should be looking around for more sponsorship opportunities had been rejected on the grounds that every company, even the highly successful CPS, was feeling the pinch financially. It was noted in the minutes that they might reconsider the idea following the next general election, after which the opinion of the majority of board members was that things could only get better. Jonny couldn't see how but didn't argue.

It was hardly worth him having an office there any more, but his son, Marcus, who was now CEO of the company, insisted that since he still had a seat on the board, his father should put in the occasional appearance and he could hardly be expected to hot desk with junior management, could he? Jonny's comment, to the effect that he and Marcus might hot desk on the rare occasions it was necessary, had not gone down well and the situation had remained unresolved. There was still an office on the management floor of the building with Jonny's name on the door. It had a pretty view over the Grand Union Canal and he could sit at his desk in a nice comfortable chair and shuffle papers, while hopefully giving the impression that he had work to get on with. He arranged some correspondence about the breakfast clubs into two piles. One for Windsor and one for High Wycombe. The High Wycombe one he'd take home and hand over to Belinda. The other he'd drop off at the Breakfast Club Detectives' office, which was where he actually did the Windsor club's paperwork. After that he took some photographs of a dog diving into the canal to retrieve sticks until it was time he could leave for home without it looking too much as if he'd just idled away an afternoon. He'd gathered up his paperwork and pulled on his jacket when there was a knock at the door and a woman with a smile came in carrying a tray with two cups of tea.

Dawn Roberts had worked for the company for years, having joined as a junior clerical assistant shortly after Jonny had taken over as chairman. She had risen to the role of human resources manager but was now cutting down her hours prior to retiring. 'Thought you could do with a cuppa and a chat,' she said, putting the tray down on the desk.

'Lovely,' said Jonny. 'I've always time for tea and a chat. One of the benefits of retirement.'

Dawn laughed. 'You've hardly retired. I hear you're solving murders now.'

'Keeps the old brain ticking over.'

'Probably better than sudoku.'

Jonny agreed that it was. 'Any plans for your own retirement?'

'I'm off to sunny Spain with a friend. We're buying a villa on the Costa del Sol.'

The CPS pension scheme must be more generous than he'd remembered. 'Very nice,' he said. 'You selling your house here?'

'I'll rent it out until I know if I want to settle out there.' She laughed again. 'I can see the cogs turning,' she said. 'You're thinking the retirement lump sum won't go anywhere near a villa in Spain.'

That was exactly what he was thinking. 'I wouldn't presume to pry into your financial affairs.'

'Well, you'd be correct, but this was a once in a lifetime offer. My friend, who is also recently retired, worked for an estate agent in Warwick. They'd been approached by a Spanish property company who sold a villa to one of their employees. It was all going well until the man failed to come up with the final payment. No one knows why, but since he'd paid all but around twenty-five percent, they offered to sell it back for a substantially reduced amount. And as my friend was an employee, she was offered first refusal on it. We've got an absolute bargain.'

Jonny's head spun. He couldn't believe his luck. He fidgeted in his chair in excitement.

'You okay?' Dawn asked.

'Absolutely. Do you happen to remember the name of the man who failed to buy the villa? It wasn't a man called Laurence Trubshaw, was it?'

'No idea, I'm afraid. Would you like me to text Helen and ask her?'

'If you wouldn't mind.'

Dawn tapped a message into her phone while Jonny sat with his fingers crossed, hardly daring to hope that the most amazing breakthrough had landed in his lap without him even trying to look for it.

'Is it something to do with one of your cases?' Dawn asked once she had sent the message.

'Probably just coincidence, but I had to ask.'

'Detectives can't afford not to follow up clues, can they?'

'That's right,' he agreed, although he had a feeling Dawn was laughing at him.

'It doesn't mean we're going to lose the villa, does it? We thought it was safe once we'd completed the contract.'

'No, nothing like that. If it's the same man, he's dead. His deal was never completed. From what I understand, he was about to fly to Spain to sign on the dotted line, hand over the final payment and collect the keys. I'm sure you don't need to worry. If you've completed the contract there's no way they can turn around and say it's not yours.'

Dawn's phone pinged and she looked down to read the message. 'Looks like you've found your man,' she said. 'Helen says she didn't know Trubshaw well, but she's given me the name of a woman who was handling his affairs over here. A neighbour, apparently. Would you like me to send it to you?'

Jonny nodded. He watched as the message pinged onto his phone. An address near Warwick. *No time like the present,* he thought, picking up his car keys. 'Dawn, it's been great seeing you again. Make sure you keep in touch. Let me know all about the new lifestyle.' He reached for the two cups; better not leave washing-up lying around.

'Don't you worry about that,' said Dawn, taking the cups from him. 'Can't let a bit of dirty crockery come between a detective and his case.'

It took him an hour and a half to reach the village where Marcia Jones lived. She'd been surprised to get Jonny's call but said she would be happy to tell him all she knew about Laurence Trubshaw.

She was standing in her garden when Jonny pulled into her drive and parked in front of a compact cottage with a tidy garden and what looked like newly painted window frames. She invited him in and he sat in a tidy if, to his taste, rather chintzy living room.

He took out his notebook and a pen. 'So what can you tell me about Laurence Trubshaw?' he asked. 'Did you know him well?'

'He was an odd character,' she said. 'Lived on his own. Divorced, I think, but no children. Not short of a bob or two, but I don't know how he made his money. I'm guessing estate agents are not that well paid and it's likely to be something illegal. I assumed that's why he disappeared. Not that any of us knew he'd disappeared. We thought he'd gone to live in Spain.'

'When did you know he hadn't?' Jonny asked.

'I had my suspicions when some mail I'd forwarded was returned, and shortly after that I had a bill from the company who were supposed to ship out some of his stuff. They'd not been able to deliver it. They tried to charge me to have it returned here, but the house had already been sold. I refused to pay and told them to keep it all. It was probably worth more than the cost of shipping it.'

'So let me get this straight,' said Jonny. 'He sold his house here and said he was going to Spain.'

'That's right. He sold the house very quickly and the new people moved in a day or two after he left.'

'Do you know where he was flying from?'

'He wasn't flying. He planned to drive there. He told me he was going to stop on the way. A friend of his had a hunting lodge in Windsor Great Park. Just a shack, he said, but he could camp for the night there.'

'I don't suppose you know the name of this friend?'

Marcia shook her head. 'I didn't know who his friends were. I don't think he had all that many.'

'Did you ever see anyone here?'

'Only the people who came to view the house and the ones who picked up his furniture. Oh, there was a woman who used to visit him occasionally.'

'Do you know who she was?'

'He didn't introduce us. I really didn't know him at all well. I thought she might be working for him, a lawyer or accountant. Or I suppose she might have been a relation, a niece, perhaps. She was a lot younger than he was.'

'What did she look like?'

'Tall, dark hair, a bit nervy-looking, if you know what I mean.'

Remembering Katya's description of the woman she'd interviewed with DI Hannington, Jonny was wondering if this could possibly have been Davina Ferdinand. He was wishing he had a photo of her to show Marcia, when the doorbell rang.

'Goodness, I am popular today,' said Marcia, getting up to open the door.

Jonny could hear voices in the entrance hall. Women's voices, he noted, although he couldn't hear what they were saying. A moment later the door opened and Marcia ushered a woman into the room. Jonny leapt to his feet in surprise as the woman approached him, holding out her hand for him to shake. 'Mr Cardew,' she said. 'You're the last person I expected to meet here.'

'I think I can probably say the same, DC Shafiq.'

MARCIA MADE A POT OF TEA, and half an hour later all three of them were sitting around a table drinking tea and eating biscuits baked by Marcia herself. She sighed as Annie asked the same questions that Jonny asked just half an hour earlier, muttering that she didn't see why she needed to go all through it again. Jonny had offered to leave, but Marcia said she preferred him to stay. Odd that she was perfectly happy to chat to a man she didn't know from Adam, and yet seemed ill at ease being questioned by a diminutive female detective constable. That was the power of the police, he supposed, not without a twinge of regret that it was not a position in which he'd ever found himself.

Annie was taking notes in an old-style police notebook. He'd assumed they now used iPads and phones when questioning people. Perhaps it had been found that actual notebooks were less intimidating. Annie covered several pages with notes and, turning to a new page, she asked a question that Jonny had asked when the doorbell had rung. 'What did the woman who visited him look like?'

'She was tall. Like I said before, younger than Laurence.'

'And when did she last visit him?'

'I'm not sure. Perhaps a couple of weeks before he left?'

'And she came by car?'

Marcia shook her head. 'She arrived in a taxi. I don't think she was local. She'd probably come by train and taken a taxi from the station.'

'Did you make a note of the taxi company?'

'No, why would I?' She giggled. 'I never expected to have police asking me about it.'

'But it was definitely a registered taxi, not Uber?'

'I think so, yes.'

'I believe he transferred some money into your bank account.'

'That's right. It was to cover the cost of cleaning the house after he left.'

Annie made a note of that and then looked up. 'Nearly finished,' she said as Marcia started piling up the teacups in a way that suggested she'd like to be left alone. 'Just one more question. Did anyone visit the house after Mr Trubshaw left and before the new people moved in?'

'Just a woman from the estate agent, arrived in a green car. She said she had one or two things to check before the final handover. She had to borrow my key to get in. I thought that was strange, but maybe she'd not come straight from the office and had forgotten to pick one up.'

'And she gave it back to you when she left?'

'Yes, she popped it through the letter box.'

'You didn't think that was odd? If the house had been sold, wouldn't they want to hand all the keys over to the new owner?'

'I didn't give it much thought.'

'Are you sure she was from the estate agent?' Jonny asked, wondering if Annie would object to him butting in.

'That's a good point,' said Annie, looking slightly embarrassed that she hadn't asked it herself. 'Did she have any ID?'

'She was wearing a suit. Dark grey, it was. That's what they wear at Hatchwards, with red ties or neckerchiefs.'

'Was she wearing one of those?'

'Now I come to think about it, no, I don't think she was. But she did have one of those clipboards with a load of house details on headed paper.'

'And can you describe her?'

'A large lady, late fifties, I'd say. Oh, and she had a brooch, one of those Chinese things. Looked expensive, sparkly stones round the edge.'

'Chinese things? A dragon?'

'No, one of those black and white things.'

Jonny opened his own notebook and drew a circle, a curved line down the middle. He shaded one side with his pencil and leaving a small circle of white. 'Like this?'

'Yes, just like that,' said Marcia. 'How did you know?'

'It's a Yin Yang symbol. A Confucian representation of the opposite but interconnected. In Confucianism I believe it carries a moral dimension.'

Annie looked impressed. 'I've seen it on so many things,' she said. 'Never really knew what it meant.'

'Is it anything to do with selling houses?' Marcia asked.

'Doubt it,' said Jonny. 'It probably had more personal meaning for her.'

'Like Christians wear crosses?'

'Something like that, yes.'

'Well,' said Annie, closing her notebook and putting it into the inside pocket of her jacket. 'I think that's all I need. We'll leave you in peace.'

Jonny, noticing her use of *we*, followed her out to where they had left their cars.

'Heading home?' Annie asked.

Jonny nodded.

'Then let's stop off at Warwick Services for a coffee. You can tell me what brought you here and we can compare notes.'

'Sure. See you there. Starbucks?' he asked.

JONNY WAS the first to arrive. He made his way through the glass-covered porch of the Welcome Break area, where he noted a sign that told him Warwick North had the best rated toilets of all Warwick motorways. A pity, then, that he was travelling south. He should have taken advantage of them on his way to visit Marcia, not waited until he was on the way home. It was a pleasure that would have to wait for another time. But how many motorways were there in Warwick?

Couldn't be that many, even if the wording was wrong and it should have said Warwickshire.

His musings were interrupted by Annie's arrival and Jonny bought them both cappuccinos – tall. That led to Jonny wondering why the smallest size was called tall. Some weird form of customer manipulation, he supposed. In his working life he'd sat through meetings with excruciatingly boring discussions about branding the sizes of CPS cardboard boxes. Why not just publish the size in metres? He'd been overruled and their boxes carried stupid names, most of which Jonny had now forgotten.

He added a couple of flapjacks to the order and carried it all to the table Annie had chosen at the far end of the seating area. Less likely to be eavesdropped, he supposed.

He explained the coincidence that had led him to his visit to Marcia, wondering if Annie would give him an earful about how he should go to the police with information rather than following it up himself. She didn't, which was a relief. 'Can I ask what brought you to her door?' he said.

'A way more time-consuming route,' she said. 'We spent a long time searching for Trubshaw's bank accounts and eventually we traced his final salary payment from the estate agent he worked for, and which is still sitting in a current account, more or less intact.'

'Don't banks close unused accounts?'

'Not always. They can lie dormant for years.'

'So that salary payment was the last time the account was used?'

'No, we were able to get a warrant for the account details. He'd paid a removal company as well as the small sum to Marcia Jones. We hoped we could trace where he'd been and also the date he'd used the account for the final time, which could help us with the time of his death.'

'So you accept that he was the victim?'

'We were fairly sure it was him. We'd traced his shoes through the maker but that wasn't final proof. He might have given his shoes to someone else. But we also traced hospital records that identified him through the injury to his foot.'

'That wouldn't have killed him, would it?'

'No, it was nothing to do with his death. He'd been shot well before that. He died from injuries he received possibly after a beating.'

'Are you allowed to tell me this?' He wouldn't want her to be in trouble for disclosing confidential evidence.

'It's not a problem. We'll be releasing the information soon anyway. And in any case, you are working with a team who all have security clearance set up by DI Lomax.'

'So were you able to trace where he'd used his cards?'

She looked excited. 'Yes, we were, and it ties in nicely with the sighting of the two women at Beedham on Midsummer's Day. He'd bought petrol at Beaconsfield Services on the evening of June twentieth. He then headed into Amersham and used his card to stock up on what I can only describe as luxury breakfast items: free range eggs; hand cured ham; a loaf of sourdough bread; hand rolled butter; a small bottle of white wine; an expensive brand of coffee and a small tub of cream.'

'He was going to make eggs benedict,' said Jonny.

'And probably not for one, unless he was planning to take it all to Spain to stock his new larder.'

Jonny shook his head. 'That would take at least a couple of days. In a hot car the butter would have melted and the cream gone off.'

'He had a booking for LeShuttle on the evening of June twenty-second. We think he was planning to stay a night or two this side of the channel, possibly with a friend.'

'He had the use of a hunting lodge in the Great Park.'

'Great to know,' said Annie. 'We thought we were going to have to go for Airbnb records or launch an appeal for witnesses. You've probably saved us a lot of time.'

'Glad to have helped. What do you think about this woman who might or might not have been from the estate agent?'

'I'll need to check with them about that,' said Annie, draining the last of her coffee. 'But right now I need to get back to the office.'

As they walked out to the car park together, something was

nagging at Jonny's brain. It was still nagging as he followed Annie's car onto the motorway and they both headed south. Nine miles and ten minutes later, Jonny made a snap decision. Junction twelve was coming up. He took the exit, driving in what felt like a full circle, crossing the motorway and then heading back onto the northbound lane. Twenty minutes later, having resisted the temptation of visiting Warwick's best motorway toilets, he parked in the road outside a house on the outskirts of Warwick. The same car he'd seen last time was parked in the drive, which he hoped was a sign the resident was inside. He walked up the drive and knocked on the front door, planning in his head what he was going to say.

The door opened and Ottilie Kent stood there, frowning at him as if puzzled about who he was. A kind of *I know you from somewhere but can't quite place where* expression. Then she smiled, in an embarrassingly flirtatious way given what he was about to accuse her of. 'Forgive me, Mr Cardew. I didn't recognise you for a moment. To what do I owe this pleasure?' She opened the door wider. 'Come in. I was about to pour myself a glass of wine. Will you join me?'

Probably better not to when he needed to keep his head clear. 'Just a soft drink,' he said. 'I'm driving.'

She led him into a living room with a well-stocked drinks cabinet. 'Pineapple juice?'

He nodded and she prised open a small bottle, pouring the contents into a glass, which she handed to him. Then she poured herself a large glass of red wine. Jonny glanced at a clock on the mantelpiece. 'Five o'clock,' she said, taking a sizeable gulp. 'Perfectly respectable time for a drink. Sun over the yardarm and all that. Never really knew what that meant. Something to do with sailors, I suppose.'

Jonny didn't know either but suspected that Ottilie took the view that the sun was always over the yardarm somewhere in the world.

'So,' said Ottilie. 'This is nice. Are you here to do what I thought you were going to do thirty years ago and make a pass at me?'

'Forty years, actually. And no. I'm here to talk about your daughter.'

'Davina? Why?'

'The last time I was here you told me how successful she was, but you also hinted that you'd had to rescue her in some way and that she was, I think your actual words were, *going through a difficult patch*. That you'd hoped she would travel to China with you but that something was preventing her.'

'Is that any of your business?'

'No, but it sometimes helps to share a worry. And a troubled daughter rather fits that description.'

'So you're here as some kind of good Samaritan? How charming. It's a pity you didn't feel like that forty years ago. All of this could have been avoided.'

Jonny felt he'd had a lucky escape. If he hadn't met Belinda when he did, he might now be shackled to Ottilie Kent, who may have been charmingly flirtatious forty-odd years ago but who was now showing signs of being not only eccentric and sinister, but with an incipient drink problem. 'What were you doing at Laurence Trubshaw's house a couple of days after he'd supposedly left for Spain?'

She sloshed some more wine into her glass with a shaking hand. 'I really don't know what you mean.'

'Oh, come on. A woman claiming to be from Hatchwards visited the house to *make a final check*. This was after the sale had been completed and she didn't even have a key.'

'Could have been anyone. What on earth would I be doing there?'

'That's what I hope to find out. You fit the description given to me by Marcia. You are unusually tall and the woman she spoke to was wearing a brooch like that.' He pointed to Ottilie's lapel.

'It's just a yin yang brooch. They are quite common.'

'The symbol may be very common, but brooches like these, with a diamond edge, are probably not. And would be way beyond the means of an estate agent. One selling billion-pound apartments in London, possibly, but not a clerk from a small branch in Warwick.'

'You've no proof it was me.' Her speech was beginning to slur.

'A neighbour saw a person who matches your description arrive in a car just like the one parked in your drive.'

'They are not uncommon. Did this neighbour make a note of the registration number?'

'The police are, probably right now, checking local ANPR records for the roads around that area.'

She sat down suddenly. 'The police are involved?'

'Of course they are. Larry's body was found in a trunk alongside another murder victim.'

'Two bodies?' She was having trouble getting her head around that.

'And both victims were known to your daughter. I believe the police are about to pull her in for questioning about both murders.'

Ottilie turned to the drinks cabinet and opened a second bottle of wine. She poured herself a generous measure and then turned towards him with an open bottle of pineapple juice. 'Another drink?' She held the bottle out to him.

'No, I should be going.' He stood up as Ottilie walked towards him. She was wearing a long, kaftan-type garment. He backed towards the door, unwilling to take his chances with whatever she might have concealed in its folds, or for that matter take a sip of the drink she was holding in his direction. If she was as experienced at disposing of dead bodies as he suspected, he didn't like to imagine where he might end up. He felt in his pocket for his car keys and slid them between his fingers. It was the only weapon he had, but it might be enough to distract her, giving him long enough to head for his car. But then he heard the door opening and a voice calling out.

'Hi, Ottilie. Sorry I'm early.'

A student, Jonny assumed, making a dash for the door, bumping into a young woman and knocking the sheet music she was carrying to the floor. He mumbled an apology, rushed to his car, clicking the lock open – he knew the car keys had been a good idea – and speeding off.

Two miles out of town, he pulled into a layby and called Annie.

41

'Seems you were right.' Annie wriggled out of her coat and slung it over the back of a chair. Then she edged onto the window seat next to where Jonny was tucking into a plate of poached eggs on toast.

Jasmine approached, notebook in hand. 'You're in early. What can I get you?'

'I'll have what he's having,' said Annie with a glance at Jonny's plate. 'And black coffee.'

'Coming right up,' said Jasmine, writing it on her pad. 'Les not coming in this morning?'

'He's not working today. Doctor's appointment, I think.'

Jonny looked up from his eggs. 'Not ill, I hope?'

'Nothing like that,' said Annie. 'At least I don't think so. He has to check in now and then with the regional health team. No idea why, and he's not talked much about it so your guess is as good as mine. But I'll take a couple of your breakfast rolls for Gary and the boss.'

'I'll have them ready for you,' said Jasmine, adding it to the list on her pad and heading for the kitchen.

'So what was I right about?'

Annie opened up her iPad. 'After you called I got Gary to get onto

DVLA again. They take their time unless you nag them. He'd already enquired about Porsche Carreras registered by women five years ago. They'd whinged a bit and said it would take time, but he called again and told them to check for Davina Ferdinand. He also dropped in the fact that they could be delaying a murder case and hinted that his next step could be a complaint to the Motoring Ombudsman or the deputy commissioner or someone.'

'They probably get threats like that every day. I've had trouble getting through to them myself.'

'You should try dropping in a few police names or threatening them with your local MP. Anyway, whatever Gary said did the job. They got back to him within the hour. A brand new Porsche Carrera was registered by a dealer in West London in the name of Davina Ferdinand on nineteenth June 2018. Gary called them and they checked their records. The car was delivered to Ms Ferdinand at her office in Hammersmith the following day.'

Jasmine arrived with Annie's breakfast. 'You two solved the case yet?' she asked.

'Actually,' said Jonny, 'I think we are well on the way.'

Jasmine pulled out a chair and sat next to him. 'Are you about to make an arrest?'

'We're not quite that close yet,' said Annie. 'But once the boss discovers all of this, and has checked with the pathologist that Trubshaw's injuries could have been the result of being hit by a car, we'll be bringing Ms Ferdinand in for an interview.'

'You think owning the right kind of car will be enough?' Jonny asked.

'That and the fact that she lied to the boss and Katya. She told them she didn't drive. What she didn't tell them was that, although she might not drive now, she was once the owner of a Porsche similar to one that was spotted at Beedham House on Midsummer's Day in 2018 and that around the same time was repaired after allegedly hitting a deer in the Great Park. The park authorities have no record of the incident. We also have the car's ownership history from DVLA. It was sold on June thirtieth of that year through an online second-hand car site. It's still owned by the same guy. Gary spoke to him and once he'd been assured that the sale was legit, he came up with all sorts of useful info about the woman he'd bought the car from. It was for sale at a bargain price and he beat it down a bit further when he noticed it was missing the Carrera decal. She knocked another thousand quid off the price and he was able to buy one on eBay for eighty.'

'Sounds like she was keen to get rid of it,' said Jasmine.

'Well, she hadn't quite got to the stage of paying him to take it,' said Annie, laughing. 'But apparently her rush to sell it had the buyer checking to make sure it hadn't been registered as a write-off.'

'And it hadn't?' Jonny asked.

'No, but he said he thought one of the wings had been repaired. Some slight mismatch in the paintwork. But he'd got it for such a good price he was happy to accept that.'

'So one of the wings doesn't match the other?' Jonny asked.

'Didn't seem to worry him. Only noticeable to a practised eye in a good light, apparently. But it does add weight to the theory that this was the car that killed Larry.'

'Wow,' said Jasmine. 'That is progress.'

'All thanks to Jonny and his theory that Trubshaw had been hit by a car. Ms Kent told him not only that Davina had owned a Porsche, but also that she'd been in a relationship with Trubshaw and was planning to visit him the day before he was due to leave for Spain.'

'Will you be bringing the mother in as well?' Jonny asked. 'She's quite creepy.'

'In what way, creepy?' Jasmine asked. 'Like a witch?'

'Not a witch, no,' said Jonny. 'The Chinese equivalent, perhaps. She had loads of Oriental memorabilia and books about Eastern philosophies.'

'Not sure that's enough evidence,' said Annie, laughing. 'That will be up to the boss. But hang on, did you say Eastern philosophies? Confucius?'

'Yes, among others. Why?'

'There was a quote from Confucius scratched onto the lid of the trunk, something about revenge.'

'You think Ottilie scratched a message onto the trunk? Why would she do that? Wouldn't they want to cover their tracks?'

'Not sure that was made public, so keep it to yourselves. Anyway, forensics said it was recent so it's probably not relevant.'

'But whether it is or isn't, we discovered Ottilie Kent owned a Fiat at the time. Same as the one spotted at Beedham at the same time as the Porsche.'

'That's a bit more of a problem, though. Little white Fiats are not that unusual, and we can't check the ANPR records for roads around Beedham because they are deleted after six months.'

'Perhaps Davina will give something away when she's interviewed.'

'That's what we're hoping. And we're also looking into the fact that Ottilie impersonated a Hatchwards employee to gain entrance to a private property. If the neighbour can identify her, that might help.'

'But that only implicates her in the Trubshaw killing, doesn't it? And she will claim that was an accident. She'll still be in trouble for not reporting it and for dangerous driving, but that's not the same as murder. And Stefan Halliwell was definitely murdered.'

Jonny took a thoughtful sip of coffee. 'That message on the trunk,' he said. 'If it's not just a coincidence, it could be something that linked the two deaths.'

'You think Ottilie was there on both occasions?' said Jasmine. 'She helped cover up Larry's accidental death to protect her daughter and then killed Stefan Halliwell? Why would she do that? And why leave a message that would lead straight to her?'

'Probably time to let us look into all of that,' said Annie, reaching for her coat. 'Any chance my rolls and coffee are ready?'

'Sorry,' said Jasmine. 'I got distracted. I'll get them for you.' She picked up the bags Stevie had been keeping warm behind the counter, waved Annie off through the door and returned to clear the table. Jonny was scribbling something in his notebook. 'I've got a theory,' he said. 'Got time to hear it?'

'Sure,' said Jasmine. 'We're not too busy yet.'

'You already know the first bit. Davina knocks Larry down with her car, calls her mother to come and help. They drive to Beedham and stash the body away in a trunk in the attic.'

'That works for the first body. What about the second?'

'Stefan Halliwell somehow finds out the truth about Larry's death and starts to blackmail Davina. She enlists her mum's help again and they lure Stefan to Beedham and kill him.'

'Hmm,' said Jasmine. 'As theories go, it's not bad.'

'But?'

'Well, first, the voices Ruth heard were men's.'

'You think we can trust Ruth? She was scared and a bit of a distance from the house. She could have been mistaken.'

'Okay, that's possible. But it doesn't explain the quote on the trunk.'

'Like Annie said, that might not be connected at all. Or perhaps Ottilie is planning on becoming a serial killer. They leave a signature, don't they?'

'You think there'll be more killings with strange bits of Chinese philosophy etched into the furniture?'

'Okay, now you're laughing at me. Forget it.'

'No, I'm not saying you're wrong. Do we try to sell your idea to the police team?'

'Possibly. Probably not the inspector or the sergeant.' Jonny had only met DS Trotter briefly and hadn't warmed to him. 'But Annie's open to ideas.'

'How would she follow them up?'

'I don't know. Check all their bank accounts, perhaps? Davina might have already paid him off and then killed him because he was being too persistent.'

'So if there's a large sum of money missing from Davina's bank account, and a matching one paid into Stefan's, then you're onto something.'

'Maybe your friend Les would be the one to go to. You've been working on online stuff with him.'

Jasmine nodded. 'He's got reports from their IT people about what Stefan was up to. He could probably take a close look with that in mind. They'd need a warrant to check bank accounts, but if there was anything to suggest blackmail they'd probably get one easily enough.'

'And not tell us what they'd found,' said Jonny. 'But like Katya says, it's justice that counts, not our own ego.'

'I'm hoping Les will drop in this evening. I can ask him.'

42

Ivo took Reggie's key out of his pocket and unlocked the cellar door. To his surprise, it turned easily. He thought after all the years the house had been deserted, that it would be rusty and stiff. He'd even slipped a can of WD-40 into his pocket just in case.

The door opened onto a flight of stone steps. He turned on his torch and led them down into the cellar. At the bottom of the steps he trod on some scrunched-up newspaper, and kicking it away, thought he heard scuffling. Rats, probably.

Kai followed him down and shone his own torch around the space. It was a big room lined with wooden shelves and at the far end another flight of steps, presumably leading to the rest of the house. 'It's horrible in here,' he said, brushing a cobweb out of his hair. 'Reggie was right about leaving the dogs,' he added, as his feet crunched on some broken glass on the floor.

Ivo shone his torch on the shelves. 'Probably a wine cellar. The Beedhams sound like the sort who'd have a lot of parties.'

'Did they leave any?' Kai swung his torch hopefully along the lines of cubby holes.

'Not likely,' said Ivo. 'There's been a lot going on down here –

squatters, parties, people on the run from the police. They'd have finished off any wine that had been left years ago.'

'I wouldn't fancy a party down here. Even after a bit of a clean-up and some candles, it's still creepy.'

'It smells as well,' said Ivo, kicking a bag of what looked like an uneaten Chinese takeaway into a corner. 'I don't envy you if this is the type of set they'll use for your kidnap story.'

'It won't be an actual cellar. They'll mock something up in the studio. That's why I wanted to see what a really manky cellar felt like.'

'Well, they don't come much mankier than this one. Have you seen enough? We should be heading back to pick up the dogs. I'm going to need a shower after this.'

'I vote we explore the rest of the house first,' said Kai. 'It'll probably be a lot nicer than this. We could take a look at the attic where they found the bodies.'

'I don't know,' said Ivo. 'We're already trespassing, and the police will have removed anything interesting.'

'No one's going to know. Come on.' He headed for the steps at the end of the room, Ivo following him unwillingly. He couldn't let Kai go alone, could he? He was only fifteen and Ivo felt responsible for him.

They climbed up to the attic and looked out at the garden spread out untidily below them. As Ivo expected, the room was empty. Even the trunk and rocking chair had been taken away. 'That'll be for forensics,' said Ivo. 'Did your mum say if they found any useful evidence?'

'She doesn't talk about it much. I suppose she wants to forget it all when she's at home. It's a pity, though. If I'm going to be in a police drama, I should know a bit about how the police operate.'

'They have special advisors, don't they? Retired police officers who hang around telling them if it seems authentic.'

'I suppose they do, but it'd be good to get ahead with some actual case notes.' He scanned the room with his torch. 'There's not much to see up here, so you're probably right that we need to get back to the dogs. Hey, what's that over there?'

Ivo followed his gaze into the corner and a crack between the floorboards. Something glinted in the torchlight and Kai bent to pick it up.

'Don't touch it,' said Ivo. 'There might be fingerprints. Here.' He passed Kai a tissue. 'Wrap it in this.'

Kai picked it up carefully and carried it to the window for a closer look. 'It's a locket,' he said, gently prising it open. 'Look, a picture of a man and a woman.'

Ivo looked at it over Kai's shoulder. 'Father and daughter, do you think?'

'Could be. Or a sugar daddy and lady friend.'

'I wonder how the police missed it.'

'It was tucked into a crack in the floor. Easy to miss.'

'Unlikely,' said Ivo. 'Scene of crime people check every inch of a crime scene. Someone must have been here since they moved out. But who and why?' He looked out of the window. Colin Sugden was coming out of his cottage door. Probably on his way to work.

'Perhaps we should take it to the police,' Kai suggested.

'I'm not sure. They'd say we could have found it anywhere. They would probably just treat it like a piece of lost property.'

'What would happen to it then?'

'I think they'd keep it for a month or two and then if it wasn't claimed it would go into a sale.'

'What if they were able to identify the two photos?'

'No idea,' said Ivo. 'I think it would be best to just leave it here and tell the police we found it.'

'Then they'd know we'd been trespassing. I'd get a rocket from my mum.'

In Ivo's opinion, that was something he should have thought about before dragging them both there. The locket was probably dropped by someone who, like them, had been snooping around. But whatever the reason, it wasn't likely to be anything to do with the murders, not if it was dropped after the bodies were removed and the police had moved out. He was about to suggest they leave it and go home, forget the whole thing, when the door swung open, crashing back against the wall behind them.

'Give me that,' said a voice Ivo recognised. Colin Sugden.

'We were just looking around,' said Kai, slipping the locket into his pocket. 'We've not damaged anything.'

'It's okay. We were just leaving,' said Ivo.

'Not so fast.' Colin was now blocking the doorway. He was carrying a crowbar with a couple of vicious claws on the end. He brandished it in Kai's direction. 'I said give it to me.'

'What would that be?' Kai asked with an expression of innocence.

'That locket you just slipped into your pocket. Stealing, that is. I could call the police.'

'Better do as he says,' said Ivo. 'Then we can go.'

'You should listen to him,' said Colin, tapping the non-claw end of the crowbar against the palm of his right hand.

'Go on,' said Kai, with rather more bravado than Ivo thought strictly necessary. 'Call the police. See what my mum has to say about you threatening me.'

'Aw, call Mummy. That's sweet.'

'His mum's a detective inspector and this was a murder scene,' said Ivo. 'That locket could be vital evidence.'

Colin considered that for a moment. 'Need to call my boss,' he muttered, brandishing the crowbar in their direction. 'Don't move. You don't want to see the kind of damage these claws can inflict.'

That was one thing Ivo definitely agreed with. How would he explain to DI Hannington, not to mention DI Hannington's mother, that he'd allowed their son/grandson to be attacked by a thug with a crowbar?

'Just stand there and put your hands on your heads while I make the call.'

'That'll mess up my hair,' said Kai.

'Just do it,' Ivo hissed at him.

Kai raised his hands reluctantly and cupped them over his temples while Colin tapped a number into his phone. 'Locket's been found,' he said when the call had obviously been answered.

Ivo could hear a voice on the other end but couldn't make out what it was saying.

'Dunno,' Colin continued. 'Young blokes.'

A few more mutterings from the recipient of the call. Again nothing Ivo could hear. Whoever it was must have ended the call. Colin stared at the phone screen for a moment and then slid it into his pocket. 'Turn off your phones and put them on the floor,' he said. 'And don't try any funny business.'

'How can I do that with my hands on my head?' asked Kai.

'I said no funny business,' Colin growled. 'You can turn them off with one hand and keep the other on your head.'

Ivo and Kai both did as they were instructed, Kai still muttering his objections.

'Now the locket,' said Colin.

Kai took it out of his pocket and slid it across the floor towards Colin, who picked it up and pushed it into the pocket of his jeans while kicking the two phones out of the door and down the stairs.

'What are you doing?' Ivo asked as Colin edged towards the door, pulling out a key on a string.

'Just locking you in,' he said, pushing the key into the lock on the door. 'And it's no good trying to escape. There are bars on the windows and a three-storey drop onto the gravel drive.'

'You can't keep us prisoners,' said Kai.

'You think?' said Colin. 'Just stop whining until my boss and I decide what to do with you.' He headed out of the door and locked it behind him.

'Now what?' Kai asked.

Ivo rattled the door, pushed it with his shoulder, then took a few steps back and charged at it, trying to break it open. It refused to budge. 'We'll have to do as he says, I suppose.' He rubbed his shoulder and glared at the door.

Kai was examining the window. There were, as Colin said, bars. Iron bars fixed sturdily into the window frame.

'Don't waste your time,' said Ivo. 'Even if you could shift them, it's too far to jump. We just have to sit it out until help comes.'

'Or that bloke's boss gets to us first. He might have a gun, and people have been murdered in here before, you know.'

Ivo knew only too well. 'They weren't shot. One was beaten to death, the other was smothered.'

'Did you know that guy? The one with the crowbar?'

'Colin Sugden. Lives in one of the cottages. Thinks he has some kind of claim on it. It would still be his granny's if she'd lived a bit longer.'

'And who's his boss? The murderer?'

That was an interesting question. Colin worked for a delivery company, and he couldn't think of any reason the boss of the likes of Evri or Yodel would have any reason to murder an estate agent with a limp or a computer nerd, but Ivo would be the first to admit he didn't know all the facts.

'Perhaps he's a psychopath, working his way through all the different ways there are to murder people.'

That was a grisly prospect. Also an unlikely one. From what he knew about psychopaths, Ivo didn't think they usually worked in pairs. And in the back of his mind, he had an idea they were quite particular about the modus operandi, and experimenting with different killing techniques wasn't something they went in for. He could, of course, be quite wrong. He looked out of the window, wondering if it might be possible to attract Reggie or Peg's attention by shouting for help. But that would also attract Colin Sugden's attention and he wasn't keen on another visit from him and his crowbar. Perhaps it wouldn't be long before Reggie started to worry about how long they'd been. But that also brought the worry that Reggie might come looking for them and find himself at the wrong end of Colin's crowbar. For the moment he'd run out of ideas.

Kai folded up his coat and settled himself on the floor, using it as a cushion. 'Well,' he said, 'if we do get out of here, it's given me some first-hand experience of what it feels like to be locked in a creepy house. That should bring a certain frisson to my role, don't you think?'

Ivo had to agree that it probably would. *If* they got out unscathed.

Right now, he'd probably settle for getting out only slightly scathed. An odd word that. *Unscathed* was familiar. He wasn't sure he'd ever heard anyone say *scathed*. But he was not a big user of words. He'd failed his GCSE English, hadn't he? It had upset him at the time, but right now it didn't seem to matter very much.

43

Katya kicked crossly at the leg of the desk, where she was supposed to be filing evidence bags ready for storage in the basement. If she'd known that helping the police as a civilian meant she was going to be a glorified clerk, she'd never have pushed her way in. They'd have been better carrying on as usual. But Jonny had been getting on well with Annie, who seemed to have no problem letting him know what was going on police-wise. Jasmine had been working closely with Les, although Katya was not sure how much of that was work and how much was bonding. Even Ivo had been able to pass on some useful info to Gary. And what was more, it was info that Gary took seriously. Apart from sitting in on an interview with Davina Ferdinand, an occasion that, in Katya's opinion, the DI could have got a lot more out of, she'd made little contribution towards solving the case herself.

So here she was, sitting in front of a box of evidence bags with little in the way of conversation. Not that she expected much from Gary, who was tapping away on his computer keyboard giving off *interrupt me if you dare* type vibes. The DI flitted between her office and the board, tweaking papers now and then but not looking as if she was on the verge of a big breakthrough in the case. Katya had no idea where Les or Annie were. A pity, because they were the most approachable of the team and might have been up for a bit of police station gossip.

And then her phone rang, Reggie Braddock's name flashing up on her screen. He sounded worried. Ivo and a young friend, the one that was on the telly, he told her, had left their dogs with them. They'd gone to explore Beedham House. Something to do with a film the lad was making. 'And that was over an hour ago,' Reggie said. 'They were going to look at the cellar, something about a film set. I went over there just now in case the door had stuck or something, but they weren't there.'

Film set? What the hell was he on about? 'Have you checked the rest of the house?' Katya asked.

'Didn't like to,' said Reggie. 'I called up the cellar stairs but there was no response.'

'Don't worry, Reggie,' said Katya. 'I'll call Ivo and see where he's got to. I'm sure he'll be back soon. It wouldn't be like him to desert Harold. Sit tight and I'll call you when I know what he's up to.'

Reggie ended the call and Katya tapped Ivo's number. His phone was turned off, which was not like Ivo at all. And who was the lad he was with? The DI strolled out of her office and Katya had a horrible feeling she knew who the lad was. Ivo had been getting quite friendly with Kai Hannington – a mutual interest in dogs.

'Okay, Katya?' Charlie asked, emerging from her office with a pile of papers that Katya was afraid were about to land on her own desk in need of filing.

'Do you know where your son is?'

As Katya expected, the DI dumped the pile of papers in front of her. 'At home with his grandmother, why?'

'Could you check? I think he might be out somewhere with Ivo.'

'So call Ivo and ask him.'

'Tried that. His phone's off.'

Charlie sighed and reached for her phone. 'Kai's not answering either. I'll call home,' she said, tapping in another number.

Katya tried not to listen to the conversation, but as the volume of Charlie's voice rose, she couldn't help it.

'So where were they going?' she yelled, and Katya had a moment's sympathy for Ms Hannington senior.

'Bloody hell,' said the DI, ending the call. 'Why on earth did they go to Beedham?'

'Shall I go and look for them?' Katya asked. 'They could still be in the house.'

'Doing what, for God's sake?'

'I dunno, but they're young. They're probably sitting with their headphones on soaking up the atmosphere.'

'And how were you planning on getting there? You don't have a car.'

That was a good point. 'I could call Jonny to give me a lift.'

'I'll drive her,' said Gary, looking up from his desk as if more than a little keen to be away from the office.

'We'll all go,' said Charlie, grabbing a set of keys and heading downstairs at what Katya felt was a dangerous speed.

It was a long time since she'd been in one of the pool cars. They hadn't improved. This one was in service long before Katya had retired, but Gary stuck a blue light on the roof and put his foot down. The old car shuddered and then took off at a surprising speed.

'Ivo's van is still here,' said Katya as they turned into the drive.

They climbed out and peered through the windows of the house as Reggie appeared in the doorway of his cottage.

'Still no sign of them?' Katya asked.

'No, but I saw that young Sugden a moment ago. He let himself into the house through the front door. Didn't know he had a key.'

'Right,' said Charlie. 'Gary, you go in through the garden door. Katya and I will take the main entrance and see if we can head him off. I don't trust him, and if my son's inside the house, well…'

. . .

THEY MET up at the foot of the stairs up to the attic. Gary had got there first and had Colin Sugden pinned up against the wall. 'Where are they?' Gary growled.

'Who?' Colin croaked, his windpipe having been blocked by Gary's fist.

'Ivo Dean and the boss's lad.' Gary loosened his hold just enough for him to take a spluttering breath.

'Dunno. Just got here, haven't I?'

Charlie had already galloped up the stairs and was rattling the attic door. 'Kai,' she shouted. 'Are you in there?'

'We're both here,' said Ivo.

'Shh,' said a voice Charlie recognised as Kai's. 'We don't want her to know we're here.'

'Too late for that,' said Charlie, hurling herself at the door to little effect.

'Here, boss,' said Gary, throwing her the key he'd just extracted from Colin's pocket. 'Try this.'

Charlie fitted the key into the lock and turned it. The door opened to reveal Ivo looking embarrassed and Kai wearing a rebellious expression. She looked back down the stairs. 'Cuff him,' she shouted to Gary. 'And get him back to the station.'

'You can't do that,' Colin wailed. 'I ain't done nothing.'

'Breaking and entering, false imprisonment, child abduction? That'll do for starters.'

'What you mean, child abduc—'

He didn't have time to finish as Gary dragged him down the stairs. 'And get a warrant to search his house,' Charlie shouted after them. 'And you.' She turned to Kai. 'I'm calling a car to take you and Meg home.'

'I can take them home,' said Ivo.

'Oh, no,' said Charlie. 'You've caused enough trouble for one day.'

'It's not his fault,' said Kai. 'I made him bring me here. It was for research. And we found—'

'Enough,' said Charlie. 'You're going home right now and you're grounded for the foreseeable.'

44

It was frustrating not being a full member of the team. Katya had enjoyed a good interview in the past, but today she'd been told not to come in until midday, and by then the interviews would be done and dusted. Oh well, her fault for retiring when she had. She'd not minded so much about not being able to arrest people. It was the crime solving she was more interested in. Sifting through evidence and working out what had been done by who.

The office was quiet when she arrived. Gary and Annie were interviewing Colin Sugden. The DI was on her way back from Warwick where she and Gregson, thanks to Annie and Jonny's latest work on the case, had questioned and charged Ottilie Kent with failing to report a fatal traffic accident. The theory was that she'd responded to her daughter's plea and helped her to transport Laurence Trubshaw's body from the road, where he'd been lying dead, to a trunk in the attic at Beedham House. It was Jonny's recent visit to Ottilie that had made them suspicious, along with the confirmation from the pathologist that the injuries received by Trubshaw could have been inflicted by a car rather than a person. Five years of lying dead in a trunk had meant it was difficult to be conclusive about a murder weapon. Katya was sceptical about that and more inclined to blame Dr Yates' impatience. A pathologist with his credentials should know the difference even after a five-year gap.

Katya had been left on her own to finish sorting the evidence bags after the interruption the previous day. There were two cardboard boxes of them still waiting to be labelled and transported down to the evidence vault in the cellar. Katya took the lighter box first. This contained only the decal from Davina's Porsche, some notes about the car itself and its current ownership, along with the till receipt from Larry's shopping trip for breakfast ingredients and a few items that had been found at the now-derelict hunting lodge in the park. There were also photos of Trubshaw's car, which had been discovered in some bushes behind the lodge. It had been set alight and was minus its wheels but was still identifiable.

No one else was in the office, so Katya decided it wouldn't hurt to catch up with what had been written up on the board. In fact, she'd do that before she sorted any more evidence bags. She stood up and crossed the room for a closer look. They'd been thorough, and much as she might like to, Katya couldn't fault them. Everything Ottilie had told them about Trubshaw's stay at the lodge and her daughter's intention to visit him there checked out. The stretch of road nearby had been searched, although after five years there was little to find. Davina's colleagues had confirmed that she'd left the party at a time that tallied with Larry's possible dawn-time death. They'd also noted that she'd been extremely drunk. She should be on a drunk-driving charge, but that was going to be difficult to evidence after five years. A visit by a couple of Warwick uniforms to Marcia Jones with a photo of Ottilie identified her as the woman who had visited the house, although they had no idea why she might have done that. Ottilie had been vague about it when questioned. Just checking there was nothing to connect Davina to the house, she told them.

Katya returned to the desk and noticed the two recently arrived mp3 interview files on the desktop. Katya had been left with instructions to forward them to the DCI at the hub as soon as they arrived. And she couldn't do that without checking that they were the correct files, could she? Katya's mouse hovered over the two audio files and she wondered which to listen to first. One was Annie and Gary's interview with Colin Sugden. The other was the DI and Gregson questioning Ottilie Kent. There was nothing to indicate which was which. Katya tutted. They should have been renamed before they were uploaded to make them easy to identify. She wouldn't be doing her job properly if she didn't see to that. Even more reason to listen to both of them. She clicked the one on the left of the screen first and heard the DI and Gregson introduce themselves. Ottilie Kent had declined the offer of a solicitor. She admitted to assisting her daughter in covering up Trubshaw's death. Davina had been at a work celebration. It had been a highly successful year for them. She had drunk excessively and should not have driven herself away from the party until several hours after her last drink. Katya listened as Ottilie claimed that Davina and Laurence had been in a coercive relationship and that if they'd reported the accident, Davina would have been charged with manslaughter. When questioned about her visit to the house Trubshaw had lived in, Ottilie explained that she'd merely gone to check that he hadn't left anything there that could incriminate Davina.

Ottilie denied all knowledge of the message left scratched onto the lid of the trunk, and they had believed her after checking the forensic report, which noted that the words on the trunk had been carved recently by someone left-handed. Both Ottilie and Davina were right-handed. Apart from the message, there was nothing to connect Ottilie to Stefan's murder. Even that bit of evidence was dubious. Being interested in Chinese philosophy hardly connected Ottilie Kent to Stefan's death. But one arrest was progress and they would no doubt be pulling Davina in on the same charge.

Then she opened the other file and listened to Gary introduce himself and Annie. He asked Colin and the solicitor to give their names and recorded the time and date of the interview. All in order so far. She could stop the playback, rename the files and get on with something else. But she didn't. She continued to listen as Sugden huffed his way through, denying everything that was suggested to him but backtracking now and then. He'd been allocated the duty solicitor. A man Katya was familiar with, nice enough and perfectly efficient when dealing with clients.

Colin was asked to explain his movements on the day of the murders. 'At work,' he told them.

'And what time did you arrive home?'

He'd cycled home and couldn't be sure of the exact time, but he'd arrived around the same time as the police car.

He was shown a photo of Stefan Halliwell. 'How well do you know this man?'

'You don't need to answer that,' said the solicitor. 'That's purely subjective.'

Gary sighed audibly. 'You do know who he is?'

'Yeah, the bloke that works for the trust.'

'When did you last speak to him?'

'Dunno. Weeks, maybe months.'

'For the tape,' said the DI, 'I'm showing Mr Sugden some objects that were found in his house. Can you tell me about this locket?'

'Found it.'

'Where did you find it?'

'In the attic.'

'And yet, according to our witness, you didn't find it. You took it from him while threatening him with a crowbar.'

'I thought he was stealing it.'

'What made you think that?'

'Trespassing, weren't he?'

'And you planned to do what with it? Hand it over to the police? Sell it?'

'Nah, I didn't, I...'

'You put it into your pocket and left with it, having locked two young men in the attic.'

'No, well, yes, I suppose...' The solicitor, Katya assumed it was him, coughed a warning to silence him.

'For the tape,' Gary continued, 'I'm showing the suspect a gouging tool.' There was a sound of something being slid across the table. 'Can you explain this?'

'What is it?' the solicitor asked. 'I don't see that it has any relevance to my client's arrest.'

'Dunno,' said Sugden.

'It's a gouger. Used for wood carving. It was found in Mr Sugden's house. Do you do any wood carving, Mr Sugden?'

'Not mine.'

'No?' Annie's voice this time. 'It has been identified by forensics as the likely tool used to carve a message into the lid of the trunk.'

'Don't know nothing about that.' He was lying, Katya was certain.

'For the tape,' said Gary, 'I'm showing Mr Sugden a bunch of cable ties that were found in a drawer in his kitchen. Can you explain why these were in your kitchen?'

'Dunno, never seem them before.'

The recording picked up a deep sigh, presumably from Gary. Katya didn't think she'd ever heard Annie sigh. 'Okay,' Gary continued. 'Your two hostages told us that you threatened them with a crowbar while calling someone you described as your boss. Can you tell us who that was?'

'Didn't call no one.'

'I'm afraid you did. For the tape, I'm showing Mr Sugden a copy of his phone records. You see the call I've highlighted? Our witnesses say you made that call at exactly the time they were trying to avoid your attack with a crowbar.'

'If I were attacking them with a crowbar, I couldn't have been on my phone, could I?'

Once again the solicitor coughed.

'Who did you call?'

'You must already know that if you've got my phone records.' Katya could almost hear the sneer in Sugden's voice.

'Enough,' said the solicitor. 'I'm requesting a break. I need to confer with my client.'

THE RECORDING BEGAN AGAIN with the solicitor reading out a statement.

Mr Sugden denies any knowledge of the killing of Stefan Halliwell, although he admits to having had an argument with him several days before his death. Mr Sugden was concerned about the ongoing ownership of the cottage that had belonged to his grandmother and in which he was currently living. He describes Mr Halliwell's attitude as aggressive and unhelpful.

Shortly after this meeting, Mr Sugden took on work as a waiter at Ascot races. While there, he was approached by a man who introduced himself as representing the interests of the Beedham House project. He offered Mr Sugden a large payment in return for a number of small jobs that would help clarify Mr Sugden's predicament. My client assumed this to mean that it could lead to the transfer of the cottage into his name. He realises now that he should have regarded this with suspicion but states that he has no experience of these matters and that he was acting in the interest of his family – Mr Sugden has a young son.

The jobs that Mr Sugden was asked to undertake seemed innocent enough and he accepted the offer, after which the sum of two hundred pounds was posted though his letter box with the promise of another thousand when the tasks were completed. These were explained to Mr Sugden over the phone and are listed as follows:

1. To collect a key to Beedham House from a flowerpot by the front door on a specified day.
2. The same day to use the key to access the house himself. That morning an envelope would be posted through his letter box containing a wood carving tool, a message that he was to copy and scratch onto the lid of the trunk in the attic, and a locket that he should leave concealed there.
3. When this was completed, he should return the key to the flowerpot.
4. He should not speak about this to anyone as this could hamper the plans for the house and delay the transfer of the cottage into his own name.

Mr Sugden completed the first two tasks but forgot about the locket.

Realising his mistake, he kept the key in order to return to the attic after the police team moved out and hide the locket as requested. He assumed this would not make any difference to the plans for the house.

KATYA LISTENED to the recording twice. Did she believe him? The man must have been a complete idiot, but Colin Sugden had not struck her as the brightest key on the ring, so it was feasible. She picked up the evidence bag that held the locket and manipulated it inside the plastic until it opened. It contained pictures of a man and a woman. Larry Trubshaw and Davina Ferdinand.

Sugden was to be held in custody for a further forty-eight hours while Davina Ferdinand was questioned. The intention was to charge both of them with Halliwell's murder.

45

Jasmine poured two cappuccinos, put a blueberry muffin on a plate and carried them to the table Les had chosen. It was nearly closing time and the café was quiet. She decided to join him, hoping he didn't think she was being pushy.

'Mind if I join you?' she asked.

'I'd be delighted. If I'm not keeping you from your work.'

'We're not busy.' She watched as the only other customer finished the cup of tea they'd been drinking and headed for the door. She stood up and turned the sign to *Closed*.

'Finished work early?' she asked, pulling up a chair and sitting next to him.

'I've been off today,' he said. 'Had an appointment.'

'It sounds like your lot have been busy. Ivo was in earlier. He and Kai had a bit of an adventure. Colin Sugden locked them into the attic at Beedham House. He's been arrested.'

'Yeah, Gary called me. They searched Sugden's house and found enough evidence to detain him overnight. They interviewed him first thing this morning.'

'Did he have something to do with the murders?'

'Possibly, and from what Gary told me, they seem to think he was working for someone. They are also bringing in Davina Ferdinand. Her mother has admitted to covering up Trubshaw's death and leaving him in the trunk. They suspect Davina might have hired Sugden to kill Halliwell.'

'Why would she want to kill him?'

'IT found some evidence on Halliwell's computer that suggested he knew about the cover up and was blackmailing her. But that's not the only evidence. They found a locket that had belonged to Davina along with a carving tool and some cable ties in Sugden's house.'

Jasmine gave him a sceptical look. 'I don't think that can be right. I suppose she might have dropped a locket, but leaving a message on the trunk, well, that doesn't make sense. Unless, of course, Davina wanted to frame her mother for the murder.'

Les shook his head. 'I agree. I think she's been set up.'

'What does your team think?'

'Like I said, they are bringing Davina in for questioning as a suspect. I don't think it's a strong case, though, and she'll have a top-notch lawyer with her who'll probably make mincemeat of the evidence. Then we'll be back where we started – without a clue about what happened. I think Davina was probably the one being framed.'

He was probably right. From what she knew of Colin Sugden, he didn't have the brains to frame someone for what looked like a carefully planned murder, not on his own. But how could they find out who he was working with? Who would want Stefan out of the way and Davina and her mother out of action? Something echoed in her brain from a film she'd watched once with her dad. *Follow the money.* And from reading murder mysteries where someone said *the first thing you should look at after a murder is who gains from it.* Then she remembered something she'd read only last week. A story Teddy had covered and titled *The Incarceration of Maureen Stratford.* She scrolled through some files on her laptop and then nudged Les. 'Look at this.'

It was a story about an elderly woman who had been living on her own but with a daughter, Marian, living nearby until she was posted to Australia for a year by the company she worked for. Maureen, a woman in her late eighties, had been in good health so Marian had no qualms about leaving her for a year. She asked a neighbour to pop in and keep an eye on her while she was away. Mother and daughter had never been good at letter writing and Maureen insisted that phone calls to and from Australia would be far too expensive, so they kept in touch through WhatsApp. The daughter sent photos and short messages about the places she'd seen, and Maureen replied with short texts usually saying little except that *everything was fine*. Marian started to worry when she realised that her mother had not been in contact for several weeks. She tried to call her mother and the neighbour, but neither were answering their phones. Not unusual for Maureen, who was deaf and hated the phone. Lack of response from the neighbour was more concerning. Marian called a colleague and asked them to call in to check up on both and was alarmed by the news she received. The neighbour had been knocked down by a delivery van, had spent time in hospital and was currently at a rehabilitation centre undergoing extensive physio. Of Maureen there was no sign. Her house had been gutted ready for renovation. Marian had no alternative. She cut her contract short and returned home. It took her a while to track her mother down but eventually found her installed in a home for those with dementia where, if she hadn't been confused before, she definitely was now. Marian tried to take her mother home but faced considerable objections from her mother's doctor – not the GP she'd been with for more than forty years, but a private one her mother had switched to for reasons Marian didn't yet understand. A legal battle ensued, and after months of expense, Marian was granted power of attorney and removed her mother from the institution. After several more months of recuperation, Maureen began to recover and she was able to piece together what had happened. She'd been drawn to a leaflet that offered her lifelong care in exchange for a large sum of money. Maureen didn't have a large sum of money, but she did own a house. After making some initial enquiries, she was persuaded to see the company doctor, who assessed her as needing full-time care and she was hounded daily until she agreed to sell the house to pay for it.

Marian was outraged and determined to get justice for her mother, but finding very little she could do, she decided to go public. She might never be able to recoup the money her mother had lost, but at least it might warn others in similar situations. She contacted Teddy Strang.

Les looked at the date Teddy had first published his piece. Three years ago. 'Did it do any good?' Les asked.

'I don't know,' said Jasmine. 'I'll give Teddy a call.' She picked up her phone and called his number.

'Still ongoing,' Teddy told her. 'There's a big legal wrangle going on, but I've had a gagging order which prevents me from naming the company and any individuals involved. Marian's lawyers told me I should go along with it or risk her losing the case. When she does win it, and I'm sure she will, there'll be a massive story in it for me.'

'A gagging order?' said Jasmine. 'Is that just if you publish anything about it?'

'Or if I do anything that leads to someone else publishing.'

'But you could give me some names? Or the police?'

'Well...'

'Please. I won't pass it on to anyone. It's just, I think I know someone who might be a target.'

Teddy agreed to text her the name of person he'd been investigating. 'Just so you can warn them.'

Jasmine's phone pinged and she opened the message and stared at it in surprise.

'What is it?' Les asked.

'That blows my theory about the motive out of the water. I thought I had it all tied up. Davina planned to make a killing by persuading the Braddocks to sell and break the covenant. The only thing stopping her was Stefan Halliwell.'

'So she kills him and tries to point the blame at her mother?'

'Jonny said he thought Ottilie was manipulative, so that could be a motive.'

'And some of the emails we found on Stefan's computer hinted that he knew what Davina was up to. But perhaps that was her property plans, rather than the fact that she'd killed Trubshaw.'

'But that doesn't work now. Look.'

She held up her phone for Les to see the name Teddy had sent her.

46

Diana Hannington was emptying the last dishes from the dishwasher and looking forward to a relaxing cup of coffee while the house was empty. She put the kettle on and then noticed a patch of oil on the floor near the cooker. It was nice that Kai liked cooking; she just wished he wasn't quite so messy. A slick of oil on the floor could be dangerous and she should clear it up while the kettle was boiling. Having a resident teenager could be exhausting. Not that it wasn't delightful having Charlie and Kai living there with her. Really the house was far too big for Diana on her own, but she'd lived there for more than forty years and she couldn't face starting again somewhere else. She liked it right where she was. She enjoyed her own company, but she also had friends in the village. Friends of all ages. She would hate to be living somewhere, however easy to manage and luxurious, if everyone she ever talked to was over sixty. No, she planned to stay right here until they carried her out in her coffin. And Kai, with all his mess and exuberance, would keep her feeling young.

She'd started filling a bucket with hot water and a squeeze of pomegranate-scented floor wash – whatever would they think of next? What had happened to those green blocks of household soap that smelled vaguely institutional? The bucket was nearly full of soapy water, when there was a knock at the door. Meg stirred in her basket but otherwise didn't respond. Good company but no guard dog, that was Meg. Diana turned off the tap, and patted the dog on the head as she made her way to the door. She wasn't expecting anyone. Ivo said he would call to replace a bolt on the shed door, but she didn't expect him yet. He had jobs to do at *Shady Willows* in the mornings. It was too early for Kai even if he had forgotten his key again. Maybe a delivery, not for her as she hadn't ordered anything recently, but Kai was always sending off for stuff. It was probably some weird outfit he'd taken a fancy to on Vinted. It could have been a mistake giving him access to her account.

She opened the door, expecting to see someone holding a parcel and requiring a signature. What she was greeted with was a man in a suit holding a clipboard and an armful of glossy brochures. 'Ah, Mrs Hannington,' he said. 'Good of you to agree to our meeting.'

Meeting? She'd agreed to nothing. The man didn't wait to be invited in but pushed past her into the hall. 'Kitchen this way, is it?'

All she could do was follow him into the kitchen, where Meg started growing softly from the safety of her basket.

'Right,' said the man, pulling up a chair and sitting down at the table. 'Just a few papers to sign and then you can start choosing what you will take with you.'

'What the hell are you talking about? What papers? I can assure you I will sign nothing and I'm not planning on going anywhere.'

'Why don't you put the kettle on, and we'll have a nice cup of tea?'

'I don't want a nice cup of tea. And I certainly don't want strange men sitting at my kitchen table.'

'I expect it slipped your mind. At your age it's not unusual to become a little, shall we say, forgetful.'

'I can assure you I'm not in the least forgetful. And I'd like you to leave right now.' She held the door open, hoping he'd get up and go away.

He didn't. He gave her the kind of patronising smile usually reserved for aging relatives. 'I promise it won't take long. You just need to sign a few papers and then I can leave you in peace.'

'I'm not signing anything. If you don't leave right now, I shall call the police.'

'Now, now.' He tutted. 'Don't upset yourself. All I need is confirmation that you agreed to sell us your house. The sooner you do that, the sooner we can settle you into your cosy little apartment.'

Things began to fall into place. 'Are you by any chance from Baverstock Holdings?'

He beamed at her. 'Well done. I've heard that people with your condition have flashes of memory. I am indeed from Baverstock. In fact, I'm the company chairman. My name is—'

'I know your bloody name. You're Monty Letward. And you'll get your hands on my house over my dead body.'

'And I believe sudden mood changes are also quite normal as the disease progresses.'

'You must have the wrong person. There is nothing wrong with my memory and I've not agreed to anything. In fact, I instructed my solicitor to stop you harassing me.'

He reached out and held her arm. 'Come now, why don't you sit down? We can have this done in no time.'

'Let go of me right now.' She tried to wriggle free to reach out for her phone that was on a nearby worktop.

Letward strengthened his grip and pulled her away. 'I said sit down,' he growled at her, pushing her down into a chair. 'Now,' he said, pulling out a knife and holding it at her throat. 'Sign this.'

He pinned her down with one hand and with the other he pushed some papers towards her while trying to force a pen into her hand.

'Or what?' she said. 'You're going to cut my throat? A lot of good that will do you. Everything I have goes to my daughter after my death.'

'Oh, I've found grieving relatives to be very accommodating. Aggravated burglary can leave a nasty mess. My company can move in and get it all cleared up in double-quick time and your nearest and dearest get a nice big cash handout before the coffin lid's screwed down.'

'No,' she yelled. 'You are not getting your filthy hands on my house. Kill me if you must, but you won't get away with it. My daughter will see to that.'

'Shush, calm down. No need to get agitated. You've no neighbours nearby. No one will hear you shouting. This is a no-win situation for you. Either you sign and move into a nice little flat, or you die. I help myself to a few carefully selected valuables, clean up a bit – don't want to leave any fingerprints, do I? And it will be investigated as aggravated burglary. Although, of course, you won't know anything about that.'

She glanced down at Meg.

'Oh, don't worry. I won't hurt the poor doggie.'

That wasn't what Diana was thinking. Meg had looked up, cocking her head to one side. She'd heard something. 'I'm in here,' Diana shouted.

Letward pushed the knife a little harder and drew a few drops of blood. 'Shut up. I told you. There's no one to hear you.'

As if on cue, the door was flung open and an angry bundle of black fur and bared teeth leapt into the room. Letward took a surprised step back, staring at the angry dog that stood snarling at him. Not looking where he was going, he stepped on the patch of oil. Losing his balance, he fell to the floor, knocking his head on the edge of the Aga on his way down and landing in an unconscious heap close to where Diana was sitting.

Harold wagged his tail and placed a paw on Letward's chest as Ivo came into the room. 'Oh, my God,' said Ivo. 'Has Harold killed him?'

Letward groaned. 'No,' said Diana. 'More's the pity. He's just stunned. But have you anything in that toolbox of yours that we could tie him up with? He was about to kill me.' She reached for a tissue and wiped some drops of blood that were making their way down her neck.

'Are you okay?' Ivo asked anxiously.

'I am now, but for God's sake get him tied up before he regains consciousness, or he might have another go.'

Ivo reached into his toolbox and extracted a length of electrical flex, which he hacked into pieces. He tied Letward's hands behind his back. Then he picked up a bike lock and fastened Letward's wrists to a radiator near the kitchen sink.

'We'd better call it in,' said Diana. 'Can you do it? I feel a bit wobbly.'

∼

GARY SCREECHED to a halt in the drive, hurling gravel in all directions. He got out of the car and rushed into the house, Annie and Katya at his heels. They rushed into the kitchen and found Diana and Ivo sitting at the kitchen table, drinking cups of tea and eating chocolate Hobnobs. The two dogs were curled up next to the Aga, chomping their way through dried pigs' ears. Letward was lying on the floor, spitting out curses and threats of revenge.

'What kept you?' Diana asked.

Gary looked at his watch. 'We were only ten minutes,' he said.

'Joking,' said Diana. 'Ivo, dear, pour everyone a cup of tea and hand round the biscuits.'

'A lovely thought,' said Gary. 'But I'd better be getting your friend here back to the nick.'

'And charge him with attempted murder,' said Ivo.

'Don't worry,' said Gary. 'We've found a lot more incriminating evidence against this guy. We were about to pull him in but couldn't find him. I guess we've got you to thank for that, along with Jasmine and some journalist chap who's been investigating cases like this.'

'And Harold,' said Ivo.

'Bloody dog,' muttered Letward from his spot next to the Aga.

Diana smiled sweetly at Gary. 'I don't suppose there's any way of keeping all of this from my daughter, is there?'

'I'm afraid not,' said Gary. 'Much as I'd like to take all the credit.'

'We'll talk to her, though,' Annie chipped in. 'Tell her how brave you and Ivo were.'

'Don't forget to mention Harold,' said Diana, winking at Ivo.

47

'They call it gaslighting,' said Kai. 'Persuading old ladies that they're losing it and getting them to sign over their houses. But Gran got the better of him,' he added proudly. 'Blini, anyone, or some more champers?'

'Just as well Ivo arrived when he did,' said Diana as she mingled with her guests. 'Or I wouldn't be here today.'

Charlie had been reluctant to throw a party to celebrate the end of the case. It didn't seem right, somehow, even if they had solved the murder of Stefan Halliwell and made a number of other arrests connected to the scam Letward was running. He'd be facing a lot more than a murder charge. But there they all were, and it was good to see her mother dressed to kill in deep red velvet enjoying every minute. It was quite like the old days when her father had been at the Home Office and parties were regular events.

She smiled at Teddy as he topped up her glass. 'A highly satisfactory result,' he said. 'You caught your criminals, and I got the story of the year. I'm still uncovering cases like Maureen's. I've been approached about fronting a TV programme to investigate the whole business.'

'Will Maureen get any of her money back?'

'Eventually. Company assets have been frozen, and not just Baverstock. There was a private medical company involved, as well as some property financiers. Your mum had a narrow escape.'

'It's unbelievable, isn't it? Happening right under our noses. I dread to think what might have happened.'

'If it hadn't been for Ivo,' said Teddy with a wink as Ivo crossed the room to join them.

'It was Harold, really,' said Ivo modestly. 'If he hadn't charged in like that, Letward wouldn't have slipped on that patch of oil.'

Charlie laughed. 'And if Kai had been more careful, there wouldn't have been a patch of oil for him to slip on.'

'It's nice to see the whole crowd here,' said Teddy. 'I told you joining up with the Breakfast Club Detectives would be a good thing. They seem to get on very well with your lot.'

Charlie could only agree. Annie's mum and aunties, who had provided much of the catering, were swapping recipes with Jonny and Belinda. Katya and Gary were deep in conversation. Charlie couldn't begin to imagine what they were talking about, probably competing with each other about who had arrested the most villains. And Les and Jasmine were holding hands and laughing at Kai's jokes. Les looked more relaxed than she'd ever seen him. Had he confided in Jasmine? Charlie had talked to colleagues and eventually uncovered the case of the little girl who had drowned. Les had dived into the river in an effort to save her but had failed. And had then been severely beaten up by the child's father and spent several months in hospital. Les had continued to blame himself for the child's death, even though it had never been suggested that it was in any way his fault. Charlie had uncovered this through unofficial sources and could never tell Les that she knew what had happened. But she hoped he was able to talk to Jasmine about it. It was too much for him to carry on his own.

Detective Superintendent Archie Groves was approaching, a bottle of champagne in one hand, his free arm around Katya, whom he had detached from Gary. 'Excellent result,' he said. 'Your father would be proud of you. Case closed, all thanks to your hard work, and this lady here, of course.'

'Oh, not really,' said Katya with uncharacteristic modesty. 'It was a team effort.'

'Well, the murderer is behind bars and facing multiple charges. That's what matters most.'

'What about Davina Ferdinand?' Katya asked. 'And Colin Sugden?'

'Ferdinand and her mother have been charged with failing to report a death, but it's a historic case. Slap on the wrist at worst. Sugden admitted he was working for Letward and helped to frame Ferdinand but swears he didn't know that's what he was doing.'

'I don't think he's very bright,' said Charlie. 'He probably doesn't even know the meaning of *framing*. He was offered cash and jumped at it. Prosecution will have a job proving he knew about the murder.'

'What's happening with the covenant?'

'Everything Stefan Halliwell owned, he left to his mother. She's going to take the covenant over and find a good lawyer to oversee it. The Braddocks are secure for the next four years and then they can do as they wish. But to be honest, the Letward business is in such a mess it's going to take several years to sort it all out. Nothing will happen at Beedham for now.'

Groves was interrupted by Diana leaping onto a chair and tapping her glass with a spoon. 'A toast,' she said. 'Kai, fill everyone's glasses, mine first.'

Kai leapt into action. He put down a plate of sausage rolls on a small table and picked up a bottle of champagne. He filled his grandmother's champagne flute and weaved through the guests, topping up their glasses.

'I'd like to thank everyone involved in this case,' said Diana. 'My daughter and her team for making all these arrests, my grandson for obligingly spilling olive oil on the kitchen floor, and to Ivo, who turned up in the nick of time with the necessary tools apprehend the criminal.'

'Don't forget Harold,' said Ivo.

'Who could forget Harold?' said Diana. 'So raise your glasses everyone and drink to the continued success of the new local detective team and their partnership with the Breakfast Club Detectives.'

Amid all the cheering and clapping, no one noticed Harold deftly tipping the edge of the dish and downing six sausage rolls.

ACKNOWLEDGMENTS

I would like to thank you so much for reading **Death in the Attic**. I do hope you enjoyed it.

If you have a few moments to spare a short review would be very much appreciated. Reviews really help me and will help other people who might consider reading my books. Just click on the link below:

https://www.amazon.co.uk/review/create-review/error?ie=UTF8&channel=glance-detail&asin=B0CW1FH9HS

I would also like to thank my editor, Sally Silvester-Wood at *Black Sheep Books*, my cover designer, Anthony O'Brien and all my fellow writers at *Quite Write* who have patiently listened to extracts and offered suggestions.

Discover more about Hilary Pugh and download the Breakfast Club Detectives prequel novella **Crime about Town** FREE at www.hilary-pugh.com

THE BREAKFAST CLUB DETECTIVES SERIES

Death in the Long walk

Death in the River

Death on the Carousel

Death at the Festival

Visit my website www.hilarypugh.com to join my mailing list and download a free copy of the series prequel, **Crime About Town** and **On the Edge,** a short story that introduces DI Hannington.

ALSO BY HILARY PUGH

The Ian Skair: Private Investigator series
Finding Lottie – series prequel
Free when you join my mailing list:
https://storyoriginapp.com/giveaways/61799962-7dc3-11eb-b5c8-7b3702734d0c

The Laird of Drumlychtoun
https://books2read.com/u/bwrEky

Postcards from Jamie
https://books2read.com/u/4X28Ae

Mystery at Murriemuir
https://books2read.com/u/mgj8Bx

The Diva of Dundas Farm
https://books2read.com/u/bMYMJA

The Man in the Red Overcoat
https://books2read.com/u/4DJRge